Henry Anderton

Life and poems of Henry Anderton

Henry Anderton

Life and poems of Henry Anderton

ISBN/EAN: 9783337206710

Printed in Europe, USA, Canada, Australia, Japan

Cover: Foto ©Raphael Reischuk / pixelio.de

More available books at **www.hansebooks.com**

LIFE AND POEMS

OF

HENRY ANDERTON,

OF WALTON-LE-DALE.

LONDON:
W. TWEEDIE, 337, STRAND.
PRESTON: FERGUSON, CANNON-ST.

MDCCCLXVIII.

PRESTON :

PRINTED AT "THE GUARDIAN" OFFICE,

CANNON-STREET.

PREFACE.

It is matter both of interest and instruction, when studying the history of the great movements which have shaped the course of the world's thought and action, to know something of the great actors, the leading minds, the master spirits, who led those movements. For truly the men are the best illustrations of their work. Interesting indeed it is to know the life and temper of Luther, and to observe its influence upon his time and work; and of our own Latimer, and the martyr-witness which he left us; to read the memoir of Stephenson—that man of the north, whose genius and labours have wrought such a mighty change in the commercial position of his country; to know something of that noble Englishman, the large-hearted Wilberforce, the champion of freedom on British soil; and deeper and stronger still than any of these, is the interest which every Christian man feels in the life and deeds of Him, the Holy One, who came "to bind up the broken-hearted, to proclaim liberty to the captives, and the opening of the prison to them that are bound."

And so, in the history of Total Abstinence, stands out in striking clearness the eager form of HENRY ANDERTON; a man whose poetry, earnestness, and eloquence, not less than the great kindness of his heart, have endeared his memory to all earnest and loving men.

Born, too, in the lovely Lancashire village of Walton-le-Dale; nursed by the banks of its beautiful river,—where stood once the hut of the ancient Briton; where the Roman formed his camp; a spot which has been the theatre of important events in our national history; whence has gone forth many a good man and true, who has done work in the world, and many another who is doing it still,—his life cannot fail to be of deep interest to some of us. There he spent his early days; there he fought some of the noblest struggles of his life; and there, now he is gone, rests all that remains of him, in the quiet churchyard grave.

But the dearest of all causes to our hearts should be the cause of truth—*truth*, the very germ of all life—TRUTH, the very attribute of the Eternal. And when, amidst mistakes, ignorance, and misrepresentations, such different impressions of Anderton prevail, it is due to those who knew him—to those who bear his name—those of his own family and kindred—that some true and authentic memoir of him should be published, by those whose position and knowledge of him enable them to fulfil the task.

For these reasons, his relatives have given this volume to the world. It comes as a light upon the early history of Total Abstinence; it comes as an offering cast upon the altar of Truth; it comes as a loving tribute to the memory of a good man.

Q.

WALTON-LE-DALE.

NOTE.

It was originally intended to publish a volume which, while it refuted the many errors contained in Mr. Grubb's edition, would give an authentic account of the life and times of Henry Anderton. The gentleman who was engaged in this work, and who had almost completed it, has rested from his labours ; and, as many friends had been earnestly looking forward to the promised volume, these short memoirs have been somewhat hastily put together, and are now sent out to the public, together with the poems, in the hope that they may be instrumental in advancing the great and good cause of Total Abstinence.

The Committee of the Bury Abstinence Society respectfully record their sense of the value of the services of the late Mr. Henry Anderton to the cause of Temperance—both by the living voice and the pen of poetic fire—in the early struggles of the great moral movement of the age. They desire to express their sincere sympathy with the bereaved family ; and, in veneration of the departed, they shall ever cherish a sacred regard for the widow and the fatherless.

CONTENTS.

PAGE

CONTENTS.

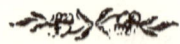

LIFE.

GES had flown, with swift yet silent footsteps, and the world had unmurmuringly, almost unwittingly, lain under the fatal sway of the demon Alcohol. Men, good, brave, and gifted, had fallen in countless numbers into dishonoured and hopeless graves; women, pure, lovely, and true, had been dragged into the deepest degradation and sin; and yet the world, age after age, was blind to the fact that it was clasping a deadly poison in its embrace, and, despite the sad havoc caused by it, continued insanely to smile upon it and to drink of its blighting streams. And, as the old man, prematurely weak, was carried to a drunkard's grave; as the strong, brave youth was cut down like a green and spreading oak; as the fair woman, with golden tresses and fairy form, fell from her lofty and pure state, like a falling star, to shame, misery, and death; and as they were followed to their premature and hopeless resting-places by a few shocked, agonised, and disgraced relatives, the world looked on and said, "Poor things, how very sad!" but continued, age after age, to hug to its bosom that which had done it all, and was day by day doing more deeds of death. Kings drank and cherished it in their lofty palace-homes; queens quaffed its feverish waters; bishops drank from its ensnaring cup; and the great and good kept it in their homes as a dear friend.

But, as years flew on, a few murmuring voices rose against this giant fallacy, this angel of death; but they were, for the time, lost in the multitude of voices which cried for alcohol. At last, a white standard was raised amidst this wilderness of misery; brave, true men held it boldly aloft, in defiance of the devil, and on it was written, in shining characters, the glorious word TEMPERANCE. As the eyes of men rested

B

upon it, some laughed, some frowned, and some—who lived
by the sale of drink—grew violently angry. Taunts, insults,
and abuse could not move the brave, dauntless standard-
bearers. After a time, finding that to touch this thing was
to be in danger of hell and ruin, they manfully determined
to change their motto ; and so, under the smile of God, and
amidst abuse and insult, they furled their first flag, and un-
folded the snowy banner of TOTAL ABSTINENCE, and bore it
through all weathers ; and, blessed be God, it is yet floating,
in all the majesty of purity, to bless a sinful world. And
did they lose anything, in health or wealth, religion or
morality ? No ! For not only were they healthier, but
better, nobler, purer, and more holy ; and, as we look upon
the glorious things that have been done by Total Abstinence
—how young men have been saved from ruin and death, and
brought back from sin and misery ; how woman has been
rescued from deepest shame ; and how the all but lost
drunkard has been brought again to holiness and God—we
turn our thankful hearts to heaven, and say,--

> " Lift up your hearts, and voices too,
>   To Him to whom the praise is due ;
> And let the glorious subject be
>   The triumphs of sobriety."

And those who lifted the standard of Total Abstinence on
high, who were the first to show to a benighted world a new
and better path, and who dragged to the light all the crimes
and abominations in which alcohol had revelled for ages,—
were they the highest, the most learned, the most exalted ?
No ! They were plain and, in many cases, unlearned men,
of whom the world knew nothing, and whose names had
never been breathed by the lips of fame. " But," you say,
" of course they were welcomed in every home, they were
surfeited with dignity and honour." Nay ; in their immediate locality many flocked to hear them, and much good
was done : but *they* were left in total, unqualified neglect;
they were laughed at and insulted, and some of the very
people they were attempting to save laughed them to scorn.
" But," you say, " of course the wise and good took them
under their protection, the ministers of the Gospel boldly
supported them, and they were granted a fair hearing."

Nay ; the wise and good turned a deaf and scornful ear to their pleadings, and many opposed them. Such is the reward of earth. Of the first men who bore the brunt of the battle some remain ; but, as more than thirty years have elapsed since then, many have gone to their little rest-ing-place in the village churchyard, where, with but a plain stone to mark the spot, they lie awaiting that day when every one shall be rewarded or punished. As you pass by their simple, unnoticed graves, can you not hear their voices speaking to you, imploring you to turn from the ensnaring cup ? Let no one disturb their ashes !

It is of the life of one who fought in the early part of the battle that this short sketch would speak : the brave, good, and gifted HENRY ANDERTON, the Temperance Poet. He sleeps peacefully in the churchyard of Walton-le-dale. His form has perished from amongst us, his voice has died away into silence, but his works ought to be remembered. Noble monuments, stately tombs, laurel wreaths, and a world-wide fame are the lot of those who fight their country's battles ; and, while men honour these, ought they *quite* to forget— ought they to pass by without some honour—the memory of those who, unpaid, fought the battle of their country's bodily and spiritual weal ? Henry Anderton fought that fight nobly and manfully ; and there are many who will not, cannot, soon forget that earnest, thrilling voice, that piercing eye, that keen wit, that resistless humour, and yet —underlying all—that deep thought and solemnity. There are many who remember sitting, as if under a spell, while he poured forth a rushing torrent of eloquence that charmed every eye and ear, and brought many to the side of the right. Many there are who look with love and gratitude on his honoured name, and who would bear a loving testimony to his earnestness, worth, and goodness.

On the banks of the Ribble, in the immediate neighbour-hood of Preston, lies the pretty village of Walton-le-dale. The church is a beautiful building, standing in a sweet spot, higher than the village, like a beacon to remind it of heaven ; overlooking on one side a lovely wood-covered eminence, and on the other a sweet green-clad valley, between which and the village winds the Ribble, " in graceful curves." It was here he was born. He was descended from a family which is "of remote antiquity in the north of England," and his ancestors for centuries have haunted the same spot. His father was a well-read, intelligent, upright, and truly Protestant man, and, at the latter end of his life, a firm teetotaller. "He died the death of the righteous." His mother was a hearty, loving, cheerful, and exceptionally kind woman, and was universally beloved and respected.

His childhood was marked, no doubt, by many things which told of his future life. He was a fine, healthy boy before the age of three years; but, unfortunately, at that age, whilst playing in the open air, he was run over by a loaded cart, the wheel passing over his chest. He was brought home for dead ; but gradually, by dint of the tender, anxious nursing of his fond mother, he recovered, but was always left-handed, in consequence, it is said, of this sad accident. We can fancy we see him seated upon a grass-clad mound, looking with childish wonder and admiration upon the lovely valley beneath ; or gazing with thoughtful eyes upon the village churchyard ; or, at night, peering with awe-stricken face into the fathomless sea of stars above him. As a boy, he was peculiar, eccentric, enthusiastic, imaginative, and sometimes boisterously fond of fun. He was like an April day, at one time dreary, dull and dreamily thoughtful, and the next moment bright, joyous, and happy, as when the sun bursts out in meridian splendour and is reflected on the pure faces of a myriad dewdrops. He was an earnest admirer of the good, true, and beautiful, and was peculiarly alive to female beauty,—ever and anon wandering among the sunlit trees, telling the sweet tales of love, or singing in poetic strains the praise of beautiful, enchanting girlhood. He wrote many such strains,—some enthusiastic, some repining, some tender. He was a strange boy : different from others,—of another stamp. They were *body—earth ;* he was *spirit.* He was always very fond of fun and jokes. There is a story that, one day in winter, when the water was frozen over, a group of boys were about a small place, disputing as to who should first slide over it, and that our hero at last determined to take the awful step. So, one ! two !! three !!! off he went ; and, as fate would have it, *in* he went too,—like Pepper's Ghost, he disappeared. By dint of a rope, however, they managed to haul him up ; and a pretty figure he was,—by no means in a poetical plight. At one time we see him with a troop of "Peace-eggers," shouting out a song ; and again we see him, with his scarcely-touched dinner before him, staring vacantly into distance, as if he were oblivious of having even an existence here. He was an excellent mimic, and had a deep knowledge of human nature ; could sympathise with anyone in any sort of distress, and could not bear to see anyone in misery of any kind. He had a tender and compassionate heart. As he grew to maturity, he became a devouring reader and an earnest and devoted man.

As in every forest there is one lifeless tree, so in the best life there are blots and stains which mar its beauty. For about one year of his early manhood, Intemperance set its foul foot upon his neck, and bowed him down beneath its hellish sway ; but, thank God, he survived the blow, and trampled the foul demon beneath his feet. What an important time is early manhood ! when the mind begins to free itself from its tethers of ignorance and frivolity, and to take up its position, to assert itself as something, to take the helm in its own hands. And oh ! through what a turbulent sea it has to steer. How careful should we be not to take a wrong stand, *or allow others to do it*, friend or foe, so far as we have any influence. How sad to have had the power of doing good, and to have left it undone !

Henry Anderton took his stand by the right ; and firmly he held it, till, after this tedious mortal life, God called him home. He had an original mind—one that took its own stand,—and a lively and beautiful imagination : he could paint bright pictures in his mind, and often mused about past and future. He had a great dislike for the discussion of small doctrines ; but he was always ready, when duty called, to say a word for the glorious Christianity which he loved, cherished, and followed, and for the noble Protestant-ism which was the pride of his father. In the days when Radicalism was rife, and when Mr. H. Hunt shone, he was a most enthusiastic Radical, and wrote some very spirit-stirring poems in a little paper then published, known by the name of the "3,730." One piece, of great eloquence, runs as follows :—

"THE POOR, GOD BLESS 'EM!"

" Let sycophants bend their base knees in the court,
     And servilely cringe round the gate,
And barter their honour to earn the support
     Of the wealthy, the titled, the great ;
Their guilt-piled possessions I loathe, while I scorn
     The knaves, the vile knaves who possess 'em ;
I love not to pamper oppression, but mourn
     For the poor, the robb'd poor,—God bless 'em !

"Let tyranny glitter in purple and gold,
     The sheen and the costly array ;
Let idiots take pleasure in what they behold,
     Till the puppet-shows vanish away ;
I turn from such pageants as these, for I know
     Whose gold bought the gewgaws which dress 'em ;
I turn from such splendour to brood o'er the woe
     Of the poor, the starv'd poor,—God bless 'em !

"Let legalized wrong domineer over right,
     And want be accounted a crime ;
Let barefaced dishonour put virtue to flight,
     And traitors exult in their prime ;
Let the pride-trampled mob feel the venomous claws
     Of the vultures who strip and oppress 'em ;
I care not : my soul is alive in the cause
     Of the poor, the stung poor,—God bless 'em.

"Let the halls of our foemen like Solomon's shine
     With jewels, and echo with mirth ;
While cellars, and dungeons, and garrets confine
     The bravest and best upon earth ;
I'll not be the slave of the upstart, who soils
     The knee which he bends to caress 'em ;
Give me the unbought gratulations and smiles
     Of the poor, the warm poor,—God bless 'em!

"And what though discretion should check me and say,
'The wrath of your foes will be roused?'
I'll fight against self, if it stand in the way
Of the cause that my heart hath espoused:
The poor are my brethren, and for them I part
With honours and those who possess 'em;
For oh! while a pulse bespeaks life in my heart,
It will throb for the poor,—God bless 'em!"

Time tempered his views, and he became a loyal and devoted subject, as he always was a deep lover of his country. He was an absent man; and oftentimes, when his body has been in the midst of business, his soul has been far, far away, pondering on things more spiritual, more to his taste. As he walked through the world he looked at it as from another country, yet he always did his duty in the business part of life.

About this time, a few men begun to ask themselves if nothing could be done to stem the torrent of waste, misery, ruin, and damnation brought about by the liquor traffic; and at last they came to the determination of establishing a society which should enforce upon its members total abstinence from spirits and temperance in beer and wine. After a fair trial, this was found to be wanting; and so, after consideration, they determined to form a new society, on the principle of total abstinence from all intoxicating drinks. At first they met with opposition, sneers, and taunts, and the publicans tried to silence them; but *their* opposition was too well understood by the Teetotallers to be taken any notice of. It is told that, one day, as the Teetotallers were speaking at the obelisk (now taken down), in Preston, the publicans brought up a band and tried to *play* them down. They did not succeed: for the Teetotallers procured four speakers, posted one at each corner of the erection, and, when the publicans brought the band to one corner, fired away at the other. We have heard the secretary of the society in those days say that he has been pelted with eggs. Henry Anderton did not join the movement at the very first, but soon after he took his stand in those invincible ranks, and at once occupied a prominent place.

Those who had the privilege to hear him, can never forget how, in those early days, his voice sounded so earnestly and so eloquently in defence of the then new principle. We could wish to take the courteous reader to the meetings in those days held in the Cockpit, in Preston,—those glorious meetings, where drunkards gave an account of how they liked the change from drunkenness to sobriety, and where brave, noble voices ably defended their cause. Here Henry Anderton poured out his heart to crowds who listened to his able addresses. Then there were those grand meetings in the Preston Theatre—great, crowded, and enthusiastic. From the *Preston Temperance Advocate*, published by Mr. Joseph Livesey (the able and veteran advocate of Teetotalism), we find that, in November, 1834, there was a meeting in the Theatre, P. H. Fleetwood, Esq., M.P., in the chair. At this meeting Mr. Anderton gave an eloquent and inimitable address—pointed, able, and sarcastic. At the third annual festival of the Preston Temperance Society, we see, by the same paper that "the flags were flying in different parts of the town, the large coffee-pot, ' Hugo' was exhibited from a window in the Temperance Hotel, and the bells of the Parish Church rang several merry peals." In the evening there was a meeting which was held, we believe, in the Theatre, C. Swainson, Esq., in the chair, at which the Preston Temperance Society was constituted an exclusively Teetotal society. The chairman made a most suitable speech, and congratulated the society upon its amazing progress, and the meeting—which was a crowded one—for its harmony. On the following evening there was another meeting, at which "Mr. H. Anderton occupied the time for upwards of an hour with the delivery of a speech replete with wit, sarcasm, and sound argument, and interspersed with pieces of original poetry. Even if space permitted, it would be a vain attempt to offer to abridge his address ; besides, the peculiarity of his delivery is such, that Mr. Anderton must be heard to be duly appreciated." He wrote nearly all of his speeches before delivery, and had a wonderful memory. His speeches were inimitable, original, and thoroughly intellectual. At one time he was deep in satire, at another, in his peculiarly forcible manner, appealing to the common-sense of his

audience, and anon to their hearts ; and all this with a master hand. He could be fierce as a lion and tender as a
mother. We have heard a gentleman who listened to him
say that he was "the best speaker in England." Then there
were his journeys (unpaid) as a Temperance missionary ;
and, as he went from place to place, he poured fresh torrents
of eloqence against the monster, Drink. He spoke with an
earnestness that touched the heart. We will trouble the
reader with an account of a journey, in his own words, from
the *Preston Temperance Advocate* :—

"I was engaged five nights last week in the Temperance
cause, and the following are a few particulars.—Chorley was
the first place I visited, and I rejoice to say that the society
there is progressing. While its rarely-occurring meetings
were held in the National School, its operations were re-
tarded, its funds were more than expended, and the members were few ; but now, since they have made Preston their
model, they have recovered from the dying condition to
which they had been reduced by the chilling policy of those
one-glass, seldom-meeting, milk-and-water advocates. Over
and above paying their debts and purchasing 2,000 tracts,
they have money in hand. The seemingly impassable gulfs
through which it had to wade have been rendered fordable
by the disinterested exertions of those who have the cause
really at heart. West-street Chapel is well attended by an
attentive audience., drunkards continue to put their names
to the pledge, and its well-wishers are enabled to go on their
way rejcicing.

"From Chorley I proceeded to Bolton. There are two
Temperance societies in this place ; one under the patronage
of the Vicar, and the other commonly known as 'The
Operative Temperance Society.' 'The Working Man's
Society' (its most appropriate appellation), with its weekly
aisle-filling audiences, runs like a giant '*refreshed with
new wine.*' Of course my visit was to this. Our friend Mr.
Entwistle was called to the chair. The place of meeting
was crowded to excess, and it was the only place that reminded me of our own meetings in the Cockpit. Indeed,
but for the different construction of the building in which

we were, I could almost imagine myself addressing a Preston audience. Abstinence and plain, homely speeches are working well for the cause.

" Manchester.—This was my next place. The place of meeting was the Independent Chapel, Grosvenor-street, Piccadilly, Doctor Hall in the chair. For an annual Temperance meeting I considered it badly attended. After the Rev. Hugh Stowell (who spoke in favour of ale-drinking) had addressed the meeting, Mr. Gadsby interrupted the proceedings by some silly objections against the 'pledge;' and I am glad to say that, although he did his best to gain the applause of the *poor* (the greatest portion of the audience) by renewing his objections, with a sneer at the gluttony and winebibbing of the *rich*, his objection was completely refuted. Mr. Gadsby, and after him another disorderly opponent. engaged the meeting so long that a medical gentleman, from Wigan, and myself could only say a few words, and this stormy meeting concluded. The cause of Temperance in Manchester I am afraid is on the wane, and were it not for the disinterested, but unacknowledged, labours of Messrs. Pollard, Wood, Candy, and a few other of the laity, the Manchester Temperance Society would soon become extinct.

" Oldham was my next appointment, at which place I was glad to meet Mr. Entwistle, from Bolton, and Mr. Candy, from Manchester,—two abstinence-preaching, Preston-like friends of the cause of Temperance. As Mr. Entwistle was the chairman of the Bolton meeting, I had not there an opportunity of judging what kind of speakers they had at Bolton, but was amply repaid by the specimen he gave us at Oldham. He occupied the meeting three quarters of an hour, and spoke feelingly, impressively, and soundly. Mr. Candy simply came to hear us, and said very little, but that little was to the point—abstinence! The society at Oldham, like all who have adopted our plans, is going on prosperously ; but as I have to be there again at a tea-party, at the commencement of the new year, I will defer till then the pleasure of describing more fully the nature of its operations and the increase of its members.

"Eccles.—At this place I closed the labours of the week; and I sincerely lament that I cannot give a favourable account of the Temperance society there, especially as it is my *Temperance birthplace*, and to the instrumentality of Mr. Woods, Mr. Langshaw, and the Misses Horsfall, residents in that village, I am indebted for the lengthened span of my existence—a reformed father,—my present hatred of intemperance, and zeal for sobriety. Why is the cause in a declining state at Eccles? Simply because it has followed the chilling, cramping example of the large towns. But they have begun afresh; they have got a new book, that those who are really interested in this 'work of love' may re-enter their names. May God speed them, and add wings to their successes!

"Thus I have lightly skimmed over the prospects and successes of the cause of Temperance at the places I called at in my week's ramble; and perchance you will be enabled to discover that where the meetings recur less often than weekly, where none but privileged and educated men are permitted to speak, and where *ale* is preached up as a *nutritious* beverage, or at least as a 'necessary evil,' the societies in those places are languid and dying, or dead; and, on the contrary, that where meetings are weekly, where uneducated, reformed drunkards have full liberty to tell their 'round, unvarnished tale,' and where abstinence—unqualified abstinence—is held forth as the only safeguard of those who are reclaimed—those societies are progressing with a glorious rapidity.

"HENRY ANDERTON.
"Walton, near Preston, Dec. 16, 1833."

As the moon bursts out in all her silver glory upon the darkness of night, so he went from place to place, shedding the light of Temperance upon those dark places. And his labours were not in vain. We have now before us a letter from a grateful old man who calls him his "father in Temperance." He is now 67 years old, and hopes to die a firm Teetotaller, "by the help of his Heavenly Father." Strangers came often to thank him for the good they had received from his speeches, which had been the turning-point in their lives. At Hulme, near Manchester, he was presented with a silver star and chain, by his friends and admirers. He acknowledged it in an appropriate and heartfelt speech, concluding with the following original and apt lines :—

"'Tis an exquisite keepsake, a beautiful present ;
And this is the chain whose bright links are to bind
Our souls in a bond, not like dew evanescent,
But like what it is, of a durable kind ;
Ay, lasting as life, for I utter no fib here,
Nor shall your kind gift from my keeping depart ;
I'll stow it, as Jack says, beneath my fifth rib here,
And there I will wear it,—next door to my heart."

His relatives were not always willing for him to go on Temperance expeditions, as they were afraid it might, as it did, injure his health, and they used to lock up his clothes to keep him back. He was a true Christian and a lover of our beloved Saviour. At one time, he was attacked by the editor of the *Preston Observer*, who actually complained before the magistrates, about some unpaid letters which he had received, and of which he accused our hero of being the author. In point-blank denial of this he wrote the following letter to the *Preston Pilot*.

" *To the Editor of the* PRESTON PILOT.

" Sir,—In the 'Notice to Correspondents' of the *Preston Observer*, dated September 9th, an 'Impudent Scamp' named Anderton is requested to keep his ' trash' at home, and not charge the editor with the postage ; and in the last week's number of the same publication, the editor threatens 'T. R. I.' of Walton le-Dale, with an appeal to the magistrates, because the said 'T. R. I.' has insulted (!) the said editor wiith three letters—each one penny. Now, Sir, my name (as you will see by the subscription hereunto affixed) *is* Anderton ; *I* was the person who originally adopted the signature of ' T. R. I.,' and I reside in Walton-le-Dale ; and, therefore, I am the mark at which these missives of the *Observer* were directed. Not being myself one of the *Observer's* 'numerous readers,' I was unaware of the calumny until directed to it by a kind friend, who wished me to reply ; but knowing that that writer was generally known to be—what O'Connell 'illigantly' terms—' a mighty big liar,' I resolved to meet him only with mute derision ; and you, Sir, would never have received this, had not this modern Maunchausen taken advantage of my silence, and accused me, publicly, of being the author of the letters complained of, to the magistrates, in the Town Hall. In order, then, to disabuse my friends and the public, allow me, Mr. Editor, through the medium of your paper, to declare that ' T. R. I.,' alias, ' that impudent scamp, Anderton, from Walton-le-Dale,' never sent, or caused to be sent, either ' trash,' letter, or article,—good, bad, or indifferent,—paid or unpaid,—to the *Preston Observer*. And permit me to add, that so long as there are two respectable newspapers printed in Preston, no composition of mine, with my good will, shall ever appear in the columns of a *Budget!* I regret, Sir—deeply regret, that sheer necessity should so 'fool me to the top of my bent,' as to compel me to write in this *Observer*-like fashion ; but how can a man touch pitch and not be defiled ? and, really, Sir, it would upset the meekness of Aaron's brother, to be handled as I have been by this scavenger of what Byron calls ' the literary lower empire,' by sweeping the very refuse of the channels of slander into that noisome, stagnant sink, the *Preston Observer* ; where *his own* lies—so much lighter than the rest—' float uppermost' like scum. But, Sir, the aforesaid sink is being rapidly dried up ; and common sense, truth, decency, public opinion, are stopping the supplies ; and when the place which knows it now shall know it no more for ever, *you*, Sir, will cease to blush for the 'fantastic pranks' of a contemporary ; and the author of (where is it ?) Columbia—the notorious ' Albion hack,' shall no longer reluctantly drag from his happy obscurity

" Your humble servant,

HENRY ANDERTON.

" Walton-le-Dale, September 27th, 1837."

After a time, business called him away from Preston to reside at Fleetwood-on-Wyre, where his spare time was very limited, and he lived a very retired life,—business, reading, and thinking, and, at very distant intervals, speaking. While living at Fleetwood, he was married to Fanny, the amiable daughter of the late Mr. Robert Snape, of

Great Eccleston, latterly of Preston, a good, honourable, and thoroughly Christian man. Mr. Anderton contributed from time to time to the *Fleetwood Chronicle* articles on passing local events and topics. After a few years' residence in Fleetwood, he was obliged to leave, on account of the failing health of Mrs. Anderton, whose frame could not stand the very strong sea-air of this, to most persons, bracing little seaport. He removed to Bury, near Manchester.

He had not the remotest talent for pushing himself forward in the world ; in fact, he did not care as some men do for riches, but truth, religion, purity, and home were the treasures he coveted. Perhaps some may be disposed to think the old spirit was dead, and that the voice which once launched forth its heavy artillery against drink was silenced in indifference ; but ah ! how much are they mistaken : the brave, noble spirit was yet alive, the voice was not indifferent ; but, in point of fact, he had scarcely any time he could call his own. He yet clung enthusiastically to the glorious principle of Total Abstinence, and his only regret was, that a blind, ignorant, and unjust world spurned it, and took in its place the viper Drink.

At the election of a member of Parliament for Bury, between the Right Hon. Frederick Peel and Lord Duncan, he wrote several capital squibs, brimful of wit and sarcasm. He was very fond of elections. Occasionally when some piece of tyranny came to his ear, or some great injustice or dishonesty came in his way, the old, glorious spirit would flash like lightning from his eyes, or escape in a few stinging words. I see him as a weary pilgrim, with brow furrowed by a thousand years of thought, toiling wearily over the few remaining steps of life's pathway, yet with the fire in the eye as of old, and the firmly-closed lip and clenched teeth of bye-gone days, looking ever and anon wistfully at the gates of the far-off city, at the peaceful bowers above, and then resuming his way, refreshed continually by the cooling fountain of God's blessing.

One day he very nearly lost his life by the falling of the Bury station, and escaped in so remarkable a manner that it has been declared almost a miracle. Had it not been for a pillar that fell over him, he would have been crushed to death. His hat was crushed completely, but he was saved alive, although the roof fell just where he stood.

Those who knew him and had to do with him think of him as a Christian English gentleman, and with feelings of great respect and deep trust. He caught a cold, which brought on his last fatal illness; the slight, worn frame made but a feeble resistance to the last enemy; eight short days only elapsed between comparative convalescence and death—time and eternity. During his very short illness he suffered patiently, and for some time very keenly. He never thought from the first that he would get better. As he drew near to the dark valley, he seemed to be full of rejoicing and praise to God for all his goodness; full of poetry, grand as if he were already with the redeemed in glory. When asked if he felt he were going to heaven, he answered, "I am there, follow me!" He kept repeating the three first verses of the 14th chapter of Revelation:—

"And I looked, and lo! a Lamb stood on the mount Zion, and with him an hundred forty and four thousand, having his Father's name written in their foreheads.

"And I heard a voice from heaven, as the voice of many waters, and as the voice of a great thunder: and I heard the voice of harpers harping with their harps:

"And they sang as it were a new song before the throne, and before the four beasts, and the elders: and no man could learn that song but the hundred and forty and four thousand which were redeemed from the earth."

Thus, amidst those who loved him, full of triumph and glory in Christ, happy in his Saviour's love, passed from this mortal, painful life the spirit of Henry Anderton into the arms of Everlasting Love.

His beloved remains were taken where the dear departed one would have wished to be laid, in the sweet, quiet, peaceful churchyard of Walton-le-dale, "and he slept with his fathers;" and there, beneath the broad blue vault of heaven, peacefully sleeping, he lies serenely awaiting the voice of the archangel. Oh! that we may all sleep thus hopefully!

Two years after his death, a few of his friends, the old Temperance advocates, including Mr. John Cassell, of London, and Mr. Joseph Livesey, of Preston, visited the spot where the departed poet was buried, and united in singing a hymn over his grave. The following is taken from *The Preston Guardian* of that date :—" The party next ascended the hill to Walton church, to see the grave where repose the remains of the late Henry Anderton, the Teetotal poet. The scene was truly affecting. Most of them had strong remembrance of his early labours. Two or three short but affecting addresses and exhortations were delivered near the grave, reminding each other of the uncertainty of life, and of the necessity of patient and persevering exertion. The party, consisting of fourteen persons, all stood on the stone at the same time." How mournful it is to think that, in spite of all the eloquence, the poetry, the argument that has been launched against the poison alcohol ; in spite of the host of souls it sends prematurely to an awful tomb ; in spite of the damning effect it has upon all classes, sexes, and ages ; we see it yet flourishing, to use the poet's words, like a " hell-planted Upas tree," running, slaying, and devastating, and—worst, most abominable of all—allowed by law, and actually fed upon by Government. Do not tell us about the spotless flag of England, about her unsullied glory! Voices from innumerable graves deny it, with bitter, inexpressible contempt. Oh! that in our own hand rested the power of removing it! Would we tolerate it, support it, live on it, pet it? No! We would crush it into innumerable atoms as we would a scorpion. God grant that it may soon be destroyed root and branch, and that our beloved England may no longer dishonour God by this abominable, filthy traffic in souls and blood. Alcohol is a poison : then why, in the name of religion and the commonest of common sense, is it tolerated?

But let us remember that Teetotalism is but a help, a forerunner to religion, and not the means of salvation. Life is short, eternity is long. *He who walks on the brink of a precipice, with closed eyes, is a madman.*

IN MEMORIAM. *

A Visit to the Grave of Henry Anderton.

(*From the " Temperance Advocate.*")

———

There is something sadly pleasing, something of melancholy sweetness, in looking upon the scenes of the lives of the great and good who have gone before us. And when the absent one has been near and dear to us, of our class, who has lived in our own time, belonged to our own circle, whose living presence and burning enthusiasm are yet fresh and green in our remembrance, the impression becomes stronger and deeper still. To see the place of his birth, the school of his youth, the river by which he played, the woods where he rambled, the battle field of his life, the spot where he sleeps in death in the quiet village churchyard, as the memory of him we loved comes over us, all this stirs within us the deepest and most sacred feelings.

One Sunday in October, we entered the churchyard of Walton-le-dale, and wending our way amongst the records of "Old Mortality," stood by the grave of Henry Anderton.

The shadows of evening were gathering. The last crimson tints of the setting sun were fading from the western horizon. Around were the spreading trees, their foliage tinted with autumn's gold. On the north stretches the wide-extended vale, through whose midst, fresh flowing from its native hills, winds the beautiful Ribble. Here and there the yellow stubble showed the reaper's track, and reminded us again that the Reaper had been here. Further yet on the rising hill stands proud old Preston, but on this holy day its busy hum is hushed ; its tall, dark chimneys pierc-

———

* The writer was considerably disappointed, on reading the somewhat barren memoirs of Anderton which are prefixed to his poems, recently published, to find not the slightest reference to his burial-place.

ing the sky ; but higher still, pointing heavenward, rises the magnificent spire of its old parish church. On the south lies the picturesque glen of the Darwen, with its wooded banks, its waterfall, and famed historic stream. In front, "beautiful for situation," stands the grand old church itself, with its venerable tower, its ivied walls, and its fine eastern window. And here, in this hallowed spot, in "God's acre," lies Henry Anderton.

Here sleeps the fair young bride, leaving a desolate home, a sad heart behind her, for she has gone to meet the Bridegroom ; the wee loved one in his narrow grave, under the little green sod, beneath the silvery birch, sweetly emblemed by the flower.

"From silken couches and beds of down,
  Through the dusky ways of the crowded town,
  By hall, and village, and moorland bleak,
  Have the angels travelled those buds to seek."

Yonder the parish priest, cut down in his bloom—dead, yet living in the memories of those who knew him and loved him ; the fragrant rose, the tender flowers, affectionately tended by loving hands, blossoming over his resting-place. Here the silent moss, upon the tombstone of a youth, lining with its velvet the very letters of his name, seems to determine that his memory shall be ever green.

Here stands the old sundial, which has told its tale to father and son for generations : they are gone, but there it stands still.

And here Henry Anderton " sleeps with his fathers."

"One place there is—beneath the burial sod,
  Where all mankind are equalized by death ;
  Another place there is—the fane of God,
  Where all are equal who draw living breath."

On a plain, flat tablet we read—

" Beneath this stone lies the body of James Anderton, who departed this life March 9th, 1836, aged 67 years. Also that of Henry Anderton, his son, who died at Bury, June 21st, 1855, aged 46 years."

Then follow that of James, his brother, and Ellen, his mother, and then—

"Be ye kind one to another."

With a brain too active for his frail frame, worn out by the struggles of a life of no ordinary toil, he died at the early age of 46 years.

No marble monument, no granite column marks the spot where this our brother rests. And he needs none. His monument is not on sculptured stone or splendid tomb, but in the hearts of those whose lives have been ennobled, and whose homes have been made happy by his earnest words and his loving sympathy. Wherever the cup has blighted the fair form of woman, and brutalized all that is noble in man ; wherever the voice of Temperance has helped a wretched one to turn from his evil way and lead "a godly, righteous, and sober life," there the name of Anderton shall be blessed.

The sweet old bells are pealing out their vesper chimes ; the sister church from the neighbouring hill, mellowed by distance, sends back the sweet refrain ; the noble organ thrills us with its swelling strain. Up the hill, by the lane, through the winding path they come,—the villagers to evening prayers. We enter. Within the sacred porch stands the massive font, and here Anderton was dedicated to God. Here he was received into the "congregation of Christ's flock." Here his Master's mark was set upon him, "in token that hereafter he should not be ashamed to confess the faith of Christ crucified, and manfully to fight under his banner against sin, the world, and the devil ; and to continue Christ's faithful soldier and servant unto his life's end." And he bore that cross. And he fought that battle. Feebly and imperfectly it is true ; sometimes through weakness, sometimes rashly, many a mistake he made ; yet right manfully he did it, right bravely he bore it, as any man amongst us.

And there before us stands the holy table. There many a weary pilgrim has been refreshed, has again renewed those promises, and received strength from God to fight under that banner and to bear that cross.

Within these noble walls, for centuries has poured forth from the "great congregation" the chant of the mighty *Te Deum*—"All the earth doth worship thee, the Everlasting Father." Here has been offered up from time immemorial the prayers of our grand old liturgy—"That it may please thee to strengthen such as do stand; and to comfort and help the weak-hearted; *and to raise up them that fall*; and finally to beat down Satan under our feet." Beneath this roof, in the olden time, have our fathers worshipped; the proud knight, the strong dalesman, the brave forester, the hardy seaman, the noble lady, the modest spinster, have knelt here together on the rush-strewn floor; their mortal bodies have now mingled with the dust around us, and we feel "it is good for us to be here."

And here still we find the living church, the youthful child of God, the aged Christian, the "holy communion." Here still the noble prayer is offered up which He taught us, "Lead us not into temptation, but deliver us from evil." The sacred page is read; the swelling chant, the noble hymn, the hearty response burst forth from the assembled worshippers. The young minister of Christ tells us the glorious evangel, "the good news of God," of Him who hath redeemed us, and who died "to save the people from their sins," and teaches us "to follow the blessed steps of His most holy life." Again rolls forth from choir and chancel, aisle and nave, the grand old evening hymn. Again we bend the knee in prayer—

"Holiest, breathe an evening blessing!"

That heavenly blessing is pronounced, "The peace of God which passeth all understanding," and we depart, with that blessing resting upon us, echoing in our hearts the prayer that it may "be amongst us and remain with us always."

We return to the grave of Anderton. And here, on this sacred spot, on this holy day, on this solemn occasion, standing by the remains of him we loved, the feeling comes over us with irresistible intensity—there is "the communion of saints." With the great and good in all ages who have felt and lived to God; with those noble Englishmen who throughout this land of ours—

"The soil where martyrs bled,
The Christian land, the free,"—

each in his own sphere and in his own way, is labouring for the physical, mental, and spiritual improvement of his fellow man; with those brave men, in every clime, under every difficulty, who are "fighting the good fight" of truth, of progress, and of God, we feel as members with them in one common bond of universal brotherhood, in the one Holy Catholic Church, and in "the household of God." We feel with them the inspiration of the same Eternal Holy Spirit, the same love to our Father—God, and to our brother—man.

But the old church clock wakes us from our dreaming. We have lingered somewhat long by the grave of Anderton, and still we love to linger there. But we have a work to do. Let us, like Anderton, learn to feel a deeper faith in God, a wider, a truer love to man. Let us recognise in the fallen one a *sister*, and in the poor drunkard a *brother*. Let us cheer the weary hour of the lone one, and drop a flower in the path of the sad one. Let us smooth the pillow of the sick one, and speak a gentle word to the erring. And let us thank God that he has placed us here, and that so he has taught us—

"Lives of great men all remind us
 We can make our lives sublime,
And departing leave behind us
 Footsteps on the sands of time.
Footsteps that perchance another,
 Sailing o'er life's dreary main,
A forlorn and shipwrecked brother,
 Seeing, may take heart again."

Walton-le-dale.   Q.

A SHORT SKETCH,

BY HIS ONLY SURVIVING SISTER.

THE late Henry Anderton, the Temperance poet, was born in the year 1808, and was a native of the once bonny village of Walton-le-dale, near Preston, Lancashire. The house in which he was born was taken down in the year 1824. At the age of three years, he was run over by a loaded cart, and was not expected to survive ; but through the skill of Dr. Sinclair, of Preston, and the careful attention of a good mother, together with the blessing of God, he eventually recovered. He attended school till the age of eighteen, and was much noticed for his droll expressions and clever intellect. My father and uncle were partners in business at Walton-le-dale, and were saddlers and harness makers. My mother also kept a shop, and sold all kinds of garden seeds and confectionery. About the time when Temperance societies first started, my father and uncle dissolved partnership, and were engaged in a lawsuit which lasted for some time. After the death of my father, we gave up the saddling business and went to live in Jordan-street, Preston, next door to my brother's friend, the late and much respected Mr. Moses Holden. My brother Henry applied for the situation of agent on the railway at Fleetwood, and through the testimonial of our friend and neighbour, Charles Swainson, Esq., the situation was given to him, although he was the one hundredth applicant. He remained in the company's service until the time of his death, which took place on the 21st of June, 1855.

We used to think that he went too much away from home after Temperance, and spoke too long. We always considered him as an invalid, through the accident before men-

tioned, and we all gave in to him being more indulged on
that account. His tenderness towards us was above proof.
I never saw anyone with such tender feelings. In 1851, he
went with my husband to the Exhibition in London. When
I asked him how he liked, he said that the Exhibition far
exceeded his expectations, but the distress he saw in the
streets of London so preyed upon his mind that he could
not enjoy it. He possessed good health generally, but was
never strong. He had so many pressing invitations to
attend Temperance meetings, that if he had attended to
them all he would never have been at home. I never saw
my brother drunk, but he has told me how he was led into
it. He had learned to dance, and, being fond of it, was led
into society which he had not been accustomed to. He
attended, for a time, an inn in the Market-place, Preston,
where there was a dancing-room, which led him very far
astray from the paths of Zion. I never let him rest until he
had given up going to the theatre. He had read Shake-
speare's plays, and was fond of seeing them acted. No sud-
den conversion took place in the case of my dear brother.
He had always a deep sense of God's great goodness to fallen
man, and great faith in the atoning sacrifice of his dear Son
our Saviour Jesus Christ. He was led by the grace of God
to serious reflection, and was at length brought back into
the blessed fold of Jesus. He grew in grace, and in the
knowledge and love of God his Saviour. We were very
much attached to each other. In the last letter which I
received from him he says : " My own dear Ellen ; to touch
her would be to touch the apple of mine eye, who first led
her Henry to Jesus. We truly 'have erred and strayed
from Thy ways like lost sheep.'" Before any of my brothers
and sisters left home, I don't think there was a more united
or happy family anywhere. No children had better parents,
and, as we grew up, we were all Sunday school teachers.
When I look back upon those happy days, it is almost, at
times, more than I can bear to think of the havoc strong
drink has made amongst us : what brilliant wit, what intelligent minds, what loving hearts, what bright, bright prospects for time and eternity have been blighted. My brother

James alludes to our once happy home in one of his poems.
He had left it for a time, when he writes :—

"Thou sweet little village of Walton-le-dale!
When I think of thee, thou never dost fail
To cause me to weep, to sigh, and repine
Because thou wert once, but now art not mine.

"On part of thy clod stands a cot so dear,
Where my parents did me and my brethren rear :
No household so happy, so loving as we ;
No family more blessed I'm sure e'er could be.

"O, for a peep through my bedchamber light,
It never doth fail to give me delight,
To take a full view o'er Bob Webster's land ;
O, how the thought does my bosom expand !

"To see the herds, lowing, as they pass along
Those banks of the Ribble : how can my tongue
Express what I feel ? and what I did then
Can't be pourtrayed by tongue or by pen.

Give my hand and my heart to my father and mother,
And do thou, for me, them with kisses smother,;
My Ann and my Henry, my Jane and my Bob,
My darling sis' Bet—they are all in my nob.

"With pangs for their welfare.
"From thy loving brother,
"JAMES ANDERTON."

On another occasion he wrote :

"Dear Ellen, 'tis Valentine time,
And thy brother is tempted to rhyme.
Dear Ellen, receive this from one
Who loves thee, although he be gone
Far, far away.
"Hypocrisy ! mark that word well !
I hope I've no occasion to tell ;
Forgive me, if I thee remind
That it runs through the limits of most of mankind,
So I'd have thee take care.
"Your loving Brother and Valentine,
"JAMES ANDERTON."

How little did he think, when writing these lines, that he would fall a victim to strong drink !

The cause of Temperance is sure to prosper. Our Heavenly Father knows everything that is done for His cause, and will, in His own good time, bless His work and His servants, and the enemies of the Lord shall be found liars. I hope that all those who have enlisted under its banner will look to the Strong for strength, and will be faithful servants in the good cause. The battle is not yet fought, but our soldiers are marching onward with a certainty of victory, "not by might, nor by power, but by my Spirit, saith the Lord of Hosts."

> " Ride on, Thou great Omnipotent ;
> On our weak efforts shine :
> Prosper the work on which we're bent,
> And make it, make it Thine !"

GRAPPENHALL COTTAGE.   E. N.

POEMS, &c.

MR. ANDERTON, when a youth, generally pleaded in rhyme, for anything that he particularly wanted ; as in the following extempore lines :—

And, after having ta'en such pains,
  Must I on pins keep sitting?
And will she keep my poor, crack'd brain
  By sad conjecture splitting !

And can a mother use me so,—
  Can she her feelings smother ?
Will she let James to Preston go,
  And keep at home the other ?

No, mother, no ! it's not thy mind ;
  Thou canst not deal thus badly ;
And thy pure heart is much too kind
  To use a brute beast sadly :

Much less treat ill thy weakly son ;
  'Twould be above digestion ;
Thou'dst rather say, " Put thy clothes on,
  And have a walk to Preston !"

This is thy very heart, I wot ;
  O may these lines impress thee !
And, whether I'm to go or not,
  May God Almighty bless thee !

On one occasion he wrote the following imaginary dialogue :—

HENRY.

Dear mother, shall I go to Preston ?
Answer me this important question.

MOTHER.

You rascal, you, pray let me know
Why you so urgent are to go !

HENRY.

I'll tell you, if you'll cease your scolding :
I want to hear old Moses Holden.

Mr. Holden was an astronomer, and was much respected
in the town of Preston. He occasionally delivered lectures
on religious subjects in Vauxhall Chapel ; and as Henry
much admired his plain and straightforward mode of speaking, he often went to hear him. Many of these lectures
were delivered on the Sunday ; but, as Mrs. Anderton did
not like her children to leave their own church, he had often
to plead hard for permission to go.

HENRY.

Mother, don't cast my spirits down,
But let me have a walk to th' town.

MOTHER.

All things are proper in their seasons :
You want to go, but what's your reasons ?

HENRY.

Nay ! do not with my feelings grapple,
But let me go to Vauxhall chapel.

Written on a Good Friday :—

This day to me could not have been worse,—
Instead of a blessing it has been a curse.
But stay ! before thou begin'st to chatter,
And endeavour to cut more short the matter :
In spite of what earth to my aim opposes,
Let me go to Preston, to hear old Moses.

On another occasion he writes :—

To-night old Moses will, in Vauxhall-road,
Show unto sinful men the way to God.
Dear mother, shall I go ?   Grant my request !
Whether I'm right or wrong you know the best.
I want to go to Vauxhall-road to-night ;
Be as it seemeth good unto your sight.

But you will, perhaps, both think and say, "Thou'rt hollow;
Thou hast some other end or aim to follow."
Believe me, mother, I have not; and so
Speak out the cheerful words, "Son, thou must go."

He appears to have been much impressed with the
preachers at Vauxhall chapel.

Away with the trash of your college-taught preaching!
    Nor prate in the hearing of me or of mine;
Let me have the truths of the Gospel, heart-reaching,
    Though blunders grammatical spring in each line.

Away with that minion of fame and of glory, —
    That man-pleasing preacher, conceited and vain!
I'd choose the poor rustic, whose plain, simple story
    Is pointing to Jesus, the Lamb that was slain.

Away, child of lucre! thou holdest a station—
    A station not far from the precincts of hell—
Who makest the work of eternal salvation
    A system of traffic, to buy and to sell.

Ye Vauxhall-road preachers, sincerely I love you;
    Your labours, I trust, will be own'd of the Lord:
For what but the love of Jehovah could move you
    To preach, without money, the life-giving word.

Whene'er from the body the Saviour shall free you,
    And raise unto glory your justified souls,
There, cloth'd in His likeness, I hope I shall see you
    Among the redeem'd while eternity rolls.

TO MR. HOLDEN, OF PRESTON, ON THE BAP-
TISM OF THE PRINCE OF WALES.

The morning dawned on which to give
    A name to Britain's heir:
To celebrate the great event,
    The good and true prepare.
And what she owes that regal house
    "Our village" can't forget;
For Walton is a loyal place,
    And glories in the debt.
Hark! through her lanes and alleys, now,
    This prayer-like shout prevails,—
"God save the Queen and Albert,
    And the Royal Prince of Wales!"

And on that day our scholars, too,
  Made up a gallant show;
With flags and banners, manfully
  They "toddled" through the snow.
Nor was good "inside plenishing"
  For their young ribs forgot;
For a cartload of buns they had,
  And coffee piping hot!
And never yet a blither crew
  On British ground was seen,
To bid a Prince right welcome,
  And to sing "God save the Queen!"

Thy aid was sought, and soon forgot
  Was all about the stars,—
How Saturn calls on Jupiter
  And Venus plays with Mars.
Discarded were the lens and tube,
  Down came thy magic glass;
And when before the children's gaze
  Thy mimic ghosts did pass,
Pure rapture filled thy kindling heart,
  With watching the surprise
Which stretch'd the youngsters' little mouths,
  And strain'd their little eyes!

We love thee, Moses Holden; for
  Old Brunswick's royal line
Could never boast a faith more true,
  A heart more warm than thine.
Respected for thy loyalty,
  As honoured in thy fame;
And in this verse thy Walton friends,
  With one consent, exclaim—
(Though Whigs may hate thee for this cause,
  And Radicals revile),
"Behold an Englishman indeed,
  In whom there is no guile!"

MOSES HOLDEN'S RECOVERY FROM SICKNESS.

In a dark and awfully stormy night,
What dreadful forebodings the traveller affright:
No light, save the lightning's lurid glare
Shooting across the sulphurous air;
Bewilder'd he falls, and yields to despair.

At this desperate crisis, as from a shroud,
The moon appears from behind a cloud ;
Her beams on the face of the traveller alight ;
His bosom is fired with hope at the sight ;
His way he resumes with unwonted delight.

Just so were we ; no rest could we find
While a stroke of affliction our preacher confin'd ;
But now he's restored, he rekindles our joys ;
The air we will rend with a thanksgiving noise,—
The heavens shall echo the sound of our voice.

The following was written on the occasion of Mr. Holden
leaving Vauxhall Chapel :—

"ICHABOD."

VAUXHALL ! thou must not hear him more ;
His labours in thy walls are o'er :
Vauxhall, the fatal die is cast,
The dreaded rubicon is past ;
No more thy fame will spread abroad,
Thy name is chang'd to "Ichabod,"
                    Thy glory is departed.

Vauxhall ! thy elders are ingrate,
Factious compounds of scorn and hate.
I saw them at the lovefeast, while
They should have pray'd, with fiendish smile,
They scowl'd upon the man of God :
These men have named thee "Ichabod."
                    Thy glory is departed.

Vauxhall ! thou hast thy preacher lost—
Of thee the glory and the boast ;
Chas'd by the ingratitude of those
Who, seeming friends, were mortal foes.
Forgive, convert them, gracious God !
They've nam'd Thy temple "Ichabod,"—
                    Thy glory is departed.

He was very fond of hearing good singing ; and, as the
choir at Walton-le-dale church was, at this time, very
poor, he often went to Trinity Church, Preston. On one
occasion, when a friend said, " Henry, don't go to Trinity
Church," he replied :—

If you will furnish me with wings,
I will not go where Arkwright sings,
But fly to some far distant sphere
Where his voice cannot reach my ear.

But, while that temple is so nigh,
Where sounds that dulcet minstrelsy,
You must not think that my torn heart
Will with that sweet enjoyment part.

He was very dutiful and affectionate to his parents, and was especially fond of his mother. On her return from a visit to Manchester, in October, 1827, he wrote :—

When morning sun appeareth
    Above the boundless sea;
When through the earth he steereth,
                I'll think on thee.

When the vast, hot, mid-day sun
    Doth pour his beams on me,
When following my vocation,
                I'll think on thee.

When evening sun descendeth,
    And night begins to be,
In dreams, while he ascendeth,
                I'll think on thee.

While we're on earth sojourning,
    While life remains in me ;
At evening, noon, and morning,
                I'll think on thee.

My love shall still grow stronger :
    Amen! so let it be!
When time shall be no longer,
                I'll think on thee.

At this period of his life, he was much beloved by a large circle of friends ; and, as he was of a lively disposition, his company was much sought after. He was often asked to write poetry, especially by his lady friends, to whom he was much attached.

SONG.

Tune—" My Girl, my Friend, and Pitcher."

YE who are fond of worldly wealth,
    Go, take your fill in hoarding treasure;
Ye sots, go wallow still in filth,
    And guzzle rum, and call it pleasure :
Go, take your fill of such like bliss ;
    But, howsoever sweet you find them,
Ye simpletons, beware of this—
    They always leave a sting behind them.

I'd choose on Sabbath eve to walk
    Down Fishergate and parts adjacent ;
And with my dear, engage in talk,
    So very sweet, so very pleasant.
May we such happiness as this
    Enjoy, in spite of wind and weather ;
And, sealing all with one fond kiss,
    We'll travel on through life together.

AH! WOE IS ME.

    AH ! woe is me ;
For my heart is prone to rove :
    As many pretty girls I see—
As many pretty girls I love.

    Ye fair ones ! why
Were ye so beautiful created ?
    I cannot tell ; but such as I
Unceasingly to love are fated.

    I wonder how
Some can, unmov'd, see beauty's eyes :
    They have not hearts like mine, I trow
They cannot love in anywise.

    Beauty can bend
My spirits into any fashion ;
    And I shall never, never mend,—
For every lass lights a new passion.

    Then, woe is me !
For my heart is so prone to rove :
    As many pretty girls I see—
As many pretty girls I love.

TO MISS ———.

I'LL lock thee, dearest, in my heart,
And thou shalt be my better part;
I'll cling to thee; and, as the dove
May die, but cannot change his love,
So shall my soul devoted be
To thee, dear girl, and none but thee.

I cannot, as the changeful do,
Make a long love speech when I woo;
I cannot, like a trifler, show
More than I feel; but this I know—
Though greater beauties I may see,
My heart desireth none but thee.

More ruby lips might pout to bless
Mine, with their ripe voluptuousness;
And eyes more flashing may conspire
To turn away my heart's desire;
Yet, from such elves secure and free,
I'll bend, dear girl, to none but thee.

Time may roll on, as it hath roll'd,
And change the scenes we now behold;
Yet, as the needle to the pole   ·
Points evermore, so shall my soul
Direct her gaze, through life's rough sea,
And find a home in none but thee.

Then cheer thee, though awhile we part;
Strange eyes shall not estrange my heart;
Though farewell tears thy cheeks bedew,
Believe me, love, as thou art true;
And think that, sever'd though we be,
My spirit yearns for none but thee.

TO BETSY METCALF AND ANNE DAY.

ON Saturday evening, I bade you good night,
With sad-looking face, and a heart not more light:
For who, after gazing at angels like you,
Could coldly and carelessly bid you adieu?

But do not imagine that Henry "took pet,"
And left you, the smiles of some fairer to get:
By all that is lovely, and charming, and fair,—
If you have no beauty, there is none elsewhere!

c 3

TO MY HEART,

ON LOOKING AT MISS B. METCALFE.

Awake, awake, my heart! and though
  Thy grief has chok'd the seeds of joy,—
Away with pain! away with woe!
  Let lighter things thy thoughts employ.

Cheer up, cheer up, my heart! for Heaven
  In pity looks on thy distress ;
And, in return for pain, has given
  A hope, thy future days to bless.

Smile on, smile on, my heart! for thou
  Hast such a girl thine eyes before,
That, gazing on her beauteous brow,
  Thou canst not wish or sigh for more!

SONG.

Yes, distance makes the love we bear
  Our cherished friends increase ;
It often calls the heart-sent tear
  To flow and rarely cease.

And thus, dear girl, does my sad soul
  Bow to respond to thine :
Oh! do thy gentle musings roll
  In unison with mine?

My heart of hearts, in its least strained
  And least impure recess—
There, friend, hast thou for ever reign'd,
  In growing loveliness !

And oft, amid the cares of life—
  Which often ruffle me—
With which our pilgrimage is rife,
  I'll breathe a prayer for thee.

Oh! does thy mental vision swim
  With hours so sweet, but gone?
And dost thou ever think of him
  Who's grieving all alone?

He was thy friend—he still is so ;
  This simple song will tell
How pure and changeless is the glow
  That warms his heart.—Farewell!

TO MARY.

My Mary! yet a little while, and I must go from thee ;
And deep will be the parting sigh that hour will draw from me.
Not often, in this heartless world, is it my hap to while
My carking cares away, with one who can so sweetly smile.

Yes, when that bitter hour shall come, I shall not so regret
Thy beauty as thy kind heart, which dares me to forget.
Would that thy heart was mine : for then, wherever I might
    rove,
Our joined souls might rest, in all the confidence of love.

'Tis sweet to have a friend indeed, in whom we may confide ;
One in whose blest companionship away my life might glide:
But sweeter far to win a soul, with pure affection rife,
In gladness, and in sorrow, too, the angel of my life.

And go I must; yet, ere I go, oh! let me call my own
    * * * and so sweet to hear, thy voice's silver tone :
Oh! let thy short and fond response with exultation swell
My trembling, scarcely hoping heart, before I breathe—
    " Farewell !"

TO MARY.

"I wish I was in heaven !"—Well, go !
    And leave my stricken soul to vent
To friendless ears her tale of woe
    And lonely discontent.

Go ! pass the bounds that separate
    This troublous speck from that blest shore,
Where mortal love shall agitate
    Thy virgin soul no more.

Go ! if the pictured scenes we drew
    Of what our wedded life should be—
If all's forgot, thy track pursue,
    Nor heed my misery.

Go ! reckless of my tears and sighs ;
    Go ! though thy absence is my hell ;
Go ! if thou'rt ready, to yon skies,
    And I will gasp " farewell !"

I ne'er was happy, at the best ;
    And what brief gleams of joy are mine
Were garner'd in a faithful breast ;
    And whose that breast but thine ?

Like a nail fast in a sure place
  Am I to thee ; and didst thou not
Vow with me to run life's brief race,
  And soothe my thorny lot ?

Oh ! by that well-remember'd vow,
  By thy given heart—a blessed boon,—
Why was it given ?   And why wilt thou
  Take back thy gift so soon ?

I bargained with thee, love for love,
  And paid mine down—warm, gushing, fond :
Discharge the debt which thus I prove,
  For " I will have my bond !"

" I wish I was in heaven," thou sayest :
  Why, that's my earnest prayer ; and when
This heart account is paid, thou mayest ;
  But stir not hence till then.

Pay what thou owest ; and, when all's right,
  And mine acquittance sets thee free,
Then, Mary, wing thy upward flight,
  And I will fly with thee.

———

TO MARY.

I NEVER must reveal to thee
What is the thorn which pierces me.
If I expose my heart, the view
Would wound thy tender feelings too ;
And, though it might my spirit ease
And make her painful throbbings cease,
Yet, sooner than afflict my friend,
I'll bear my sorrows to the end.

Thy importunity give o'er,
And of my fate enquire no more.
At that eventful, awful day,
When God will take the veil away,
Then, my dear Mary, shalt thou know
That I have had my share of woe ;
But not *till* then my woe-worn heart
Will with her well-kept secret part.

TO POLL.

I'VE one request, sincere, yet droll,
To make to thee, my pretty Poll—
In after times, if it should be
That thou should'st ever think of me,
Thy sweet harp from the willow take,
And sing this song for Henry's sake. :—

Long, but in vain, I've sought for rest,
But I am restless still ;
There is a void within my heart,
Which one alone can fill :
Dear girl ! if free to choose thou art,
As for thy love I pine,
Take, claim, and keep my wayward heart,
But give, oh ! give me thine.

Through the world's garden, like a bee,
I've hunted far and wide,
A being that would cling to me,
When all were cold beside :
Thy heart, my Mary, is the bower
To which I could repair,
Content to linger from this hour,
In blessed bondage there.

My love is fixed as it appears,
As durable as deep ;
Believe me, girl, and let these tears
Lull thy dark doubts to sleep.
He, who from nothing form'd this ball,
Knows that I do not lie ;
Thou art my earthly "all in all,"
And shall be till I die.

How the proud world would envy me,
The bliss it would afford
To hear thee whisper—" let it be
According to thy word."
Now, Mary, now the grace impart,
Around my stem entwine ;
" I give thee all I can"—my heart ;
Then, give, oh ! give me thine.

TO ————.

If thou hast faults, then it is true
　　That "Love is blind ;" for I can see
Nothing to give me cause to rue
　　For having fixed my love on thee.

Thy looks speak for thee, that thou art
　　As void of guile as thou art fair :
I've prov'd thee so,—come to my heart !
　　And "reign without a rival" there.

TO MISS METCALF.

Thy face has no dimple, dear Betsy, but thou
Hast two lovely eyes shining under thy brow ;
And well may the dimple be slighted by thee,
For thou art as perfect as mortal may be.

So perfect, dear Betsy, that had I at hand,
To choose from, the choicest of every land ;
And were it thy fortune the foremost to try,
Dang it, if my feelings would let thee pass by !

TO MISS MACHRAY.

Just look at my Peri ! How sweet she appears,—
With her graceful, fair ringlets encircling her ears !
But where is the shine of her sparklers ? Some ill
Has dimm'd them, and made them with sorrow-drops fill.

What ails thee, my Peri ? It may be the thought
Of Marg'ret's mishap has this languishing brought ;
Or, thou art regretting that Death could not spare
A sister so loving, so youthful, and fair.

Oh ! weep not, my Peri ! for she is exempt
From sorrow, and shame, and her traitor's contempt.
Let the days of thy mourning for Marg'ret be o'er ;
For she is where her weakness condemns her no more.

My sorrowing Peri ! make Jesus thy friend ;
And, when this frail state of existence shall end,
Immortal and happy, in mansions above,
You shall see her again, and establish your love.

TO MISS BETSY METCALF.

I LOOK'D, and look'd, and look'd again,
To find some fault with you—in vain !
Thou wert before my eyes confest,
A soul with winning sweetness blest.

Those ornaments, which I before
Had so despised, I scorn no more :
Thy beads so gracefully bedeck
The snowy whiteness of thy neck ;

Those droppers, which I scoff'd at once,
Forc'd me that judgment to renounce ;
Because they give a careless grace
To thy sweet, ever-smiling face.

Dear Betsy ! thus I felt when I
First met the glances of thy eye ;
And thus can every beauty move
So easily my heart to love.

" A general lover !" you will say :
Well, you may have it your own way ;
I'm such a love-begotten elf,
I really can't defend myself.

What is the " general beau's" desire ?
What makes him seem all smiles and fire ?
What is the object he's pursuing ?—
To pride himself in your undoing !

But, my dear Betsy, you will not
Cast on my name so foul a blot :
You know, as well as I can tell,
I love you all, and wish you wel'.

Betsy, I have some papers here :
Will you accept of them, my dear,—
From one who is, and means to be,
The friend of woman, and of thee ?

TO THE SAME.

THE natural bent of my spirit is gloomy,
But recklessness chases reflection away ;
And, though in the winter of life it may doom me
To sorrow and pain, I will smile while I may.

While woman enlivens my heart with her glances,
And ev'rything round me is griefless and gay,
Shall sadness oppress me ? No! though it enhances
My sorrow and pain, I will smile while I may.

AN ASSIGNATION.

Oh! leave me, oh! leave me, dear Ellen, alone;
The night is approaching, and I must be gone;
And, while thou art ling'ring, I cannot but stay:
Then leave me, oh! leave me, and let me away.

Oh! weep not, oh! weep not, at parting with me;
Not long will thy lover be absent from thee:
And, if thou wouldst lighten a sorrowing heart,
Oh! weep not, oh! weep not, but let me depart.

Smile on me, smile on me! and when thou shalt see
The next Sabbath dawn,—oh! be looking for me;
And I will be there, love, to feast on the sight:
Smile on me, smile on me! and bid me "Good night!"

TO MISS E. BESWICK.

Another fleeting year has flown,
    But Time is foil'd in the endeavour
To make thee old; for he must own
    That thou art beautiful as ever!

He thought to spoil thy pretty face,
    But little evil he has done thee;
So fair art thou, that all my days
    I could, delighted, gaze upon thee.

And sure thy guardian angel would
    Be punish'd for a breach of duty,—
And he'd deserve it—if he should
    Let that youth-killer mar thy beauty.

But well thy bright protector knows
    That he might roam from town to city,
Ere he could find thy match, because
    Few are so exquisitely pretty.

And it would be a loss to him,—
    For angels love to look on mortals;
And oftentimes their eyes wax dim,
    With eyeing them through heav'n-bright portals.

Then rest thee, Betsy, while there is
    A loving thing of light to guard thee;
Enjoy thy share of earthly bliss,
    Till everlasting joys reward thee.

TO MISS B. METCALF.

This life is productive of beautiful things,
　Whose charms are sufficient to move me ;
But none have such magic as Bess, when she sings
　" Oh ! why hast thou taught me to love thee ?"

Some may with grimaces our senses impress,
　But none—round, beneath, or above me—
Can sing so expressively tender as Bess,
　" Oh ! why hast thou taught me to love thee ?"

I could throw (if I had it) a crown at her feet ;
　Though the world for the act might reprove me :
She's so pretty, and warbles so meltingly sweet,
　" Oh ! why hast thou taught me to love thee ?"

TO THE SAME.

Once, we could feast our eyes upon
Thy eyes ; but all their light is gone ;
The light they shed has vanish'd now,
And left a cloud upon thy brow.

Dear Betsy, wilt thou let me know
What can depress thy spirit so ?
And I will do what in me lies
To dry thy tears and quell thy sighs.

Say, Betsy, art thou doom'd to prove
The pains of unreturned love ?
Or art thou grieving for a friend
Untimely hastening to her end ?

Thou canst not help it—sigh no more,
But let those looks of woe be o'er ;
Cheer up ! and let thy eyes express
Thy spirit's wonted liveliness.

TO THE SAME.

There was a time when moments were
　Too long to be away from thee ;
And thou wast warm, and soft, and fair,
　And dearer than the world to me.

Yet *now*—we might have never met,
　So passing cold our glances grow :
Perchance thou wishest to forget
　The heart that prized thy friendship so.

But I forget. Thy lover droops,
  And that may mar thy buoyant trim ;
And all thy thoughts, and all thy hopes,
  Are fix'd unceasingly on him.

Dear Betsy, if 'tis so, forgive !
  'Twas not my meaning to offend :
Thy coldness forc'd me to believe
  That I had tir'd my early friend.

TO THE SAME.

I share in thy sorrows, so hand me the cup,
And gladly I'll quaff the dark sediment up ;
For, balefully rank as the potion may be,
Yet wormwood is sweet when partaken with thee.

So much for thy sorrow ;—but this is not all,
For anger has blended thy honey with gall ;
And beauty's sweet blandishments cannot control
The wrath which embodies itself in that scowl.

I share in thy anger ; and fiercely return,
With merciless hatred, thy enemy's scorn :
For, though it is sinful in " worms of the dust,"
Yet God taketh vengeance ; and is God unjust ?

Oh ! cursed be they who engender'd the clouds
Whose tangible darkness thy loveliness shrouds ;
For richly they wrought for the reprobates' place,
Who shaded with sadness thy beautiful face.

BETSY.

Her quiet is fled ; for the lover in whom
  She trusted is bound to another :
Not long will her body be kept from the tomb ;
  For nothing but dying can smother
The freezing remembrance of suff'ring and wrong,
  From him unto whom she was plighted—
Who left the poor girl, after being so long
  In the hearts of each other united.

Her visions of pleasure are o'er ; and her eyes—
  So languid, and dim, and dejected—
Convince us that Betsy is seeking the skies,
  Where her presence is hourly expected.
Her cup of affliction is fill'd to the brim,
  And angels are come to translate her
From mortals and sorrow, to glory and Him
  Who purchased the joys that await her.

ART THOU NOT DEAR?

ART thou not dear unto my heart?
 Oh! search that heart and see;
And from my bosom tear the part
 That beats not true to thee.

Yes, to my bosom thou art dear,
 More dear than tongue can tell;
And, if a fault is cherish'd there,—
 'Tis loving thee too well.

My breast did once a heart contain;
Ah! now no heart does there remain:
Resign'd, I must thy loss endure—
You, you alone, can give the cure.

TO MISS ANN H——.

WHEN I am sad, I fly to thee,
 To lull my heart to rest;
For, in thy presence, none can be
 With weariness opprest.
Yes, thou the angel art who frees
 My spirit from a train
Of heavy thoughts, and makes them cease
 To banquet on my brain.

Thy sprightliness disperses all
 The sorrow, pain, and care
Which long have held my heart in thrall,
 And reign'd supremely there.
Peace with thee, Ann! and if there be
 A God of perfect love,
He will reward thy love to me
 With happiness above.

THAT HOUR! THAT HOUR!

THAT hour! that hour can I forget,
 When on the Ribble's banks we stray'd;
Oh! no; too deep its power is set
 In fond remembrance e'er to fade.

O'er Ribble's vale, so fair and broad,
 The silvery moonbeams mildly glisten'd;
The night-bird's song melodious flow'd,
 And earth and heav'n in silence listen'd.

That lovely scene, at that still hour,
　E'en from a child, was dear to me;
But O! I ne'er felt half its power,
　Until that hour I spent with thee.

And, since that hour, I've stroll'd again,
　At moonlight hour, midst that bright scene;
But turn'd from all its beauties then,
　And fondly thought on what had been.

Oh! think not I can e'er forget
　That hour when we together stray'd;
No; in my heart its power is set
　Too deep—ah! *much* too deep to fade.

THE ROSE IS WITHERED.

How little he knows Rose's heart, who could deem
　It was careless, or fickle, or cold!
Had he lov'd, he had seen, in her eye's quiv'ring beam,
　A tale that her lips never told.

He had seen—in her joy, in her silent distress,
　In her look of confusion—her heart,
When she met him: and oh! in her hand's ling'ring press,
　What she felt, when she felt they must part.

If she ever said love was a trifle, a jest;
　If she smiled at the dupes who could feel;
She had cause;—but, thank Heaven, that cause was unjust:
　'Twas to hide what she dared not reveal.

In the hours when her thoughts seem'd to wander away,
　In a dance of delight, there was pain
In her bosom, that seem'd to the laughter to say,
　She should never be happy again.

She had dream'd such deep dreams of the hours that were yet
　To lead her through life by your side;
But the roses are wither'd, and she must forget
　By whose coldness 'twas done—they have died.

TO MARY.

Mary, I love thy sparkling eye;
　I love thy gently-swelling breast:
How oft they've caused me to sigh,
　And wish that I with thee was blest!
Come, Mary, come, no more depart;
　But dwell for ever in my heart.

Mary, I love those locks of thine,
  Which negligently round thee stray ;
How have they pierc'd this heart of mine !
  In sighs it wears itself away.
Come, Mary, come, no more depart ;
  But dwell for ever in my heart.

Come, Mary, come, and condescend
  From my poor heart no more to rove ;
Come, and be something more than friend,
  And let us live a life of love.
Come, Mary, come, no more depart ;
  But dwell for ever in my heart.

TO FANNY.

(Afterwards Mrs. Anderton.)

" ACTIONS speak louder far than words :"
How sweet a hope this truth affords !
To doubt thee now would be unjust ;
Thy whisper'd tenderness I'll trust ;
Thy actions shall my surety be
That, as I love, thou lovest me.

Thy father kind, with anguish torn,
Will grieve to lose his youngest born ;
An honest sigh will Rachel heave,
When thou shalt take thy lifelong leave ;
And sad the moment when ye part
Will press on Lydia's gentle heart.

"And shall I make this sacrifice ?
For 'home, sweet home,' I fondly prize ;
And grief will wring my heart to hear
The last farewell of friends so dear :
Yet I can freely all resign,
To have thee here, and call thee mine."

Yes, Fanny, we must all forsake,
But sweeter, stronger ties we'll make ;
And here, upon the ocean's breast,
We build our temporary nest,
And to the heartless worldling prove
How blest are they who truly love.

Yet think not, dearest, to attain
A lot, on earth, exempt from pain ;
Sin hath so marr'd our prospects fair,
That pain and pleasure, joy and care,
Are mingled for us—since the Fall ;
But Love will make amends for all.

And if the God of grace, the while,
Should bless our union with His smile,
Nor choicer favour shall we need,
Till from this narrow prison freed ;
When to our native home we soar,
To live and love for evermore.

"LOOK BEFORE YOU LEAP;"

OR,

TOM AND CECILY : A TALE.

Now, Henry, make thy windpipe clear,
And sing aloud that all may hear ;
Like Stentor, cry, and make folks wonder
By shouting in a voice like thunder.

Nay, pr'ythee stop, for my mild muse
A different way to this would choose;
Blown by a mild and steady gale,
She tells her simple, artless tale.

One night I went down "Cinder Pad,"
When lo ! I saw a farmer's lad ;
With equal steps he trudg'd along,
And sung this sweet, nocturnal song—

"I am a merry, brisk young lad,
And I'm in love quite mellow;
My spirits high, but never sad,—
A hearty, jovial fellow.

There's ne'er a lass that I have seen
But loves a jolly farmer ;
And if just now I'd England's Queen,
I'm sure I could quite charm her.

And now I'll have a bit of sport ;
Away with farm and tillage ;
For I this very week will court
With every lass i'th village.

I like a smacking hearty kiss,
On lips not so soon yielding.
Egad! egad! yonder there's Cis,
Who lives with Mr. Fielden.

Yes! Yes! it's her, it is no joke;
It's her, depend upon it:
Look at the scarlet on her cloak,
And yonder's her black bonnet.

To her I'll run, and oh! her lips
I'll press and squeeze them neatly;
I'll have, by numberless of sips,
My fill of love completely."

He finished, and away he ran:
Thought I, "egad! I'll watch the man,"
I followed close, and in a crack
I heard him give a hearty smack.

Just like one whose blood had been suck'd,—
Just like one who was ill bemuck'd;—
Like one whose boastings all were levell'd;—
Like one, also, sadly bedevil'd:—
The youth slunk back, and with slow pace
Returned with marks of sad disgrace.

Oh, Tommy Hacking, was it Cis
Thou gavest such a hearty kiss?
And did thy charming Cecily slight thee,
And 'stead of kissing did she bite thee?
And did that bite, Tom, make thee cry,
And cause thee from thy heart to sigh?

"No, biting, no! biting be blam'd;
I was most damnably asham'd—
Asham'd, I say, and am so still:
It was not Cis,—'twas "*Pedder's Will.*"

Young men, and maids, here ends my song,
I hope I've not kept you too long;
Young men, and maids, my council keep,
And always "look before you leap."

Sometimes, when at home, he would write a line or two
for his brother or sister, on a slip of paper, and hand it to
them unexpectedly. To his sister Ellen he wrote:—

Temptations now are in thy way,
To lead thy youthful steps astray;
Satan is using all his might
To lead thy heart from what is right.

And at another time :—

> I love thee, dearly, sister Nell,
> As dear as heart and tongue can tell,
> I love thee, Ellen, as a brother
> And sister should love one another.

TO MY SISTER ELLEN.

EIGHTEEN years have rolled away,
Sister Ellen, since that day,
When the light of day did rise
First upon thy little eyes.

No more, Henry, James, and you,
With Ann, will wander up Church brow,
By the church up Cuerdale-lane,
A picking flowers, and back again.

Childhood's past, and all its deeds ;
Youth, the prime of life, succeeds ;
Autumn will come on apace,
And Winter, with his meagre face ;—
Each will come, with errless dart,
And wing it hissing through thy heart.

O ! my dear sister Ellen,
Think not earth a lasting dwelling ;
Henry wishes that you may
Find acceptance, in that day
When the Lord the Judge shall come,
And fix on all their final doom.

TO MY SISTER JANE.

My dear sister Jane,
  A little I'll indite,
And now take up my pen,
  A verse or two to write.
I think the subject of my lay,
Dear sister, shall be thy birthday.

How swiftly flies each year !
  They roll on like a flood ;
Each cries aloud, " Prepare,
  Prepare to meet thy God !
Though thou be'st young, yet thou mayst see
That thousands die as young as thee."

May each succeeding year
Bring some new happiness!
When the last foe draws near,
May'st thou depart in peace;
Then, with the wings of seraphs, fly,
To spend eternity on high!

ON MY OWN BIRTHDAY,

DEC. 3RD, 1828.

THE dreary month, December, now appears,
Which makes my sum of days full twenty years.
Time imperceptibly our moments steals—
How swiftly fly his noiseless wheels!
And, as he flies, to us he cries, " O man!
Thy days on earth are dwindled to a span!"

While I am spared unto the present day,
How many younger have been call'd away;
How many this short year have found their tomb,
And sleep now in the dread, sepulchral gloom;
While I'm upheld by that Almighty power
Who watches, guards, and keeps me every hour.

'Tis but the thread of life—the slender thread—
That keeps me from the silent, sleeping dead;
Life's not at my command, or in my power—
My time appointed may be any hour:
Learn, then, my soul, this moment to be wise;
Haste to secure a mansion in the skies.

Mortal, awake! the day will soon appear
When thou must stand before the bar severe:
While sinners then are fill'd with dire dismay,
May'st thou, with all the ransom'd, wing thy way,
And soar aloft, above the fiery void,
And sing of man redeem'd and Death destroy'd.

Once, when in a plaintive mood, while walking in Walton
churchyard, which he often did, he composed the following:

Walton-le-dale! thou place to me most dear;
Thou little speck on this terrestrial sphere!
Walton-le-dale! thou place that gave me birth;
To me the dearest spot in all the earth.
Can I forget thee, Walton? Not till when
I cease to live among the sons of men.

D

I went to the churchyard, to view each tomb
I cast my silent eyes athwart the gloom ;
I said nought ; but, methought, I heard a sound
Say "Thy forefathers sleep beneath this ground !"
Can I forget thee, Walton ? Sooner must
This mortal body mix with kindred dust.

Such things as these my frenzied fancy fill :
But view yon rural church upon the hill ;
The parsonage, the river Ribble, too,
Are scenes which burst upon and fix my view.
Can I forget thee, Walton ? The fierce dart
Of death as soon shall quiver in my heart.

But turn and view yon little, whitewash'd cot ;
To me this is a most endearing spot :
Here I do live ; I've spent my whole life there—
Reason sufficient why it is so dear.
Can I forget thee, Walton ? Sooner will
The glorious sun its office cease to fill.

Walton, I love thee, as my native place,
With such a love as time cannot erase !
Walton, I love to see thy church and steeple ;
I love thy all—save thy queer, dirty people !
Walton ! though they may cause me to regret thee,
I never, never, never can forget thee!

ON SEEING A HEAP OF MORTAL REMAINS IN WALTON CHURCHYARD.

THE sun's last ray had fled the western mountains,
And Cynthia sent on us her softer light.
The village din was dying on the ear ;
'Twas in that calm and solemn hour most fitted
For lonely meditation. I was taking
A solitary ramble round the church.
I saw that night what I shall ne'er forget—
A thrill of horror as I look'd ran through me :
For, plac'd against the tower, met my view
An undistinguish'd mass of human bones.
"Alas ! alas !" cried I. " and were these once,
Like my flesh now, abodes for deathless spirits ?"
These words were scarcely utter'd, when I heard,
Or thought I heard, a melancholy voice.
An overwhelming fear o'ertook me, when
That awful voice address'd these words to me :—

" Being cloth'd with mortal flesh,
We for life look'd fair and fresh ;
But the King of Terrors came—
Death is that destroyer's name ;
He, by one resistless stroke,
Our life's brittle thread has broke.
O, repent ! for just as we
Thou thyself must shortly be."

"And must," thought I, " these lie for ever here—
A heap of mouldering and loathsome relics ?"
To which that deathlike murmur of a voice,
Responsive to my question, thus replied :—

" Son of mortals, we must not
In the grave for ever rot.
Though our several limbs are driven,
Scatter'd by the winds of heaven,
Yet, when the last trump shall sound,
Then our bodies will be found,
Incorruptible, to meet
Christ before His judgment seat.
Son of mortals, go thy way ;
    Let this thy thoughts employ—
    Eternal grief or joy
Depends upon thy spending life's precarious day."

POLICITAL PIECES.

M R. ANDERTON was at one time a member of a political union in Preston, which held its meetings at public-houses. Seeing much drunkenness resulting from this source, he endeavoured to do away with the custom of "drinking for the good of the house," by proposing payment for the use of the room. The following are the political pieces which he composed :—

THE MARCH OF MIND.

THE march of mind will level all
  That infamous partition,
Which severs, like a mighty wall,
  Plebeian and Patrician!
And *pride* of "blood," and *pride* of "birth,"
  Those "glories" of the *well*-born,
May take a pilgrimage from earth—
  To hell—for pride is hell-born!

Pull off your glittering coronets!
  The times are rather funny ;
And he is "scant o' grace" who frets,
  Because they're not *all* sunny.
Ye perch too high! the people sue
  For Title-resignation ;
Comply, and 'twill enable you
  To work out your salvation!

A little while—ye *might* have worn
  Your gay armorial trappings ;
Had your imperious "caste" forborne—
  Their tyrannous kidnappings.
But ye have slighted all our prayers,
  So ruin shall befal you ;
And, maugre your majestic (!) airs,
  The "swinish herd" shall maul you!

"KINGS ARE BUT MEN."

The Bible.

BRITONS! equip you for the war !
  The Constitution's rotten ;
Let not your pride and duty jar ;
  Be " Loyalty" forgotten ;
For what allegiance is due
To those, who starve and fetter you !

Are ye not men ? and what are they ?
  They might be superhuman :
Look at them ! they are nought but clay !
  Rise ! and let every true man
Shew to " the higher powers that be,"
The freedom of equality.

Tell them your vassalage is o'er ;
  Demand a retribution ;
Threaten that bulwark of their power,—
  " Our glorious Constitution !"
Point them to France, whose sons o'erthrew
Their tyrants, " and made all things new."

And if they " turn their ears away,"
  Act like determin'd freemen ;
Deprive these Molochs of their sway,
  And prove that you can be men !
Compel their godships to confess—
Their more than common helplessness.

"RENDER UNTO CÆSAR THE THINGS THAT ARE CÆSAR'S."

I GRANT it is right to give Cæsar his dues ;
But why does our " Cæsar" the tribute refuse?
We've promis'd to pay him ; but Cæsar looks sore,
And hopes we shall mention " the tribute" no more.

He treats us like dogs ; and there's no other way
This portion of crown-levied tribute to pay,
But leaping the parson-dug reverence gulf,
And saving the sheep by attacking the wolf.

He drives us like slaves ! and we wrathfully burn
To yield our oppressor a handsome return ;
But England is known to be frightfully slack
In owning her debts, and in paying them back.

He lightens our purses, as though we were blind ;
But Cæsar shall never want tribute in kind :
From royalty's cock-loft we'll tumble him down,
And lighten his noddle by taking the c——n.

Oh ! if this won't silence the voice of a thing
Which tyranny's servitors christen " the K——g,"
We'll tell him his "order" is widely abhorr'd,
And prove the assertion by "logic or sword."

A REPUBLICAN SONG.

Tune—" The King of the Cannibal Islands."

Oh ! cast such nicknames overboard
As Earl or Marquis, Duke or Lord ;
For we are sadly overstor'd,
  For a title-abolishing nation.
What can a free republic do
With such a domineering crew ?
For they can hatch no good unto
  A title-abolishing nation.

Chorus.—Then cast such nicknames overboard,
    As Earl or Marquis, Duke or Lord ;
    For we are sadly overstor'd,
      For a title-abolishing nation.

What have they done for you, my friends,
But brought you to your latter ends ?
Then, seize the hour that fortune sends
  To a title-abolishing nation.
America has smooth'd the way,
And Frenchmen wonder at our stay ;
Awake ! the friends of freedom say,
  To a title-abolishing nation.

Chorus.—Then cast, &c.

Oh, Liberty ! arise ! awake !
Make every towering earth-worm quake,
And their eternal farewell take
  Of a title-abolishing nation ;
Bid every true-born Briton see
The loveliness of thine and thee :
So shall enslav'd Britannia be
  A title-abolishing nation.

Chorus.—And cast such nicknames overboard,
    As Earl or Marquis, Duke or Lord ;
    For we are sadly overstor'd,
      For a title-abolishing nation.

"THE POWERS THAT BE."

Some men, lest interest be hurt,
The Scriptures fearfully pervert ;
And their atrocities gild o'er,
Beneath, above, behind, before,
With Moses, prophecies, and psalms,
Unhurt with *conscientious* qualms !

This glaring truth before our eyes
Example daily verifies ;
For, when a Briton strives in vain
To snap his fellows' galling chain,
He on the rebel list appears,
And ever and anon his ears
Are stunn'd with, " Disaffected clod,
How dare you vex that type of God,
Our gracious King ? Did not Saint Paul,
The most unyielding saint of all,
Admonish and exhort that we
Be subject to the powers that be,—
For crowns and thrones and powers are given,
To none but those ordained of heaven !"

Such is the Scripture-twisting guise
Which raises dust in people's eyes ;—
But did the saint, whose words they use,
Bend to the unbelieving Jews ?
Did he, afraid of losing life,
Give up the world-o'ercoming strife ;—
No, at his risen God's command,
He preach'd the cross in every land,
He spurn'd the tyrant Nero's power,
In persecution's blackest hour ;
And, in defence of truth, laid down
His life, and gain'd the martyr's crown.

In Britain's annals, there's a man
Poison'd by every blast of fame,
And made by constitution loons
The subject of their flash lampoons;
While our be-deafen'd sounders ring
With praises of the martyr-king.
But men of judgment will extol
The lawless deeds of poor Old Noll ;—
Yes, though it was his chiefest care
To floor the reigning powers that were ;
Yes, though the hero never shrunk
Till Charles's head forsook his trunk ;—
Yet, they who make the least pretence
To honesty or common sense,

Will justify the " Roundhead stir,"
And their unflinching chief prefer
To him, who, for a little breath,
Doom'd his devoted friend to death,—
And think Charles only got his due,
When robb'd of crown and noddle too !

Ye truth-perverters, view the shores
Beyond where the Atlantic roars,
The sons whereof, untam'd and free,
Breathe the pure air of liberty !
Yet they awhile, to bondage broke,
Endur'd Britannia's galling yoke,
Till Washington the Good arose,
And rid his country of her foes.
He fought against the powers that were ;
But he does not exist who dare
The hero of the West defame,
Or brand him with a traitor's name.

Hurrah for France ! who would not raise
For her brave sons the meed of praise ?
Who, reckless of the powers that be,
At once determin'd to be free ;
And, to the joy of most beholders,
Toss'd the incumbrance from her shoulders ;
As freedom sway'd them, fighting on,
Till Charley tumbled from his throne.

" Be subject to the powers that be."
" No !" cry the dauntless Poles, "not we :
By all the orphan tear-drops shed,
For fathers in our battles dead ;
By Freedom's bloodshot eye which laves
Her tears for us—a land of slaves ;
While the pure tide of life shall roll,
And warm each freedom-loving soul ;
While we have any strength to fight,
We'll use it in our country's right :
For we would rather bravely fall
Than pine in languishment and thrall ;
But God will help us to reclaim
Our stricken heritage from shame."

" Be subject to the powers that be."
Yes,—while they rule with equity ;
But should they on your rights encroach,
Britons, resist their first approach !
For imitations, cast a glance
Upon the fearless sons of France ;
And, with one desolating bound,
Hurl your oppressors to the ground.

The following pieces were written in connection with the Preston Election of 1830. The candidates were the Hon. E. G. Stanley (the present Earl of Derby) and Mr. Henry Hunt :—

ON YOUNG STANLEY'S CANDIDATURE FOR PRESTON.

WE want a reformer, and Hunt is our man, lads !
  The close of the struggle we need not to fear ;
For—in spite of his money, his dad's, or his grandad's—
  We'll send the lad home with " a flea in his ear."

'Twould be well for the brutes who (for lucre and swilling
  The drink of the lordling) their birthrights despise,
To keep from the hustings—'twould save them a milling,
  And wearing a pair of tricolour'd eyes.

But cheer up, my hearties ! our prospects are glorious ;
  Keep watch on the villains, and Europe shall see
That freemen can be over tyrants victorious ;
  And Preston the watchword of freedom shall be.

ON THE DEFEAT OF THE HON. E. G. STANLEY.

Though strange it may seem,
Yet, in famine's extreme,
And tempted with silver and dinners,
Young Stanley's good cheer
Has met with a sneer
From half-famish'd weavers and spinners.

With their hands and their hearts
They have acted their parts,
And the fruits of their labours are glorious ;
Their glory and pride
Shall triumphantly ride,
For the " sprig" is no longer victorious.

He deem'd not to meet
Such a signal defeat,
But content in their thraldom to find 'em :
Let him tremble for fear,
For the era is near
When "placemen" no longer shall grind 'em.

ON THE SAME.

CORRUPTION seeks her native hell again,
   But not without a struggle has the foe
Been trampled on ; nor was that struggle vain—
   Unto a prying world if but to show
That (though the "lords of cotton" threw a chain
   Around their men) some hundreds were not slow
To raise the glorious tricolour, and manly
   Confront the boasting pension-hunter, Stanley.

Stanley ! Who is he ? One in whose opinion
   Reformer is synonymous with brute ;
A youth whose ancestors have great dominion,
   And heavy-coffer qualities, which suit
The sycophants who swarm round fortune's minion.
   Of their descendants' virtues fame is mute ;
But people say there is a great sterility
   Of feeling in this "sprig of the nobility."

Perchance they're not far wrong ; fools may observe
   Him eye the poor with an infernal sneer.
What do those sneaking hirelings deserve
   Who sell their birthrights for his worldly gear ?
That *he* should be elected to preserve
   Their "rights and liberties," seems rather queer :
For how can young, hard, heartless lordlings know
   To plead for those whose heritage is woe ?

Is Hunt like him ? No,—quite the reverse ;
   A patriotic spirit, who evinces
A wish to live in freedom ; and no worse
   A friend unto the Brunswick race of princes,—
Who hopes they will not reap a people's curse
   By mocking them with Gouldburn's silly minces ;
But win their love, by granting them their wishes,
   In sharing honestly the "loaves and fishes."

But, to proceed, our hopes were almost drown'd
   In Stanley's drink ; "With bribes," corruption cried,
" I'll try the hearts of Radicals to sound,
   Or else this blacking-man is sure to ride."
But gold and everything were useless found,
   Against the freeman's chief and country's pride.
Let Knowsley hide young Stanley's rueful face,
   For Hunt and Liberty have won the race !

ON THE SAME.

Young Stanley's tongue has lost the power of wagging ;
  The uncorrupted "sweepings of the street"
Have taught the " noble sprig," in lieu of bragging,
  A veneration for the "brave black fleet."

" Yes, yes," he cried, " the masters will elect me ;
  My gentle blood secures me from defeat ;
The poor have not the courage to reject me,
  For gold will soften down the ' brave black fleet.'"

He never dream'd of the unheard-of mauling,
  Which made him like a damless lambkin bleat,
When rose the cry of " Stanley, thou art falling !"
  The jest of freedom and the " brave black fleet."

Shame will o'erwhelm this advocate of slavery,
  Wherever he and rounded jackets meet ;
For fame will trumpet forth the matchless bravery
  Of his triumphant foes, the " brave black fleet."

SONG.

The people have conquer'd! the man of their choice
  Is duly and truly elected, declar'd.
And none but oppressors refus'd to rejoice
  When the Radical Hunt was triumphantly chair'd ;
For this was the shout of the overjoy'd crowd,—
  " Proud Preston has something whereof to be proud."

Yes, Preston may boast ; for her poor have done wonders—
  They've taught us the tide of corruption to stem.
The children of Israel crouch'd less, when the thunders
  Of Sinai belch'd forth, than young Stanley at them
When the multitude shouted exultingly loud,
  " Proud Preston has something whereof to be proud."

So long had the overgrown tyrants reign'd o'er them,
  They deem'd it the easiest thing in the world
To drive, same as cattle, the sweepings before them :
  But themselves from their long-held high places are hurl'd.
If the tyrants at Liberty's footstool are bow'd,
  Proud Preston has something whereof to be proud.

TO JOE MITCHELL AND IKEY WILCOCKSON

On the arrival of H. Hunt, Esq., M.P., in Preston,
Nov. 5, 1831.

RETIRE to Sod Hall, idiotical prater !
Lest envy and madness thine optics bedim ;
For he unto whom thou hast turned the traitor
Is coming, and thousands are welcoming him.

You said you could lead us by twisting your thumb, sir,
To place our affections on bone-grubbing Bob ;
But, traitor, I think you had better be "mum" sir ;
Nor stir up the wrath of a resolute mob !

Be "mum," while the friends of the hero surround you,
And smother the flames which your treachery lit ;
Or children will sing (and their song shall astound you),—
"The Yorkshireman's diddled ! the biter is bit !"

And thou, Isaac Broadrim, who printest a paper
Whose columns are soil'd with such palpable lies ;
Dance, dance up Old Shambles a fairy-like caper,
And cast adown Church-street thy baleful grey eyes !

The hero advances ! "the remnant" is coming !
And if thy old ribs aint sufficiently stout
To bear on their surface a Radical drumming,
'Twere wisdom in you to be facing about.

"The 'remnant,' indeed !" Speak soothly, for once, sir ;
Nor suffer your name to be link'd with a bribe ;
And own that you'd rather be dubb'd for a dunce, sir,
Than damn'd with the curse of a money-led scribe.

Farewell, Messieurs Traitor and Liar ! for flaming
The flambeaux announce that *our* Member is come ;
And I must be joining the crowds, who are claiming
Their sonship in him by outsounding the drum.

———

For the Preston Election of 1837, Mr. Anderton composed the following :—

A BRAN-NEW ELECTIONEERING SONG FOR PRESTON.

"'Tis your country bids."—*Cowper.*

THE conflict's at hand, and the look-out is glorious,
Predicting success to the banners of blue.
If Truth be all-potent, we shall be victorious,
For ours is the cause of all good men and true.

He who loves not his country, loves nothing that's "jannock;"
  And is not the Church her best stay and renown?
Let our "plumpers" unnerve, like a withering panic,
  The Rumps and the Papists, who cry, "Pull her down!"

Hurrah! for the man of your choice—not Jack Crawford;
  Alas! for poor Sawney—his hope-star is dim;
He had better "turn tail," for from Preston there's no ford
  Through the sea of despair to St. Stephen's for him.
There's nae luck for thee, mon! so don't raise a pother;
  Will a hundred electors respond to thy call?
Try—and get Joey Hume, thy Malthusian brother,
  To scan the *Observer*, and "bottle" the whole.

Hurrah! for the man of our choice—not O'Connor—
  We're o'erstock'd with the "emerald" breed and their
    tricks.
"Six hundred per annum" he wants, 'pon mine honour—
  The Rads of this town cannot muster him six!
Away wid ye, Feargus! That "O" to your name, sir,
  Sounds like the "big beggar's"—it suiteth us not.
Walk off wid yerself to the place whence ye came, sir—
  Wherever you plase; but trot, bog-trotter, trot!

Hurrah! for the man of our choice; for we've hit on
  A champion, and triumph shall hallow his claim.
No mongrel cross-breed, but a thorough-soul'd Briton,
  A fine English gentleman—worthy the name;
A Protestant, firmer as fortune grows darker:
  For the altars he would not pull down, but amend.
Hurrah! for our brave representative, Parker!
  Our neighbour, our brother in breed, and our friend.

Ay, this is our champion—the lov'd of the poor man,
  Who scatters his bounty with hearty good will;
No check-populationist, no! but a sure man
  For driving slap-bang at the "coarser food" bill.
He's the man of our choice; for behold he is rearing
  A temple of God on his princely domain;
He's the man we will have as our helmsman, for steering
  Our bark past the rocks, and the haven to gain.

Come, Wesleyans! come, with your votes; for we need 'em;
  These foemen of ours would connive at your fall;
You can study your Bibles, and worship in freedom,
  And these thieves, leagued with Rome, would deprive us
    of all.
Act, Wesleyans! act like your excellent founder—
  A Churchman he lives, and a Churchman he dies.
His Church is assail'd—for his sake gather round her,
  And fight for the shrines which his name sanctifies.

Conservatives, up !   By the deaths fierce and gory
　Which our Cobhams, our Lamberts, and Latimers died ;
Which ungagg'd the conscience, establish'd our glory,
　And check'd the "red w——" in the flush of her pride !
While these aliens pollute the dear Church of the people,
　Arm, arm her with strength their worst rage to withstand ;
Return, oh ! return him who loves the grey steeple,—
　The bulwark of truth, and the grace of our land.

A PEEP AT WHIG LEGISLATION.

SURELY, wonders never cease,
Valk up, gemmen, pins-a-piece !
Pins-apiece ! 'tis quite dog-cheap,
Such a field of fun to reap ;
Pins-a-piece to peep at things,
Which the march of freedom brings.
Pins-apiece to look at a show,
Modern wonders all in a row.

Freedom's tricks in '37
Have made England just like heaven ;
Public faith without a flaw ;
Wages high, provisions low ;
Penny cobs like shilling loaves ;
Baked in Jock's No-Corn-Law stoves.
Pins-apiece to look at a show,
Cobs, where are you, all in a row ?

Mark the Whig's Dead Body Bill !
When a pauper's pulse stands still ;
" Dust to dust" is hardly read,
O'er the friendless, unclaim'd dead,
Ere the student's glittering knife,
Maims the form yet warm with life.
Pins-apiece to look at a show,
Whigs, like butchers, all in a row.

See how well these Whigs requite
Those who work for labour's right !
Dorset men sent o'er the waves,
For no guilt, by Whiggish knaves ;
Then call'd back again, no doubt,
By the pressure from without.
Pins-apiece to look at a show,
Whigs turn'd tyrants, all in a row.

Lo! yon Babel just arisen!
Gemmen, 'tis a Poor Law Prison!
Rectangle of gloom profound—
Hidden by thick walls all round;
Who are they that press thy floor?
Englishmen, because they're poor!
Pins-apiece to look at a show,
Whig-built dungeons all in a row.

In these ultra-blessed times,
Want and child-breeding are crimes!
" Husbands to your partners cleave,"
Says the God whom we believe!
" Part, and no more paupers breed;"
Says Malthusian Crawford's creed!
Pins-apiece to look at a show,
Whig-born comforts all in a row.

Paupers starve alone, to wit,
As commissioners think fit;
" Best to part," says Brougham Hal;
" And," cries Little John, " they shall!"
Classified must paupers dwell;—
Dad, mam, lad, lass,—each a cell.
Pins-apiece to look at a show,
Whig-made hermits all in a row.

They may meet at prayer; but all
To the pauper's church must crawl;—
There, where three partitioned aisles
Baulk their recognizing smiles;
In one place, yet made like three;—
Trinity in unity!
Pins-apiece to look at a show,
Whig-plann'd temples all in a row.

They may meet at table, but
There the pauper's mouth is shut!
By the silent system nurst,
All are mute, though fit to burst;
What can still groan, sigh, and sob?
Stocks and nine-tails do that job!
Pins-apiece to look at a show,
Whig-gagg'd Britons all in a row.

Does plum pudding bless their maws?
Does roast beef extend their jaws?
Beef and pudding! Nay, nay, nay!
That's the hell-born Tory way!

"That would yield no treasury grist,"
Says our Scotch economist.
Pins-apiece to look at a show,
Whig state-tactics all in a row.

Hear the Board its will pronounce—
"Weigh their diet ounce by ounce !
We must save them, so contrive,
Just to keep their souls alive ;
Let them have the coarsest stuff,—
Fifteenpence a week's enough !"
Pins-apiece to look at a show,
Whig-spread banquets all in a row.

Whigs don't kill their slaves at once,
By a blow upon the sconce ;
But they starve with right good will,
Piecemeal, bit by bit they kill ;
Thankful when we go to pot,
In the paupers' hole to rot.
Pins-apiece to look at a show,
Whig-like murderers all in a row.

Thus Whigs stop the pauper's breath ;
Save, by clamming men to death ;
Scrape from British blood and bones
Brass to pay their salaried drones.
What do these sage Britons ? zounds !
Nothing ! save the pension pounds.
Pins-apiece to look at a show,
Whig retrenchments all in a row.

Is this merry England ? Yes :
She who was earth's queen ? It is.
Look on this, and look on that ;
While I just unpoke the cat !
'Tis the work of thimblerigs !
Jock says, " Rally round those Whigs !"
Pins-apiece to look at a show,
Jocks and Melbournes all in a row.

Heed not Crawford's Liberal prate,
He's a leech, I calculate ;
And he'll follow in thy track,
Otty's filly ! Stamphouse Jack !
Place he'll buy ; and, as to price,
Sawneys are not over nice !
Pins-apiece to look at a show,
Jocks and Lollies all in a row.

Some say I'm a turncoat, oh !
Poor old Cobbett curst this law,
So did honest British Hunt,
So does Oastler plain and blunt ;
Parker's curse has found a vent,
But Jock's " silence gives consent."
Pins-apiece to look at a show,
Jocks and Russells all in a row.

Valk up, gemmen ! Gaze your fill !
You who loathe this cursed bill ;
Bury all your party gall,
" Extremes meet:" for sake of all,
Join to throw throw this Scotch bug out ;
And, your showman, I will shout,
" Pins-a-piece to look at a show—
Nothing-uttering, ' Cheesecake Joe !'
Crawford, muttering, ' It's no go !'
Segar, sputtering, ' Curse the foe !'
Barker, stuttering, ' Dit-dit-to !'
Four tamed Mad Dogs all in a row."

THE FINALE.

Preston Election, 1837.—*Fleetwood,* 2726 ; *Parker,* 1821 ;
Crawford, 1562.

"Fallen, Fallen, Fallen, Fallen !"—*Dryden.*

Let the " imbeciles" look upon THAT, and on THIS,
For their prime speculation has turned out a MISS,
And sure we were right when we prophecied thus :—
" This *stranger* shall never misrepresent US !"
And NEVER he shall, hark ! the multitudes shout,
For the "blue un" is IN, and the " green un" is OUT !

And though ilka Sawney cam ower wi' his pock,
With "red-necks," and " round-heads," to help canny Jock;
The mon is clean daft, for he's got for his pains
A great muckle hole in his Singapore GAINS!
And, to " tottle the whole," he must face " right about."
For the " blue un" is IN, and the " green un" is OUT !

And though Misther Feargus, (who put Dan in print,
Kaase *that* " broth of a boy" would'nt share that same *rint ;*)
Be-blarney'd the " pisints" like one of the TAIL,
Linking lovers of *praties* with lovers of KAIL;
How *powerless* what fell from his illigant spout !
For the " blue un" is IN, and the " green un" is OUT !

Jock "hoped against hope," for they told him fine tales,
But Jockey's credulity—Jockey bewails!
And, says he, unto Feargus, when at the coach door,
"I've put up FOUR TIMES, but I'll put up no more!"
Were Jock's *canvass'd promises* seized by the gout?
For the "blue un" is IN, and the "green un" is OUT!

Our *church* was the butt of our foes—one and all,
But nobly her children uprose at her call!
Untemptably honest, through faction they broke,
And flew to the rescue, like brave "hearts of oak!"
And pushed from her precincts the Westminster scout,
For the "blue un" is IN, and the "green un" is OUT!

Hurrah! for the enemy's vauntings were hushed ;—
Hurrah! for ONE joint of the "TAIL" we have crushed ;—
Hurrah! for "reaction" in Whiggery's despite ;—
Hurrah! for our banners, "true-blue and snow-white ;"—
Hurrah! for the blue welkin rings with the shout ;—
For PARKER is IN, lads, and Crawford is OUT!

———

The following was written for the election of 1841, conse-
quent on the Dissolution of Parliament on the Free Trade
Question. The candidates were Sir Peter Hesketh Fleetwood, bart., Sir George Strickland, bart., Mr. R. Townley
Parker, and Mr. Charles Swainson. The two first named
achieved an easy victory :—

NO GO.

SHAME, where is thy blush? for the government prigs,
Conceiving that Preston is bound to the Whigs,
Have sent down two locksmiths our fetters to forge,—
Sir Peter the Rat, and the Yorkshireman George!
Are the wires of our minds, then, so easy to pull?
Is the cup of the Whigs not sufficiently full?
Will ye smile upon him who is toss'd like a cork
From the duped but awaken'd West-riding of York?
Or welcome Sir Peter, the British "Jim Crow?"
In the name of Proud Preston, I prophesy, NO!

We'll spurn these Whig spaniels, though as a last shift,
Their masters have promised Free Traders a lift ;
A measure, propos'd with exceeding ill grace,
Not to benefit us—but for salary and place!
What men or what class would the benefit reap—
If corn is made taxless and sugar dog-cheap?

Not the workman of England, I think, is quite clear ;
But the planters of Cuba ! and the cotton lords here !
Cheap bread would force labour and wages as low !
And will ye be gull'd by such quackeries ! NO !

We've not yet lost sight of that merciful bill,
Which questions the wisdom of "Thou shalt not kill !"
And, with God's holy law and our nature at strife,—
Tears parent from child, and a man from his wife !
Makes strangling a child by its mother, no crime !
And poison'd, at Bridgewater, scores at a time !
And shall new Whig nostrums, cheap sugar and corn,
Prevent us from shewing our loathing and scorn
For the tools of the fiends who concocted this law ?
In the name of our God and humanity, NO !

Get home, Sir George Strickland, thou man of slight brains!
And persuade that big Liar,—*Leeds Mercury* Baines,
To tell us how bribes, and all that sort of thing,
Compell'd thee, from hence, like a goose, to take wing !
We've Parker and Swainson, who act as they feel,
Who, hating the Poor-law, will cede its repeal ;
And shall we throw overboard men we can trust,—
Old Neighbours, true Churchmen, frank, bountiful, just,—
That a brace of Whig Rooks may the winning dice throw ?
What ! Strickland for Preston ! No ! Yorkshireman ! NO !

Hie to Rossall, Sir Peter, and give the Whigs thanks,
For a Baronet's place in nobility's ranks !
And for making a port (?) at thy pressing request—
Of Fleetwood,—a sand hole ;—thy own rabbits' nest !
And for granting such loans as thy needs might require,
To sink in a serpentine ditch call'd the Wyre ;
Which in puffing, thy scribes have thought fit to cry down,
The river which waters our beautiful town !
But to represent us art thou likely to go ?
Damn'd pitiful, self-seeking weathercock, NO !

The following pieces were written at the time of the
Bury election, when Lord Duncan and the Hon. F. Peel
were the candidates :—

IN SUPPORT OF THE CANDIDATURE OF THE RIGHT HON. F. PEEL,

(Son of the late Sir Robert), for Bury.

DUKE Richmond mock'd a nation's woe,
    And hugg'd his corn-law hobby ;
And what could Cobden, Bright and Co.
    Have done without Sir Bobby ?

The " League" subscribed a good round sum,
  And printed tons of paper ;
While farmers dubb'd it " all a hum,"
  And our petitions " vapour."

Loud was the noise without the " House,"
  But stagnant the interior,
There needed one the state to rouse,
  To party ties superior ;
The efforts of the " League" were great,
  But paralysed in action ;
There lack'd a chieftain, good and great,
  To burst the bonds of faction.

Though Duncan's penny gun was cock'd,
  And fired amongst the number,
Monopoly had firmly locked
  The Mersey, Clyde, and Humber ;
Protection grinn'd when Liberals fumed,
  And Villiers launched his " measure ;"
To empty bellies we were doom'd,
  For bread was at high pressure.

Sir Robert left the " House" no choice,
  He captured young and hoary,
And link'd by his bewitching voice,
  Whig, Radical, and Tory ;
And, with this weapon multiform,
  By dint of mere persuasion,
The hero quell'd the rumbling storm
  Which shook the startled nation.

He welded brains of adverse sorts,
  And solder'd all their quarrels ;
Till by their aid, corn fill'd our ports,
  In French and Yankee barrels ;
And while this gallant game he played,
  State quack and swindler rumpling,
He opened Britain's doors of trade,
  And doubled Britain's dumpling.

Her statesman's death the realm laments ;
  The poor his praise are singing ;
While unto him brave monuments
  Are everywhere upspringing ;
While Europe ratifies his fame,
  The man of huge endeavour ;
And coming times shall bless the name,
  And honour Peel for ever.

Shall Bury then reject his son,
　And prove herself ungrateful ?
His native town shall never don,
　A character so hateful ;
Sir Bobby changed our dismal notes
　To ditties brisk and merry ;
And by our grateful, hearty votes,
　His son shall go for Bury !

THREE THOUSAND A-YEAR.

Tune.—" Rory O'More."

"Short Parliaments, Ballot, and Household Franchise,
Yes, I am your man, Bury Bricks, if you're wise !
I march with the times and am up to the mark,
I'm brother, by marriage, to Bob of " the park ;"
And Bobby, ye know, hath found grace in the sight
Of good Richard Cobden and pure minded Bright,
And Camperdown's heir to his country is dear
For England allows me Three Thousand a-year

Ye like a big loaf and can heartily laugh,
At fools for preferring protectionist chaff ;
Ye seek to secure it, and I am the boy,
To vouch that the masses their boon shall enjoy ;
In free-trade Crusades I have knuckled to none,
From Cobden the victor to zealous Lord John,
I've personal reasons for being sincere,
My buttercake costs you Three Thousand a-year.

You all might have kicked up a national row,
And wheedled and blustered in vain until now ;
You needed a Statesman to shape your crude plan,
To carry it forward, and PEEL was the man ;
The son of that statesman of world-wide renown
Might gracefully sit for his own native town ;
But I am the pet ye most highly revere,
And pay me, to prove it—Three Thousand a-year.

I, Hercules Duncan, will fearlessly drive,
The non-working drones from the treasury hive ;
I'll show you what vile Tory uses are made,
Of eggs which poor Goosey, the Public, hath laid ;
I'll spin you statistics as well as Joe Hume ;
And, seizing my true economical broom,
From undeserved pensions I'll sweep the state clear,
Except my own cannie—Three Thousand a-year.

The Premier will laugh to himself at your split,
And take his advantage as he may deem fit ;
Sly Chancellor Ben may triumphantly grin,
If through your divisions a Tory creeps in !
What care I for that ! I'm more liberal than Peel,
As votes in the House and my speeches reveal !
A Radical son of a tax-eating Peer,
A Patriot who pockets Three Thousand a-year.

SWIG AWAY !

A NOBLEMAN witty,
Post-haste for Bath city,
In language not pretty,
And tones very gritty,
Pours forth this wild ditty,
And " whops" his committee :—

My committee came out as Simon Pure—
     Simon Pure.
How they chew these tickets for drink, for sure—
     Swig away !
But I, their gaffer, am not so nice ;
I must walk to the Senate, whate'er the price :
     Draw the spigots, and swig away'!

The "jaw" about "morals" is all my eye,
And he who scribbles it writes a lie.
     Swig away !
To act on a mob with a telling force,
You must fuddle the noddle and line the purse.
     Draw the spigots, and swig away !

So chatter away, my virtuous scribe ;
If Peel gives tipple, my " pals" must bribe.
     Swig away !
The hammers to clench outstanding votes
Are yellow Queen's heads and five pound notes.
     Draw the spigots, and swig away !

In the city of Bath we'd glorious fun,
When " rhino" and "penkey" the battle won.
     Swig away !
And the " Mosses" shall honour the foaming brim,
For in lashings of " lush" my geese shall swim.
     Draw the spigots, and swig away !

IO TRIUMPHE!

OR, LORD DUNCAN'S FINALE.

SCRATCH the Scotch fiddle from Stand to Pigslee ;
The boasters are worsted, and Bury is free !
 Barebones, parading his true Brunswick breed up,
  To vote for Lord Sawney, was thrash'd for his pains ;
 And vainly was Freetown commission'd to lead up
  Her riff-raff batallions—all sheawt and no brains.
Scratch the Scotch fiddle, from Stand to Pigslee ;
Lord Duncan has vanish'd,—and Peel is M.P.

Swell the shrill bagpipes, from Stand to Pigslee ;
The Humbugs are routed, and Bury is free !
 Pack-poising pedlars—Scotch, clannish, and feudal—
  Would vote for a devil, " in tartan and kilts ;"
 But thin was their phalanx, for Duncan Mac-Noodle
  Has dropp'd with a whack from his gingerbread stilts.
Swell the shrill bagpipes, from Stand to Pigslee, ;
Lord Duncan has mizzled,—and Peel is M.P.

Twang the big banjo, from Stand to Pigslee ;
The quacks are well physick'd, and Bury is free !
 Tied in " the sack" and impaled on fame's stretcher,
  Young Camperdown struggles, grimaces, and grins,
 With the spikes of the war-club of brave Dr. Fletcher
  Tattooing his carcase, like Brummagem pins.
Twang the big banjo, from Stand to Pigslee ;
Lord Duncan has bolted,—and Peel is M.P.

GANG BOCK.

Tune.—" Jenny Jones."

YER luck was at ebb, when yer local committee,
 An' doubtless the een o' yer " Lancashire lass,"
Seduced ye from Bath —that maist elegant city—
 To stick up for Bury yer visage o' brass !
Yer ears mun be langer than those o' puir Neddy,
 A welcome to seek fra' implacable foes ;
Nae mair o' your gammon, our hearts are wi' Freddy—
 Gang bock, ye Scotch loon, to yer bannock an' brose !

When merciful Ten-hours' enchantments were mooted—
 The hope of white slaves in each hamlet and town—
Like Mammon's own Flunkey, that measure he hooted,
 A muckle black pill which we canna wash down !
To wealth, as to power, your allegiance is steady,
 As ony puir bairn in this borough weel knows ;
Nae mair o' yer gammon, our hearts are wi' Freddy—
 Gang bock, ye Scotch loon, to yer bannock an' brose !

I doubt, Duncan dear, ye're addicted to lying—
 Ye promise sae muckle, and naething ye do ;
Ye stink o' corruption, as there's nae denying—
 Let Coppock and Roebuck deny—if not true !—
Mak' wa for yer betters, and tak' yer fine leddy,
 She canna bide here, while her laird we expose ;
Nae mair o' yer gammon, our hearts are wi' Freddy—
 Gang bock, ye Scotch loon, to yer bannock an' brose !

The deevil possess'd ye wi' fule-hardy courage,
 To dream that yer clap-trap in Bury wad take ;
Mair wise ye were acting, while supping meal porridge,
 With braw wooden spoon by a wild highland lake.
A stout Shetland pony, this instant get ready,
 And when ye are mounted use rowels and blows ;
Nae mair o' yer gammon, our hearts are wi' Freddy—
 Gang bock, ye Scotch loon, to yer bannock an' brose !

TEMPERANCE POEMS, &c.

T the commencement of the Temperance reformation in this country, a Temperance or Moderation Society was formed in the village of Walton-le-dale ; but, as in the case of all similar societies, it did not answer the purpose for which it was intended, namely, the suppression of drunkenness. A Total Abstinence Society was then formed, at a meeting of which, held in the National Schoolroom, Mr. Anderton, the poet's father, delivered the following address :—

"I stand before you a transgressor, and an unworthy member of the Walton-le-dale Temperance Society. The Walton-le-dale Temperance Society did I say ? What a beautiful sound it has in my ears ! It is surprising to me that anything in human shape can oppose this glorious name. Our advice from Scripture says, 'abstain from strong drink.' A generation, in olden times, never drank strong drink in all their life, and was favoured by the Almighty. I believe that those in opposition to this good cause are opposing the Almighty, who is to be their Judge at the last day. The Temperance Society has already saved a great deal of misery and havoc in many families, and is likely to do more good than any institution I ever heard of. I have now lived sixty years within a short distance of this room, and have wasted a deal of valuable time in drunkenness. I have been in great danger many times, and have had many a providential escape ; but have been saved until this night, by the hand of the Almighty, to be able to say to you all that I have lived thirteen months without liquor, strong or weak. I will not drink small beer, because it is a relation to the strong ; and, relying on the strength I have received, I will never drink anything stronger

E

than water ; and I here defy the temptations of the devil
and the craft and ingenuity of man. It is about ten years
since I went publicly to the public house ; but it has
chancely happened, foolishly thinking I could not do without.
I practised having a pint every night ; and what did this
pint do ? I entered this society with very good intentions,
and, in about three days, I fell a victim to the greatest
enemies mankind has—the devil and strong drink. My
situation the next morning was dreadful. I had sinned
against the Almighty, and given a great offence to this
society—which I ought to have supported, in its infant
state,—and was going to be an outcast from all Christian
society ; and here I had great sorrow of heart. In my
dreadful situation, I applied to the proper quarter for the
forgiveness of my great sin which I had committed, and
hoped that this society would forgive me the offence which
I had committed against them. Now, here I wish to be set
as a mark. I remember, when the British fleet was going
into action at the mouth of the Nile, one of the foremost
ships ran aground. This appeared to be a bad job ; but it
served as a mark for the rest to keep off. Of course, the
captain and crew, when they got off, would never go there
again ; therefore, I hope that any of us who have run
aground will bear in mind this ship of war, and never fall a
sacrifice any more to that dreadful enemy, strong drink.
Admiral Nelson would never strike to the enemies of his
country ; and I will never strike to that great enemy of
mankind, strong drink. I have had a great deal too much,
but I will have no more. I could wish all to embrace the
useful science—to be good, and strive to stop the torrent of
eruption's fluid—I mean the flood of drunkenness—which
has risen to a very high tide. I wish it may keep ebbing,
and ebbing, till there is not one drop of strong liquor left on
the whole face of the earth ; and that we may all live in the
fear and love of God, and die glorying in the blood of the
Lamb."

Henry Anderton composed the following four hymns for
the first Temperance tea-party, held in Walton-le-dale Schoolroom in 1834. They were very much approved of by the then

incumbent, the Rev. II. W. Mc.Grath, and Charles Swainson, Esq., of Cooper hill, who presided :—

OH ! TEMPERANCE IS AN INSTRUMENT.

On ! Temperance is an instrument
   In God's all-potent hands,
To thwart the serpent's fell intent,
   And break the drunkard's bands ;
And pow'rfully Jehovah sways
   This instrument, and well :
For drunkards leave their evil ways,
   And baulk the prince of hell !

There was a time, an awful time,
   When earth was one wide mart—
A huge emporium of crime,
   From man's deceitful heart ;
And there intemperance rear'd a stall,
   And millions widely quaff'd
Her honey-sweetened fire and gall,—
   Her spirit-damning draught.

And famine claim'd those votaries ;
   And shame, disease, and strife
Dissolv'd their household charities,
   And marr'd the joys of life.
And, oh ! where is the drunkard's lot ?
   In after being, where ?
Where hope and mercy are forgot,
   In limitless despair.

But God hath dealt a mighty blow ;
   The monster's course is check'd ;
And, with our trophies from the foe,
   The wond'ring earth is deck'd.
What are those trophies ? List yon lay,—
   Is it a reveller's song ?
No, no ! the drunkard learns to pray,
   And praise inspires his tongue.

Look at the cottages around,
   Where squalid hunger dwelt,—
The fruits of abstinence abound,
   And piety is felt.
Ride on ! Thou great Omnipotent !
   On our weak efforts shine !
Prosper the work on which we're bent,
   And make it, make it, Thine.

THE BURNING RIVER.

Lo ! a dread, a burning river,
  Overwhelms the land by stealth !
And its headlong currents shiver
  All the props of cherish'd wealth ;
    All affection,
Reason, piety, and health.

In this frightful, flowing terror ;
  This dread feeder of the tomb !
Myriads, ere they see their error,
  Perish in its death-fraught womb !
    Thus unpardon'd,
Rushing to their ENDLESS doom.

Where is this destructive water,
  Ruinous to a world so fair ?
Where these victims of self-slaughter,
  Wooing hell's unmix'd despair ?
    Find a drunkard,
And behold a victim there !

Yes ! Intemp'rance is that torrent !
  Mortals quaff its direful wave,
Rush to crimes the most abhorrent,
  Plunge into a hopeless grave !
    Madly heedless
Of the Saviour's power to save.

Could I tamely see another
  Sink the roaring waves beneath ?
Can a Christian see a brother
  Prematurely stop his breath,
    Without striving
To prevent the " second death ?"

Men ! this vice has spoil'd man's beauty ;
  From its blight your country purge :
It is every Christian's duty ;
  Sure 'tis needless more to urge ?
    Free your country
From this desolating scourge !

God ! beneath Thy broad protection,
  Let the cause of Temp'rance be :
Fill the drunkard with reflection,
  Set his spell-bound spirit free !
    Save him, Jesus !
Fit him for eternity.

WHAT IS A DRUNKARD?

WHAT is a Drunkard? One who quaffs
Reason-expelling drugs, and laughs
 At every holy thing ;
The " Prince of Air's" unquestioned prize ;
At whose approach religion flies,
 With an affrighted wing.

What is a Drunkard? Passion's dupe,
Whose more than brutal cravings stoop
 " To drain the maddening bowl ;"
Who gratifies his swine-like lust ;
And, when he does it, knows he must
 Ensnare his deathless soul.

What is a Drunkard? Read his life
In the dejection of his wife,
 His children pale and wan ;
And looking, thief-like, at his feet,
With dire remorselessness replete,
 Behold, behold the man !

What is a Drunkard? One who dares
God's fierce displeasure, and whose prayers
 Are "curses loud and deep ;"
Whose callousness increases still,
Albeit, he knows his madness will
 Undying tortures reap.

What is a Drunkard? One for whom
The Lord descended to the tomb,
 For whom our ransom died ;
And shall we not, who bear the name
Of Jesus, labour to reclaim
 The gradual suicide ?

God, thou art merciful as just !
And for our sins we lick the dust ;
 Yet, for thy Firstborn's sake,
O bless the cause of Temperance here,
Stop drunkards in their mad career,
 And let Thine arm awake.

LIFT UP YOUR HEARTS.

LIFT up your hearts and voices too,
To Him to whom the praise is due :
And let the glorious subject be,
The Triumphs of Sobriety !

What has it done ? Delightful things,
Beyond our best imaginings :
The Ethiop's white,—the lion's tamed,
And hoary drunkards are reclaimed.

No more the sun, in morning's hour,
To such has lost its fresh'ning power ;
Nor the bright moon, nor twilight's glow,
Unheeded come and thankless go.

He seizes all, and all enjoys ;
And ceaseless praise his tongue employs ;
And to his newly-waken'd eyes
The earth appears a paradise.

And oh ! his home, where Famine reign'd,
And impious revelry profan'd,—
'Tis now with social joys complete,
The focus where his comforts meet.

No more he lives in bitter strife
With the poor partner of his life :
So different this to by-gone years,
Her eyes are filled with joyous tears.

At school, the pledges of their love
Learn how to wend their way above ;
And they sing Temperance songs, and bless
The God that pitied their distress.

This is the great deliverance
Achieved by God through Temperance ;
And can the Christian ever cease
To pray, to work for its increase ?

Christians, this very hour begin
To check our land's peculiar sin ;
And seek His aid, who can afford
The aid of an Almighty Lord.

HOW QUIET THE PUBLICANS ARE.

How quiet the publicans are,—not a word now
From the rascals in public and private is heard now;
'Tis better for them that their talkers are quiet,
That they keep their loud clackers from breeding a riot.

They know that their cause is a villainous bad 'un;
They know that the life of the sot is a mad 'un;
This makes them quite dumb, for we've learnt them to think,
　　lads ;
The more they are urged, and the more they will blink, lads.

The more they oppose us, the more we perplex 'em ;
The more they look big, and the more we shall vex 'em ;
Opposition just suits us ; for, sure as it grumbles,
Another big stone on the jerry-shop tumbles.

Then, let the proud villains breed strife and confusion,
It cannot long prop this detested delusion ;
Ere long will the drunkards of Todmorden waken
And learn, not to drink, but to save their own bacon !

THE SOVEREIGN REMEDY.

WHEN a rotten tooth aches in an old woman's "munch-hole,'
Sure Miss Noddy, surgeon, is sent for; who comes,
And bathes and foments with a tincture-dipp'd sponge, all
The insides and outs of her agonized gums ;
But all would not answer,—she finds she has mocked her :
Her gums are still swelled, and her rotten peg shoots ;
So she hurries away to a regular doctor,
Who cures her by plucking it up by the roots.

Such a tooth is strong drink in the head of the nation,
Racking Johnny with pains that are felt to his tail ;
And long has that maidenly quack " Moderation,"
Been trying his nostrums, but all of them fail !
We're not a whit better,—in vain we have sought all,
And tried all his tinctures,—we're worse every " bout,"
And worse we shall grow, until doctor " Teetotal,"
Shall cure Johnny's munchers by pulling them out.

FAIR DOWN :

A TALE.

A DRUNKEN man is very foolish,
Thick-headed, muddle-soul'd, and mulish ;
If there be any sceptics here,
They'll think the epithets severe,
And frown.   Well, let them frown their fill,
I'll tell the truth on't, that I will.

'Twas on a sunless, rainy day,
And, as a Darwen chap would say,
          " 'Twas varra weet,"
Two drunken men came blustering and swaggering,
And belching, * * * * and hiccuping, and staggering
          Up Preston-street ;
Like two acquainted, friendly pigs, they waddled on together,
Despising shame, and staring eyes, and slutch, and dirty
    weather.

These drunken men,
Could they have seen themselves just then
In that foul plight,
They would, themselves, have sickened at the sight ;
They would have thought it wrong work,
It would have stopp'd their tongue-work,
And spoil'd their maniac laughing,
And cur'd them of their quaffing,—
At least it would have done't for one short while,—
They were besplashed in such a finished style :
But the drunkard cannot see himself, he's blind, completely
blind
To bodily defects, or imperfections of the mind.

Now, hear me, what I mean,—
I wish you could have seen
Those drunken men
Just then ;
It seem'd as though the sky,
Convinc'd these sots were dry,
Resolved to slake and wash their outward skin,
While they were pouring " Tom and Jerry" in ;
For the rain fell down and soak'd them,
And the mire sprang up and chok'd them nearly.
So they paid, I must think,
For their crops full of drink,
And their staggering walk,
And their blustering talk,—
They " paid for their whistles" too dearly.

You have look'd at a dog
Which has been in the water,
With a twist, and a spring,
What a villainous splutter
He makes when he shakes his sides :
So, if these sots had wrung their attire,
Their drenching had been so sound,
They'd have scatter'd commingled rain and mire
For many a yard around,
So drenched were their garments and hides.

In this unseemly plight,
They caught my sight ;
As they were trudging on their reeling way,
Their conversation grew quite warm;
And, as I thought there could be no great harm
In hearing what these " rum 'uns" had to say,
I followed near,
Close in their rear,
To hear if things who really look'd like swine,
Could talk like men,—whose origin's divine :

"Jack ! Jack !" bawl'd out the first,
 And then he stopp'd to hiccup,
 At which he stamp'd and curs'd,
  Which forced the wretch to "pickup ;"
And then he tried to find his tongue again :—
"Jack !" he resumed, " I never yet was vain ;
But tell me, as thou lovest a brimming cup,
What dost thou think of me—arn't I fair up ?"

 In speaking loud to make Jack hear,
 He lost his balance then and there,
 And tumbled in the mire ; and flat
  He flounder'd there, like a dead bat.
Just when this sprawling sot essay'd to rise,
A smile lit up his fellow toper's eyes,
 Which made the slutch-embracing fellow frown ;
" Fair up !" cries Jack, with a sarcastic leer ;
" Fair up ! old Jackey, you are out on't there,
 For, dash my wig, if you are not fair down !"

 This is my tale,—I've nothing more to tell ;
 Reader, reflect upon it, fare thee well !

THE SOT.

What is a sot ? A heartless, perjured knave.
 Ask his poor partner whom he should have cherished.
He is a slave,—to that vile lust a slave,
 On whose fell shrine domestic love hath perished.

What is a sot ? His children's deadliest curse ;
 Oh ! such a man the certain prey of hell is :
He spurns their guileless love, and, what is worse,
 Laughs at their clotheless backs and foodless bellies.

What is a sot ? The landlord's veriest thrall,
 Who robs himself to line his fleecer's breeches;
Who gives him health, and wealth, and time, and all,
 To drink his drugs and hear his canting speeches.

What is a sot ? The devil's willing tool,
 Who earns enough of means to live in clover ;
And yet is never satisfied—blind fool—
 Unless when reeling drunk, or " half seas over."

What is a sot ? A youthful, aged man,—
 At thirty, worn and superannuated ;
His vigour sapp'd, eyes blear'd, and visage wan,—
 Grey-haired, affectionless, and muddle-pated.

What is a sot ?   That's rather hard to know,
  A nondescript in habits, form, and station ;
That wears the form of man, yet ranks below
  The speechless, soundless, animal creation.

What is a sot ?   A monstrous thing and queer,
  Which good men loathe, and worldly wise men hoot at ;
Which Satan welcomes with a willing sneer ;
  A mark for mocking ridicule to shoot at.

What is a sot ?   A self-willed wanderer, whom
  The hellish hireling fastens to his tether ;
A sickening mouthful for the gaping tomb ;
  A lump of filth and vices rolled together.

What is a sot ?   A thing that walks erect,
  That should for many a murder-causing bout hang ;
A dish which hungry tigers would reject ;
  A nasty, stinking, British Ourang-outang.

What is a sot ?   Yon luring ale shop search ;
  And if you see a wretch whose skin is yellow,
Whose eyes are black, who cannot keep his perch
  Upon the chair, but tumbles,—that's the fellow.

A TEMPERANCE SONG.

I LOVE my ease, and ne'er denied
The comforts of a warm fireside ;
Fair woman's beamy smiles impart
A thrill of rapture to my heart.
But are these only to be found
In the hotel's enchanted ground ?
Yes, in that happy cot serene
Where my dear wife presides as queen.

I love the burning thirst to quench,
But not amid the tavern's stench ;
I'd rather take a hearty swill
Of water from yon gurgling rill,
Or lap the pure and snow-white juice
Which ruminating herds produce ;
While often, as I read the news,
My wife a cup of " Samson" brews.

I like good living ; but not mine
Are costly draughts of ruby wine ;
Brown ale with folly may go down,
But I prefer roast beef done brown.

Away with porter's bitter froth !
Give me a bowl of starry broth ;
Health needs no stimulants like these,
And wine must bow to bread and cheese.

I welcome laughter, but my laugh
Depends not on the cups I quaff ;
My mirth is gushing, guileless, wild
As the clear chuckle of my child.
I loathe the dull, galvanic grin
Which reaches not the soul within,—
Wrung from the nerves, the face to dress,
By the vile force-pump of excess.

I am no niggard, though I strive
To keep some honey in the hive :
A bag of gold to fall upon
Is a nice thing, when age comes on ;
Bright independence is a prize
Excelled by none beneath the skies ;
And, in her stern and rigid school,
The spendthrift is a pitied fool.

The ruling passion which pollutes
Our native land with reeling brutes,
Like other despots, had his day,
But dwindles now his ancient sway.
How blest the hour when I rebell'd,—
From lip and home the foe expell'd !
Short was the conflict—brief, but hard—
And freedom is my rich reward.

A FAREWELL TO DRUNKENNESS.

Farewell to strong drink, whether spirits or ale !
For me they may dry, or grow sour, or turn stale :
I've done with the bowl and the midnight carouse,
I'm sick of the madd'ning and brain-stealing "pouse."
   Farewell, Jerry ! farewell, Jerry !
   Farewell, Jerry ! I'm out of thy book.

Farewell to " my uncle's !"—I've money enough,—
My earnings will purchase our family stuff ;
And having no old nor new drink-shots to pay,
The o'erplus I'll save for a " slattery" day.
      Chorus.—Farewell, &c.

Farewell to the dram-store and Jerry-shop! Why?
No more shall their picture-signs dazzle my eye ;
My pocket, and conscience, and health are still sore
From the scratches I got at those hell-holes before.
Chorus.—Farewell, &c.

Farewell to the landlord, his lingo and phiz!
His house is hell's church, and the parson he is ;
He praises those drugs which he knows very well
Will ruin the drunkard, and send him to hell.
Chorus.—Farewell, &c.

Farewell to "blue devils!" (thank Temperance for that!)
I've shrunk many a time from these imps of "old Scrat;"
For oft, on a morning succeeding a spree,
These blue-visag'd phantoms have terrified me.
Chorus.—Farewell, &c.

Farewell to swell'd eye, bloody nose, and black shin,—
The sure fruits of swilling rum, Jerry, and gin ;
I guzzle none now, and my "brain-pan's" unrack'd,
My "lookers" unswell'd, and my "walkers" unblack'd.
Chorus.—Farewell, &c.

Farewell to my rags! for, at one time, my coat,
And waistcoat, and breeches no buttons had got ;
So I dress'd on a morning, with needle and thread,
And doff'd them with scissors, when ready for bed.
Chorus.—Farewell, &c.

Farewell to the devil, the drug-shop, and all
The things which conniv'd at and hasten'd my fall !
I'll play this black junto a comical trick,—
I'll drink Adam's Jerry, and battle "old Nick."
Chorus.—Farewell, &c.

OH! NOW FOR A TUG.

On! now for a tug with the glass and the jug ;
   Let's arm for the struggle like Turks !
And join in the quarrel with bottle and barrel,
   And bung-hole, and vent-pegs, and corks.
Let us fire our "bomb shells," until Beelzebub swells
   With anger—the sooty old thief ;
Away with their jerry !—and make yourselves merry
   With ham, and plum-pudding, and beef !
Give the proud landlords a lash ;
Guzzle no more of their trash !

The landlord's puff'd crew, and the jerry-lords, too,
　We'll make 'em bestir their fat shanks ;
Oh ! yes, we'll make all, both great ones and small,
　Asham'd of their drug-vending pranks.
Though they swagger so now, we'll take them in tow ;
　And clip them before—ay, and aft :
At one mighty swoop, we'll level the troop,
　And ruin their villainous craft.
　　　　　　　Chorus.—Give, &c.

When the trade is all fled, let 'em work for their bread,
　With more honest and likelier tools ;
For no longer they'll dine, and grow fat, and look fine,
　With the labour-wrung pennies of fools.
Those fools will grow wise, when we open their eyes
　To the rogueries of ale-selling quacks ;
And they'll lay out their "jink"— where?—where do you
　　　think ?
On their children's poor bellies and backs.
　　　　　　　Chorus.—Give, &c.

And their children, the while, and their wives shall beguile
　Their labour and toil.　Would not this
Be a beautiful earth, if our dwellings gave birth
　To pictures so teeming with bliss ?
" Old Harry" would grin, and death, hell, and sin
　Would mourn their " unmendable" fall.
God help us to fight with these monsters of night,
　And make us triumphant o'er all !
　　　　　　　Chorus.—Give, &c.

TO DRUNKARDS.

WHAT loggerheads these drunkards are !
　The mortal foes of empty glasses ;
Their reason hardly on a par
　With geese, and pigs, and sheep, and asses ;
Drinking " brown stout" to make 'em strong
　Which knocks 'em down, and makes 'em take up
Their this-side—that-side way, along
　The far-too-narrow streets of Bacup.

Strong ale, indeed ! yes, strong enough ;
　Too strong by far, for those who venture
To cram their muzzles with such stuff ;
　It knocks a fellow off his centre !
'Tis true about his strength he raves,
　Yet in this village I could rake up
A host of strengthless, helpless slaves,
　Who crowd the jerry-shops of Bacup.

For this the drunkard wastes his time,
  And spends his coppers and his shillings,
And taints his soul with deepest crime,
  And dines, too oft, on "murphy" peelings!
For this he plagues his partner's life ;
  Pops his best coat, that he may make up
A present for the landlord's wife :
  This is not " jannock," lads of Bacup !

Where, drunkard, dost thou put thy eyes ?
  The landlord's rich, and thou art poor, lad ;
Learn from this lesson to be wise,
  And darken not his open door, lad.
Thy body is a total wreck ;
  I come, thy energies to wake up ;
Abstain ! for that's the way to check
  The purse-proud jerry-lords of Bacup.

Our plan of cure is prompt and brief—
  Heed not the landlord's hollow proffers ;
Turn o'er another, better leaf,
  Put your own " brass" in your own coffers :
Look closer after "number one,"
  Your dry bones from this slumber shake up ;
The landlords may not like such fun,
  But never mind 'em, lads of Bacup.

Jerry can't " stick," lads, " in your ribs,"
  (Though 'tis the drunkard's darling, pet stuff,)
And they can mouth uncommon fibs,
  Who say that drunkards feed on wet stuff.
What did God give you teeth for, eh ?
  To drink with ? no! to munch a steak up ;
Then cast the landlord's slops away,
  And stick to solids, lads of Bacup !

———

TO TOPERS.

Are not topers hoodwink'd mopers
  Through this vale of tears,
Growing madder, growing sadder,
  As they grow in years ?

Are not drinkers daily sinkers
  In the mire of sin ?
What's undone them ? Out upon them !
  Brandy, rum, and gin.

Lo! the swiller, the self-killer,
　Where can reason be ?
Drink o'erthrew it, and he knew it—
　What a wretch is he.

When a fellow gets " right mellow,"
　Turn your eyes that way ;
See him " pickup," hear him hiccup,
　Hark his ass-like bray !

With their wives all, woe survives all,
　Death steals on apace ;
Sorrow's traces on their faces
　Wither every grace.

And their young ones, prattling-tongued ones,
　Hang the drooping head ;
Curse the father, who can rather
　Drink, than see them fed!

The All-seeing made this being,
　Never more to die—
Form'd his spirit to inherit
　Bliss beyond the sky.

But can drunken men, so sunken,
　Tread this upward path ?
No, they're flying, rushing, hieing,
　To eternal wrath.

Hell is watching, arm'd for snatching,
　Their poor souls away :
Foes of evil, foil the devil,
　Rob him of his prey!

THE ROBBER, THE LIAR, AND QUACK.

I wonder if these landlords
　Hope to die in their own beds ;
I wonder how such precious scamps
　Can raise their guilty heads ;
I wonder how our " righteous laws"
　Can legalise the sale
Of " Mountain Dew," " Jamaica Cream,"
　And sparkling " Nut-brown Ale."

The landlord argues with himself :—
　" While there are fools to swill,
I'll dose them with my devilries ;
　If not, my brethren will." .

And, with this sop to conscience,
   He pursues his baleful task,
A robber, sanction'd by the State,
   With " licence" for a mask.

The landlord cheats throughout the day,
   The felon prigs at night ;
The landlord murders gradually,
   The felon stabs outright :
The landlord is the greater pest,
   Yet, while he waxes fat,
His brother dances on the air,
   And sports a hemp cravat !

Mine host can tell a pleasant tale,
   And would his dupes persuade
That sleek and hearty all must be
   Who taste his stock-in-trade ;
And, pointing to his goodly paunch,
   His cheeks so plump and flush,
He'll trace their " rise and progress"
   To a bellyful of " lush."

Just step within his cosy " snug,"
   Behold him at his lunch,—
How he tucks in the " solids,"
   Which he qualifies with punch.
Your money bought that fat sirloin—
   Yes, *yours*, you gaping geese—
Which plasters on the glutton's ribs
   A triple coat of grease.

If we might credit Boniface,
   There's virtue in his swipes
For every mortal malady,
   From typhus to the gripes.
Yes, " barley broth" is sovereign balm
   For bruise, and throb, and smart ;
There's convalescence in a pint,
   And rapture in a quart.

Behold you' starv'd anatomy,
   Our nature's saddest blot ;
In him your orbs may recognise
   A poor, demented sot ;
His rheumy eyes, his wheezing lungs,
   His frame upon the rack,—
These are thy work, oh ! man of " drops,"
   Thou unexampled quack !

Experience damns the loathsome craft,
  And frantic nature storms
At the dark frauds man practises
  Upon his fellow worms ;
Yet, what avail a nation's cries,
  The prayers of high and low ?
The " tap" brings grist to Government,
  And tapsters rob by law.

A curse on these decoctions !
  If the sot would close his lips,
The tavern's bad prosperity
  Would undergo eclipse ;
The tavern knave would cease to thrive
  On folly's spongy throats,
Or spin from our elastic guts
  His rolls of five pound notes.

My spleen boils over when I think
  What noodles fuddlers are :
Behold the landlord's ladybird—
  The empress of the bar !
To buy a brooch for that fat neck,
  Which swells with vulgar pride,
The sot has pinch'd his own poor wife—
  His once-exulting bride.

Return to us—once more return—
  Insulted common-sense !
Let tavern hogs grow fat no more,
  At better men's expense ;
No more let tyrant appetite
  Make havoc of our wits,—
Make butchers' shops the fashion,
  And give *us* the " choice bits."

Back to thy vaults, John Barleycorn !
  A day is coming on
When fools shall learn to save their " tin,"
  And cherish " number one ;"
When every sturdy artisan,
  As on he blithely jogs,
Shall follow Shakspere's maxim,
  And " throw physic to the dogs."

A PEEP INTO THE TAP-ROOM.

WHILE follies abound and drunkards are found,
  Can pity and scorn remain neuter ?
Our tongues shall break loose at the pitiful goose
  Who glories in handling the pewter.

The wretch has downtrod the image of God
And sunk it below the brute level ;—
As much like a man as chaff is like bran ;
He looks and he acts like the devil.

We'll just have a quiz, at the sot as he is,
The moral " black cattle" he herds with,
As seated in rows, like strings of scarecrows,
Which husbandmen frighten the birds with.
You enter the room, and snuff a perfume,
Compared with which essence so frightful
Bone-dust is a treat, guano is sweet,
And garbage extremely delightful !

We've stood at the door, ten minutes or more,
The swine have done nothing but guzzle,
Each covered with stripes of " 'bacco " and swipes,
From his gooseberry eyes to his muzzle.
That bloated old prig has dropped like a pig,
And in the rank puddle he wallows ;
His crony, still up, with snout in the cup,
Alternately vomits and swallows !

With long, snarling face and awful grimace,
There growls a political patriot ;
Yon brace with black eyes and lips of such size,
Are " good uns " at tapping the claret !
Those scheming old rooks, in opposite nooks,
Fresh tricks with dice box are playing ;
That wild-looking youth is "spouting," forsooth,
And rivals the jackass in braying !

A couple of boars are down on all-fours,
Each other most ruefully eyeing ;
They swear to be trumps, the precious old frumps,
And finish by hugging and crying.
Yon spectre so grim, with eye glazed dim,
Death grins at yon perishing noddy ;
His limbs bend and shake,—the worms will soon make
A jolly good feast on his body !

The rest are mere mutes, poor commonplace brutes,—
Suspicion itself cannot wrong them ;
A fourpenny bit will break the whole kit,
You cannot raise twopence among them !
This addle-brain'd throng roars out for a song ;
" Jim Crow" is the idol they stick up ;
When, mad as March hares, pipes, glasses, and chairs,
Are smash'd in the shindy they kick up.

What squabbles and fights, what stomach-pump sights,
  Assail the astonished spectator ;
His nose takes offence, and faintings commence,
  If there he remain any later !
What litter and spew, what a horrible crew,—
  Delirium destroying their features ;
What lunatic mirth, what a hell upon earth ;
  And these are your rational creatures !

But here's the police—the keeper of peace—
  He bawls through the door " turn those men out ;"
At the word of command, mine host waves his hand,
  And waddles to clear his foul den out.
The clock has struck " one," he mutters, "begone,"
  When lo ! what a clamour he raises :
They call for more tick, but stiff as a brick,
  He bids them " go home or to blazes."

" Go home !" how absurd ! to spend that sweet word
  On four crumbling walls is a mockery !
The " bum" has been there and stripp'd them quite bare,
  " My Uncle" has taken the crockery !
In closets below, on trusses of straw,
  Exposed to the wind and the weather,
Enclosed in old rugs, wife, children, and bugs
  Are lovingly huddled together.

As ragg'd as a colt, or bird in the moult,
  And lean as a winter cock robin ;
No pan on his hob, no brass in his fob—
  The skulking and penniless gobbin !
His skull a crack'd jar, his brain below par,
  And stunning our ears with the rackets ;
Old Bedlam's the spot, fitted up for the sot,
  For madmen are best in strait jackets.

A PUBLICAN'S THREAT.

The landlords of Bacup, a short time ago,
Thought to down with our cause with a finishing blow ;
And this is the way they began the alarm :
" If you won't drink our ale, you shan't have our barm."

"What a hobble they're in," said these scamps in their souls,
And they made the town ring with their hisses and howls :
As if they could bring irretrievable harm
To our good cause, by shouting, " You shall have no barm."

What narrow-soul'd fellows these landlords must be ;
Our pledge we admire, and our lads would agree
To fight in our ranks,—heart to heart, arm to arm—
Though they forc'd us to live upon bread without barm.

But let these fat-bellied impostors give ear,
Their threat is deserving of nought but a sneer ;
We tell the swell'd, lazy, and bitter-tongued elves,
Our chaps will have barm, for we make it ourselves !

Remove an effect by removing the cause,—
That's the rock upon which we have founded our laws :
And therefore, if drunkards are made by strong drink,
Our pledge is the offspring of reason, I think.

Then—barm or no barm—I may venture to say,
The trade of the landlord shall dwindle away ;
And, before we have done, without asking, we'll crack
Our Teetotal whip on his very broad back.

Do ye hear what we say, ye brave lads of our town ?
Let us bring Jerry-wag and old Beelzebub down ;
Let's save the poor drunkard, by hook or by crook,
And stop him from going to " Mitchell-field-Nook."

TO THE PEOPLE OF FLEETWOOD.

A PENNYWORTH'S food in a gallon of ale,
And what food there is, is both bitter and stale ;
Yet you pay for this pigmeat, and swillings. and fire,
Two shillings per gallon at Fleetwood-on-Wyre.

One dose for a chap would be more than enough,
If the devil himself had not got in the stuff ;
For none but old Nick and the landlords desire
To gain by your folly at Fleetwood-on-Wyre.

Yet you sots are so keen, and so gross is your taste,
Your earnings in jerry you recklessly waste—
The brass which your far-away families require—
To make yourselves swill-tubs at Fleetwood-on-Wyre.

Wife and child left at home is a part of your plan,
They " scrat up a living" as well as they can ;
So starv'd in their looks, and so ragg'd in attire,
You can't for shame bring them to Fleetwood-on-Wyre.

Not only his brass, but his tools and his clothes,
The drunkard will give for a " jolly red nose;"
George Swallow can tell all who please to enquire,
The tools he has *swallowed* at Fleetwood-on Wyre.

Four masons (who acted, in this, like four geese)
Pawn'd their every-day coats for a shilling apiece,
And work'd (as I'm told by a man who's no liar)
A week without jackets at Fleetwood-on-Wyre.

And when you have done all your money and "strap,"
The lawyer is ordered to give you a rap ;
And, for every fresh sheet which he draws from his quire,
You pay six-and-eightpence at Fleetwood-on-Wyre.

A week or two after your very last spree,
You got from the "Scotchman" some blankets and tea ;
And Sawney's keen-fisted, and never will tire
To "ca' for his siller" at Fleetwood-on-Wyre.

Now what do you get for your brass and your pains ?
Destruction of health and confusion of brains ;
Knocked down by policeman, and trail'd through the mire,
Of which there's quite plenty at Fleetwood-on-Wyre.

Yes, drunkards give all for crack'd skulls and nak'd hides,
Starvation, and ruin, and "wartching" insides :
We've proof upon proof, in town, village, and shire ;
We've lots of such gobbins at Fleetwood-on-Wyre.

Lo ! while you are beggar'd, that worst of all thieves,
The tub-gutted landlord, the profit receives ;
Shcots up like a mushroom, and struts like a squire,
As proud as Sir Hesketh, through Fleetwood-on-Wyre.

Fat Dobson invites you to call at his trap ;
Big Edmondson tempts you to call at the tap ;
And fine Mr. Hornby with these doth conspire
To fleece the poor natives of Fleetwood-on-Wyre.

The "Hotel" is just let, to a Frenchman, I hear,—
One Monseiur Vautiegu, for some thousands a-year :
Who says (but in language politer and slyer),
"I'll cheat dese sly English at Fleetvood-on-Vyre !"

Sign the Teetotal pledge, and his prospects you'll mar,
And Monsieur would shuffle and mutter, "Begar !
I can't pluck von goose, so from hence I'll retire—
John Bull is old slyboots at Fleetvood-on-Vyre."

Two hundred and fifty per annum Tom Lunn
Has promis'd old Parker for sharing the fun ;
And, beside paying this, Tommy Lunn doth aspire
To wax independent at Fleetwood-on-Wyre.

Place your name in our book, and the mischief prevent ;
For, if you refuse to pay Tommy's big rent,
Like a jackass whose side has been prick'd with a briar,
He'll soon "cut his lucky" from Fleetwood-on-Wyre.

Ah! poor Number One ! you've not used him so well ;
Sink lower you could not, unless into hell ;
Teetotal would raise you a step or two higher,—
Then try it, ye drunkards of Fleetwood-on-Wyre.

Remember that time is the artisan's wealth,
And time's of no use, if a man have no health ;
And sickness will vanish, and want will expire,
When sots become sober at Fleetwood-on-Wyre.

The landlord may sneer, but "let those laugh who win ;"
To-day, lads, the blest reformation begin ;
And England shall see, and, beholding, admire
The glorious example of Fleetwood-on-Wyre.

We've made a beginning ; and, some of these days,
We'll set the whole town in a Teetotal blaze :
The faggots are kindled,—may God stir the fire,
And spread it like lightning through Fleetwood-on-Wyre!

AN APPEAL TO DRUNKARDS.

Come, drunkards, we've good news for ye,
  Dispense with that derisive smile, men ;
There's freedom for you,—come and see,
  And try your luck,—it's worth your while, men.

Jerry has made your "lookers" wink ;
  Aren't you a set of precious ninnies,
To let the landlord "fork" your "jink,"
  That he may "flare up" with the guineas ?

You, and your suction-liking "pals,"
  Have given him wealth, and, with the bonus,
His lady buys her "fal-de-rals,"
  And "comes it" like a marchioness.

And, on his rising, upstart breed,
  Your hard-won, ill-spent brass displayed is :
The proud son mounts his gallant steed ;
  The jewell'd daughters dash like ladies.

And with your threepences, for which
    You drain his slop-containing chalice,
The brigand goes to pasture, rich
    As Nabob, to his country palace.

And, worst of all, you're in his debt ;
    For in his black-book there's an entry
For shots unsettled, which to get,
    He hands the "six-and-eightpence gentry."

And then you have to run a race
    With Bob, the "bum," that "come-and-fetch" man ;
"My uncle," with his Hebrew face ;
    And Mister "What's-your-will !" the Scotchman.

My eyes ! but you may well look glum,—
    Your ribs so bare, your cheeks so bony ;
Worried by landlord, shark, and "bum,"
    And "twa-for-one" exacting Sawney.

It's worth your while to turn this scale,
    With resolution firm as Cato's ;
To give this pack of wolves "leg bail,"
    And make them work for their potatoes.

It's worth your while, my lads, if you
    Some good fat beef your ribs would toss in,
And cease to glut those lubbers, who,
    As Tummus says, " are welly brossen."

It's worth your while, my lads, to hush
    Their daughters' sneers, their ladies' snarlings ;
The tears from your wife's eyes to brush,
    And clothe, like theirs, your own poor darlings.

It's worth your while to save your pence,
    To lay your spare uns altogether :
They'll serve you twenty winters hence,
    When age creeps on, and rainy weather.

It's worth your while to make your homes—
    By "bums" unstripp'd, by duns unpress'd—
Edens, where discord never comes ;
    Snug, cherished, cheerful, pure, and blest.

Too long you've liked this here brown pap,
    And cried like babbies for your "suckey ;"
It's worth your while to stop that tap,
    And make Old Jerry "cut his lucky."

Stop it ! and give "old Nick" the sulks ;
    Make Tom-and-Jerry's bulwarks rock again ;
Drive to their spades his bull-neck'd hulks ;
    And make the Sawney tribe "gang bock again."

THE PURGE.

Said a man to the "gemman" who told us this tale,
" You may say what you list against drinking good ale ;
Your efforts are vain, and 'tis bootless to urge,
For still I think ale is an excellent purge."

" You're right," quoth my friend, "'tis a purge, sure enough ;
Let the penniless pockets of drunkards give proof :
It makes them to vomit their 'silver' and 'brass,'
And he who denies it's a genuine ass.

" Not only does ale purge its swillers from wealth,
It purges a man from contentment and health :
Pray look at the drunkard ! his visage so blue
Proclaims that the dose was unerringly true.

" 'Tis a purge from the boasted enjoyments of life :
Look, look at the drunkard's poor children and wife !
His offspring's wan looks, and his wife's startled throes,
Evince that the purge is too powerful—God knows !

" It purges its patient from freedom ; nowhere
Is this purge so incredibly potent as there :
It makes the poor slave (the sheer wisdomless elf)
In love with the chains of the devil himself !

" It purges from life—and oh ! there is its sting :
How many poor souls has it forced to take wing ?
And where could they fly to ? Where sinners must go
That die unredeem'd, and with God for their foe !

" A purge ? To be sure, 'tis an excellent purge ;
But is it not also the deadliest scourge
That ever laid man so successfully low,
Or spread lamentation, and wailing, and woe ?"

Sobriety ! come, with thy health-mantled brow,
Counteract this vile purge with pure abstinence now ;
Thine advocates bless, and thy children inspire
With some of thy god-like, benevolent fire.

God ! rouse thy faint-hearted disciples at length,
Supply us with wisdom and sin-scourging strength ;
And grant that this pest may be banish'd and hurl'd
From our circles, our country, our homes, and the world.

IRRATIONAL BEINGS.

IRRATIONAL beings! your senseless career
  Will speedily lead you to misery's brink ;
And yet ye rush onward, untortur'd by fear,
  Nor pause on the threshold of hell ere you sink.

Forsake, oh ! forsake the foul paths you have trod ;
  Repent in the dust, or be fearfully driven
From hope, and the smiles of a merciful God,
  And lost to the consummate glories of heaven.

Ye rush to the tomb, unredeem'd, unprepar'd,
  With God for your firm and inflexible foe ;
And hell is the pardonless sinner's reward,
  And thither the unreclaim'd drunkard must go.

Yet Jesus invites you ; His messenger waits
  To carry your tardy repentance on high ;
Oh ! sue for a passport through Salem's bright gates,
  And cease to do evil, for " why will ye die ?"

The pleasures of drunkenness cannot repay
  The hearts she has stabb'd to the innermost core ;
Nor her peril-fraught brimmers of death charm away
  The fire she infuses through every pore.

This vice is the parent of fear, and remorse,
  And madness, and ruin, and shame, and despair ;
Which brand on the heart an indelible curse,—
  A venom which bubbles eternally there.

If Zion has beauties to draw your desires,
  Why, why do you run in an opposite path ?
If hell's unconceiv'd and unquenchable fires
  Affright you, why waken God's measureless wrath ?

I command, I entreat, I implore you,—by all
  Heaven's infinite joy and hell's terrible pain—
This moment emerge from the drunkard's dark thrall,
  And wake to the sunshine of mercy again.

WHAT ARE THE DRUNKARD'S BOASTED HOPES?

WHAT are the drunkard's boasted hopes,
  Which his besotted soul relies on ?
For surely they are falling props,
  If they are bas'd on drinking poison.

F

Tell me what joys a man can own
 Who spends his leisure on the bottle,
And pours fermented liquors down
 His satisfied, unthirsting "throttle."

Drink may—it does—its dupes beguile
 From toil, or care, or pain, or sorrow ;
And thus it will bewitch them, while
 Those dupes can beg, or steal, or borrow ;
But when resources fail, oh ! then
 Listen the sighs the drunkard fetches ;
The after-clap is unmix'd pain,
 The sot a wretch above all wretches !

And drink exhilarates the man
 While it exists within the body ;
But, when its fumes approach the brain,
 It makes that man a senseless noddy.
And drinking is the soul of fun,
 And jollity, and wit, and laughter ;
But soon as these effects are gone,
 It makes him smell of hell fire after !

Yon public-house looks snug and neat,
 But how can landlords bait that hook so ?
Sots help those robbers to complete
 That snugness ; and, to make them look so,
They rob their own domestic cots
 Of joy and comfort which adorn them,
And part with independent lots,
 To fatten publicans who scorn them !

The drunkard fills the landlord's purse
 And clothes their haughty, purse-proud wives too ;
And (this is positive and terse)
 He makes them easy all their lives through.
But where's his wife ? his children, where ?
 He knows not—recks not what they're doing ;
Dead to their accents of despair,
 And callous to their utter ruin !

Hell gapes for him : oh ! strive to win
 The drunkard from a state so awful !
Reclaim him from this frightful sin ;
 Snatch, pluck him, from a state so woeful !
God of the world ! prepare our way ;
 Forgive the drunkard's oft rebellings ;
Resume thy sovereign, moral sway,
 And drive the monster from our dwellings.

THE FELLOW WHO CUDDLES HIS TALLY.

THE public-house tattler, the Teetotal band
    From Bridge-Mill, at Whitworth are halting;
The lads in the neighbourhood stretch out their hand,
    Against their old habits revolting.
" We're dish'd any moment !" the publicans bawl ;
    " 'Tis ruin one instant to dally ;
So Dicky must fetch out a plan for us all"—
    The fellow who cuddles his tally.

The Teetotal band was playing, one night ;
    Poor drunkards a many were list'ning ;
The eyes of their wives, betwixt fear and delight,
    And sweet expectation, were glist'ning :
When, proud of his horse, of folly as proud,
    The madman cries, " Now for a sally !"
And dashes rough-shod through the peaceable crowd—
    The fellow who cuddles his tally.

He thought he had carried the meeting by storm,
    And star'd, till his eyes strain'd their sockets,
As we laugh'd at his antics—the pitiful worm—
    And jingled the brass in our pockets.
By sticking to that, we shall chase the vile crew
    From city, and hamlet, and alley ;
And then, lack-a-day ! what will mad Dicky say ?—
    The fellow who cuddles his tally.

Who kept the nice house—the old name painted out ?
    A woman it was—out upon her !
Yet, though the vile slut has no conscience about
    Her guilt, or her partner's dishonour,
She fears lest a cuckold, though tame as a louse,
    His courage and manhood may rally,
And drive, in the name of the law, from the house
    The fellow who cuddles his tally.

What man will be bullied by vermin like these,
    And forc'd their potations to guzzle,
Their pockets to fill, and their whimsies to please,
    Till " penky" runs out of their muzzle ?
Submit to them ! No ! we are thoroughly sick
    Of mixtures that gripe a chap's belly ;
We'll starve out the landlords,—especially Dick,
    The fellow who cuddles his tally.

THE LANDLORDS.

No DOUBT the fat publican laughs in his sleeve,
 And winks at his glasses well rang'd round his bar ;
He crows o'er Jack Sheppard, and cries, " By your leave,
 My goose-plucking system is safer by far."

Yet though the fat bully has law at his back,
 Though Government dubs him a "good man and true,"
The greasy delinquent would look rather black,
 If Justice had eyes, and the Devil his due.

It's stunning to think that, with eyes open wide,
 John Bull should be blind to this pitiful case ;
And suffer the legalised prig at his side
 To bleed him, and skin him, and grin in his face.

" Mine host" is a butcher ; much blood he has spill'd :
 How filthy his shambles ! how deadly his tools !
And when he invites you to come and be kill'd,
 You do as he bids you, like staring Tom-fools.

The villain contrives to get pursy and sleek
 On the solids he eats,—not the slops that he swills ;
While you might have fasted seven days in a week,
 Or swallow'd a shopful of Morison's pills.

While men take their glasses, and women their drams,
 The fly from the spider will never get loose ;
The wolf of the tavern will pounce on the lambs,
 The fox of the beershop will ravage the goose.

What think you, ye greenhorns, and ye Johnny-raws ?
 Our system the wise and the prudent extol ;
The simple expedient of shutting your jaws
 Would thin the dominion of grim Alcohol.

Touch not, taste not, nor handle one drop of their trash :
 This feasible, simple, and rational plan
Would settle in no time the publican's hash,
 And force him, as ye do, to sweat for his " scran."

How foolish the effort, by method more soft,
 To break up a system upheld by the law !
You've follow'd this milk-liver'd system too oft ;
 Your chains must be shiver'd and snapp'd at a blow.

No matter what plans the land pirates may hatch
 To keep you in bondage, like cattle in pens ;
Our pledge, like a blazing artillery match,
 Can scatter these robbers and blow up their dens.

Why unto yourselves the worst enemies prove ?
 Your homes and your children, your parents and wives,
Have sacred and paramount claims on your love,
 The sweat of your brows, and the toil of your lives.

Poor objects of pity and footballs of wit,
 Cast hither and thither—now up and now down ;
Like so many joints of roast beef on a spit,
 The landlords have done you uncommonly brown.

The landlord, poor sot, is thy direst of foes :
 Reject, then, his bumpers—bright, ruddy, and clear ;
Raise gently thy thumb to the tip of thy nose,
 And bid him march off, with "a flea in his ear."

TEETOTAL FOR EVER SHALL WEATHER THE STORM.

OLD England! though wildly thy sages have blunder'd ;
 While lopping the branches, forgetting the stem ;
Though vainly thy priests from their altars have thunder'd,
 While sharing the guilt which their sermons condemn ;
Though vainly thy statesmen have rais'd our position
 By suffrage extended, and sweeping reform ;
Thy sons shall be rescued from social perdition,—
 Teetotal for ever, shall weather the storm!

Let biblical sophists pervert revelation,
 And force it to warrant pollution so foul ;
Let sensible fools who adore "moderation,"
 Applaud a procedure which hallows the bowl ;
Let flaming professors, suspiciously pious,
 Rank rebels to conscience, to custom conform :
The priests and the Levites pass scornfully by us ;
 Teetotal for ever, shall weather the storm !

Hurrah for the future! The system is shaking,
 Intemp'rance is shorn of its primitive strength ;
Opinion is with us ; the isles are awaking
 To reason, and virtue, and freedom, at length.
Old England! rejoice in thy latter-day glory,
 When vice shall not shame thee, nor folly deform ;
When preachers and people shall blazon the story,—
 "Teetotal for ever has weather'd the storm !"

THE STING.

YE who are fond of worldly wealth,
    Go take your fill in hoarding treasure ;
Ye sots, go wallow still in filth,
    And guzzle rum, and call it pleasure ;
Go, take your fill of such like bliss,
    But, howsoever sweet you find them,
Ye simpletons, beware of this,—
    They always leave a sting behind them.

SONG OF TEETOTAL FREEDOM.

WHAT means this exulation,
    That glitters in our eyes ?
It is because the sparkling bait
    We laugh at and despise :
Yet once we were poor, sensual slaves—
    Few even such, so low—
In the days we went a revelling,
    A long time ago.

Our household gods are happy,
    Our wives and children dear ;
And peace, and love, and rapture, now
    Their mounting spirits cheer ;
Yet want had lengthen'd every face,
    And every heart was woe,
In the days we lived as revellers,
    A long time ago.

As those who live by labour,
    (No better we desire),
Our homes are snug as homes can be,
    And decent our attire.
Like Falstaff's ragged regiment,
    We cut another show,
In the days we went a revelling,
    A long time ago.

Now God be thanked for freedom
    From raging appetite !
Describ'd by one of wise renown,
    As worse than serpent's bite ;
A close-shut mouth, a manly will,
    Disarmed our subtle foe,
On the day we left off revelling,
    A long time ago.

A fig for moderation,
  That web by Satan spun,
Which tempts the half-recovered slave
  To be again undone ;
In abstinence our safety lies,
  As our whole lives will show,
Since the days we left off revelling,
  A long time ago.

WATER.

SEE ! our glasses are not fill'd
With fermented or distilled.
'Tis a liquid fools refuse—
That which Jah-Jehovah brews !
What with water can compare !
Pure as ether, free as air,
Bright as drop in pity's eye,
Sweet as breath of Araby.

Here's a bumper ! drink it up !
Life is lodged within the cup :
Quaffing this, you waste no wealth,
Brace your nerves, and guard your health.
Boon most common, yet the best,
Harmless as a mother's breast ;
Ever welcom'd with delight
By the sterling Rechabite.

Tempt no more, 'tis labour vain,—
Sherry pale or red champagne ;
Give me water,—Hermon's dew—
Clear as yon wide arch of blue.
Nature's recipe for thirst,—
Ne'er did man, by act accurst,
Remedy for that invent
Like our virgin element.

Stimulants exhaust the frame ;
Drunkards play a losing game ;
Purchase, by their beastly whims,
Aching heads and shaking limbs :
But the draught that in the wild,
Cheer'd poor Hagar's fainting child,—
Life, and strength, and freedom brings,
Like the source from whence it springs.

Laughing in the mazy rills,
Leaping down the giant hills,
Sleeping in the glassy lakes,
Where no breeze a ripple makes ;
Or in teeming showers of love,
Dropping fatness from above,
On the scorch'd and arid sod,—
Best of all the gifts of God.

Fount ! whose droppings did suffice
Sinless man in Paradise ;
Blessed cup which once did quell
Jesu's pangs at Jacob's well ;
Type of what His grace imparts
To believing, broken hearts ;
Well of life, whose running o'er
Those who drink shall thirst no more.

HARWOOD LEE.

Too LONG our drunken neighbours
    Have sham'd the mindless brute ;
But Heaven has crown'd our labours
    With a rich crop of fruit :
The vice which long did cover
    Our land begins to flee,
And now we can discover
    A change in Harwood Lee.

Drink made our place a poor hole,
    Its natives ragg'd and wan ;
But when we brought our "Cure-all,"
    They came and tried our plan.
They found it milk and honey ;
    No badge-shop slaves are we,—
They trade with ready money,
    The lads of Harwood Lee.

Our neighbours' wives were beaten,
    Their best affections chill'd,
Their flesh by hunger eaten,
    Their eyes by sorrow fill'd ;
But now, in town nor city,
    No happier dames we see ;
They're clean, and neat, and pretty—
    The wives of Harwood Lee.

The drunkard's little darlings—
  So sunk in look and deed—
Provok'd the bitter snarlings
  Of Jerry's upstart breed;
But now they look so stately,
  As poor man's child should be ;
And trudge to school quite gaily,
  The lambs of Harwood Lee.

The drunkard's house was empty—
  No bacon on the hooks ;
But now there's peace and plenty,
  And oh ! how nice it looks.
No quarrels, so unsightly,
  Disturb domestic glee ;
But love illumines brightly
  The homes of Harwood Lee.

And, best of all, our lasses
  The drinking trade condemn ;
And lads who like their glasses
  Will have small chance with them.
Temp'rance must blow Love's bellows,
  Or they will ne'er agree ;
They'll not have drunken fellows—
  The girls of Harwood Lee.

Great things are done already,
  And God our cause does own ;
Be ready, and fight steady,
  Till Jerry be o'erthrown ;
Mind not the toil or danger,
  And victors you shall be,
And drunkenness a stranger,
  Not known in Harwood Lee.

TO THE LADIES.

" Woman is the weaker vessel,"
  But her sweet endearments can
Qualify the fair to wrestle
  With the stronger might of man ;
And if every lovely woman
  Should display her welcome strength,
Arm'd with loveliness uncommon
  That bright morning dawns at length.

Fathers, husbands, sons, and brothers,
　Bow'd beneath the drunkard's curse ;
Weeping sisters, wives, and mothers,
　Make the frightful picture worse.
Dungeons fill'd, asylums crowded,
　Homes dispoiled, and thousands, too,
By this frightful sin enshrouded
　In their graves,—appeal to you.

By the hearts this vice hath riven,
　By the homes this sin hath marr'd,
By the crowds that it hath driven,
　Unreclaim'd, to their reward ;
By the earth, which it is thinning,
　By the hell, which ends its track,
Use your influence with the sinning,—
　Lead your blinded brethren back.

Down your cheeks are grief-drops stealing
　For the drunkard's woe and pain ;
By those gushes of true feeling,
　Let us not appeal in vain.
Tears enhance your power and beauty,
　Tears will your best weapon prove :
Woman, now perform your duty !
　Speed their efforts, God of love.

A WARNING TO MAIDENS.

BEFORE by your sides you permit me to strut—
　Ye whose beauties attract the beholders,—
I've a word for your ear, though 'tis hard work to put
　An old head on a young pair of shoulders.

Pray what sort of fellows have tipp'd you the wink ?
　To know that is a girl's first of duties :
Are they fond of a drop—are they slaves of strong drink ?
　Get to know, bonny Todmorden beauties !

Don't you know that to love every drunkard is dead ?
　And can ye, ye lovely ones, bury
Your beauties with men whose affections are wed
　To stink, and to spue, and to " Jerry ?"

I'll never believe it : now, therefore, my dears
　If your lads visit " Jerry-wag" benches,
Oh ! be masters for once, and, with fleas in their ears,
　Send them home, bonny Todmorden wenches.

Honest men ! modest daughters, I'm sure, will conform
To the rules of a nunnery, rather
Than marry ruffians, who cannot perform
The duties of husband and father.

Then, pester your chaps with Teetotal attacks ;
And if they abandon their glasses,
Well and good ; but, if not, with the bag on their backs,
Send them off, bonny Todmorden lasses !

A FAREWELL TO THE PUBLIC-HOUSE,

A DRUNKARD I was,—I'm a drunkard no more ;
And the change, let me tell you, is glorious ;
No more at the ale-bench I hiccup and snore,
Nor join in their revels uproarious.
My last pot of " Jerry" was long ago quaff'd ;
No landlord can call me his debtor ;
I have learnt to eschew him, his shop, and his craft,
And to like " Number One" a bit better.

I'm out of their books ; for the lawyers and " bums"
Have long ceased to kindle my passion ;
For now neither master nor "serving-man" comes,
In the old six-and-eightpenny fashion.
Having no "shots" to pay, to my pockets nor me
The arm of the law never reaches :
Good bye to the " bums ! and (I say it with glee)
Ta-ta to the " borough pros." leeches !

I've done with the tap-room : that dear little cot
Is the sweetest resort of my leisure,
Whose inmates are thankful to God for their lot,
And never lack innocent pleasure.
Our household is truly a bundle of love ;
And, to put a top-stone to my story,
Call'd up by his King to a palace above,
I've a Teetotal father in glory.

This Temperance can do—it has done for me,—
And if, like a sceptic, thou smilest,
Or doubtest the truth of my tale,—come and see !
For I'm sober, who once was the vilest ;
I've my full share of health, peace, and rational bliss ;
I can weep with my friends, or be merry ;
And you must confess, if our doctor does this,
That his physic is better than " Jerry."

TO MR. GADSBY.*

I WONDER, friend Gadsby (that title should do,
For puff, I suppose is distasteful to you),
That a man of your calling, experience, and sense,
Should set yourself up as a rock of offence.

If you thought, by presenting your impudent front,
To thwart us, 'twas Briton-like, reckless, and blunt.
You were wrong.   When unprivileged persons intrude
On a meeting, in spite of the chairman, 'tis rude.

Our annual meeting was but for our friends,
To strengthen our cause, and further its ends,
And you know, at such times, that the voice of the chair
Should be sacred and cloth'd with omnipotence there.

You slighted that voice; and, with motives as base
As would actuate friends in a similar case,
With language unfeeling, unlovely, and rash,
You spouted your frothy, irrelevant trash.

You marr'd our proceedings, and made them quite rife]
With wrath and contention, and clamour, and strife ;
And gave him a license, whose infidel din
Seem'd forged at the den of the father of sin.

Thus, sir, you dishonour'd the cause and the name
Of your peace-loving Master—the sacrificed Lamb ;
And, maugre our friendly entreaties and prayers,
Brought shame on your office, your name, and grey hairs.

And what was your motive ? (to those who were wise,
That motive was seen in your sinister eyes) :—
To sneer at our pledge ; and, by sapping that prop,
The tide of our brilliant successes to stop.

What was the objection you pleased to allege
Against our distinguishing feature—the pledge ?
If you signed it you could not conform to its rule ;
Because he who trusts his own heart is a fool.

We know he's a fool ; and, if that be the ground
Of our members' fair hopes, 'tis unsafe and unsound ;
But have we no Saviour ? and is not His power
Sufficient for man in his loneliest hour ?

---

* Written after a meeting at which Mr. Gadsby opposed the pledge.

And can't we trust Him ? in this life's trying scene,
Man is not a passive and soul-less machine—
A will-less automaton ; free his is will
To close in with grace, or do what is ill.

Yes ! man's a free agent ; no creature of fate,
Nor doom'd to the fire of God's merciless hate ;
If he has no will to obey what is writ,
God loses His power to condemn or acquit.

Like you, we believe that poor mortals have stray'd
From the image of God in which first they were made ;
Like you, to that self-crushing truth we're alive,
That its useless with inbred corruption to strive.

And does not the pledge you have scoffed at imply,
That our friends are too wise on their hearts to rely ?
And, breeder of discord, we fear not the rod
With which thou canst scourge us : our strength is in God.

OUR OBJECT IS GRAND.

Our object is grand : don't you know what we wish ?
'Tis to make men not bottom the glass, but the dish ;
Not to guzzle strong ale, and when swallowed, to spew,
But to buy some roast beef, and when that's done to chew.

Our object is grand : 'tis to make men to think,
Both to look what they eat, and to know what they drink .
To tell them that beggars at ale-shops are made,
And that none but the landlords grow rich by that trade.

Our object is grand : 'tis to banish the glass,
Which turns a nice man into worse than an ass ;
An object of pity, a tub full of sin,
Which angels might weep at, and Beelzebub grin.

Our object is grand : 'tis to give the sot sense,—
To which he at present can make no pretence ;
To put in his pocket his own hard-won pelf,
Not to work for the landlord, but "fend" for himself.

Our object is grand : 'tis to give sots a hint,
That landlords are wealthy from "jerry's" foul mint ;
And—fast as the landlord to competence jogs—
The drunkard, poor noddy, must "go to the dogs."

Our object is grand : 'tis to show the poor sot,
That, while sorrow and penury darken his lot,
The landlord just now, in the valley hard by,
Is building a house at least five storeys high.

Our object is grand : 'tis to show two-legg'd pigs,
That while landlords whirl past in their coaches and gigs,
The drunkard, in weather, wet, windy, and dank—
Trots by on a " tit " that belongs to " John Shank."

Our object is grand : 'tis to show ale-fill'd hacks,
That, while their own wives have no clothes to their backs,
The landlady—finest in fashions gay throng—
Like another queen Jezebel, trollops along !

Our object is grand : 'tis to show him who swills,
That while his own babes toil in steam-propell'd mills,
The landlord's spoil'd young ones, with elegance dress'd,
Like ladies and lords, strut as proud as the best.

Our object is grand : you have heard what we want ;
You to save your own brass, which at best is but scant :
Too long you've been robb'd by that brown-coloured thief ;
But now you may learn to " turn o'er a new leaf."

Our object is grand : and though landlords deride,
They know we've your weal and good sense on our side ;
Then drunkards, resolve that these mountains of puff
Shall rob you no more, for they've " cabbage" enough.

Our object is grand : and we call upon all
Who as drunkard's, have tasted this wormwood and gall,
To shun their worst foes—the decanter and cup—
And by signing our " pledge," turn the world right side up.

TO THE PEOPLE OF TODMORDEN.

LANDLORDS told us from the first
This would prove a stubble :
They must alter, ere they burst,
Our Teetotal bubble.
Kindled in the heaven-taught fire,
'Twill go out they tell us :
Disappoint their fell desire,
Todmorden's brave fellows !

As we march, our ranks increase
From the mere beholders ;
As we march, domestic peace
Pats us on the shoulders.

At strong drink we aim the blow,
  By his dreadful slaughters ;
Help us now to lay him low,
  Todmorden's fair daughters !

Evil reigns ; the churches weep ;
  Christ is vainly bleeding ;
And can God's own servants sleep,
  Careless, cold, unheeding ?
Rather up and meet the fray ;
  War with these Philistines ;
Cast the "little sup" away,
  Self-denying Christians !

Now to make sin's temples nod,
  Brethren, do not dally !
For the sake of man and God,
  Round this standard rally.
Other towns for Heaven and man,
  Fearlessly combine, lads !
Foremost in the godlike van,
  Let your valley shine, lads !

THE DOINGS OF "JERRY."

The "Jerry Lords" tell us what good there's in drink,
But they'll be wise fellows to prove it, I think ;
These sellers are liars in praising their stuff,
And this the poor drunkards have felt long enough.
Ye drunkards, bethink you what "Jerry" has done,
And that will unblink you, as sure as a gun :
For, if not too puzzling, ye slaves of the pot,
O tell us by guzzling what good you have got.

  The pleasures of drinking.—O my ! O my !
  You rate them, I'm thinking, too high, too high ;
  For "Jerry" deceives you ; and, give it fair play,
  It beggars, and leaves you the piper to pay.

Can drink make you merry ? It may for a night ;
But, in a great hurry, this pleasure takes flight ;
To-day it brings laughter, makes enemies friends ;
But oh ! the day after, what horror attends !
Still "Jerry" pursuing, rank madmen you prove,
But stung with the ruin of all you should love ;
The knife and the halter lay ready, you find ;
But there your hands falter, for hell is behind.

Is this to be merry ? O fie ! O fie !
I tell you what, "Jerry," you lie, you lie !
You heighten the fever with proff'ring relief ;
You barefaced deceiver, you legalised thief !

Whilst poverty scatters your last spark of pride,
And patches and tatters your skinny ribs hide,—
These swipes-selling vermin, as if by design,
Have spick-and-span garments, oh ! bless us, how fine !
And while you sit grumbling—alive, and but just,
Voraciously mumbling a butterless crust,—
With your precious money those rascals command
The milk and the honey—the fat of the land.

Your figs are but thistles, I fear, I fear ;
You pay for your whistles too dear, too dear ;
The price makes you tremble,—health, money, and
   peace ;
And just you resemble so many pluck'd geese.

A pitiful pickling your brains are, I think,
To cling to that tickling Iscariot, strong drink ;
To welcome starvation, their coffers to swell
Who death and damnation are licensed to sell.
Yes, " Jerry" hath made you the laugh of the town ;
Beguil'd and betray'd you, and you are " done brown ;"
Yet still to the slaughter like sheep you depart,
To buy this spoil'd water, at sixpence per quart.

From glasses and revels—oh fly, oh fly !
Bid " bums" and "blue devils" good bye, good bye :
The cap of reflection this moment put on,
And show some affection for poor " Number One."

AMBROSE BROOK'S THIRTEENTH TEETOTAL
BIRTHDAY.

WHAT ! thirteen years ? and his health as good
As when he mix'd " old stingo" with his blood ?
Have not his nerves grown shatter'd, trembling, weak ?
Has not the rose deserted his wan cheek ?
Does not the wind pierce through his ghost-like frame ?
Do not his friends with such a kinsman shame ?
What has he gain'd by his Teetotal whim ?
What has the " water system" done for him ?

Ask his dear partner ; and her glance implies—
" Look at our Ambrose, and believe your eyes !
No more his appetite for ' Jerry' yearns,—
He saves the pittance which his labour earns ;
Of cheerful men he holds the foremost rank ;
He owes no debt,—my pocket is his bank :
And thus we pace the downward slope of life,
A loving husband and a happy wife."

Ask his dear children ; and methinks I hear
Their blended voices mingling loud and clear :—
" The bliss he caused no mortal tongue can tell,
When first he bade the poison-shops farewell ;
And, though we all have left the parent nest,
Where once we nestled peacefully and blest,
His bright example on his brood abides,
And cheers and purifies our own firesides."

ON THE SIXTEENTH TEETOTAL BIRTHDAY
OF THE SAME.

Of winters and summers sixteen have roll'd by
Since Ambrose our system determin'd to try ;
A system whose principal doctrines are these :—
Drink milk, tea, or coffee, whichever you please ;
In choosing your solids, exert your best skill—
From bread to plum pudding—whatever you will ;
Retain a firm grip on the strings of your purse ;
And banish "spoil'd barley," the Englishman's curse.

This common-sense system my father has tried,
And to make it advance is his glory and pride.
Behold him enthron'd, like a cock on a perch,
As proud as a king, and as stiff as a church ;
A sterling Teetotaller, firm to the core,
As warm as a stripling, though sixty and more ;
A soldier of virtue, unstain'd by disgrace ;
The blessing of Heav'n on his jolly old face !

The soul of content in his countenance shines ;
There happiness writes her indelible lines :
Both able and willing to work for his bread,
The equal of any he holds up his head.
Without being rich, he is not very poor ;
The awful " dun-horse" never stops at his door ;
No creditor frowns, whether heavy or small,—
My father can " shake a loose leg" at them all.

As husband or father, as neighbour or friend,
His children are ready his name to defend.
How grateful they are that kind Providence spares
So long his example, his love, and grey hairs.
I speak it to friends, I proclaim it to foes,—
There breathes not a being more true to the cause :
Father Mathew's renown more extensive may be,—
Father Brook is the model and pattern for me.

His frank, smiling face makes a capital speech ;
And these are the lessons my father would teach :—
" A purse in my hand has a pleasanter look
Than my name written full in the publican's book ;
A man looks as well, as he trots o'er the flags,
In a suit of broadcloth as in tatters and rags ;
And a loaf of wheat bread, with a pound of nice chops,
Will feed a man better than barrels of slops."

The valley of Todmorden boasts not a few
Of men, like my father, to principle true ;
Who righteously war with that thief of the pot
Which ruins the shiv'ring and penniless sot ;
Who visit his wife in her seasons of grief,
On errands of pity, and promise relief ;
The wrath of the wicked and careless outbrave,
One drunkard to rescue from guilt and the grave.

Poor slaves of intemperance, crush'd and downtrod
Beneath the foul wheels of a vile belly-god !
By signing our pledge, with a good will and strong,
You shatter the chains which have bound you so long ;
By this, and this only, is freedom ensur'd ;
Thus only can life-foster'd habits be cur'd.
Abstain for the future, past follies deplore,
And landlords shall riddle your pockets no more.

***

FOR THE TWENTIETH TEETOTAL BIRTHDAY
OF THE SAME.

(Written about four months before the Poet's death.)

A LOVELY place is Todmorden, when wintry tempests lower,
Or the bright sun illumes her with vivifying power.
In shaggy rock or whimpling brook, green wood or smiling
    dell,
I know no spot in other climes which her sweet nooks excel.
Her hillocks into mountains rise, as fair, if not so grand,
As thine, enchanting Windermere, and prouder Switzerland.

God's lavish hand hath beautified the captivating scene,
And swarming hives of labour rise the wildest glens between ;
Blithe human voices strangely blend with sounds of lowing
herds,
And childhood's laughter emulates the music of the birds ;
A life pervades the landscape which in foreign views we miss:
Alas ! that sin should desecrate a paradise like this !

Yes, here man's deadliest enemy has sown his baleful tares,
And innocence on ruin's brink, stands trembling unawares ;
Fell habit, with strong links of lust, like a grim tyrant binds
The aspirations of the soul—the pinions of the mind.

TO AN OLD MAN.

READ it, old boy ! to child and man,
    And, happen, they'll grow steady ;
As for thyself, thy knowledge-pan—
    Has learnt that trick already.

Go on ! for thou hast well begun ;
    And, though the landlords bellow,
Their rage will cause us lots of fun,—
    And fun suits thee, old fellow !

TO AMBROSE BROOK.

GOOD BYE, old chap ! not oft we've met ;
But, Ambrose, you're a jolly set :
Homely and hearty ; such to find
Is a hard task, among mankind.

I can't say but I rather grieve
Such comfortable folks to leave ;
Not, Ambrose, that I wish to cry,—
Or that I could do, if I'd try.

But who does like to leave a spot
Where all his cares were half forgot ;
Not many, I should think, feel so ;
Nor so do I—but I must go !

Well, if I must I must ; but then,
Ere long, I'll be with you again ;
And then, old friend, along with thee,
We'll have a brave Teetotal spree.

Oh! yes, we'll learn folk not to brew,
Nor drink, nor stagger,—but to chew.
Though now 'tis stiffer than a rock,
We'll give the foe another knock.

May great success our efforts crown !
May sin's great bulwarks tumble down!
May drunkenness to fly be made !
May landlords find a better trade !

And now, good bye ! old chap, stick fast !
Thanks, Ambrose, for the favours past ;
While it shall be my hope to dwell,
I'll wear thee in my heart,—Farewell !

WE FEAR NOT OUR FOES.

WE fear not the number, nor might of our foes ;
Our hands and our hearts are engaged in this cause :
The weal of our fatherland urges us on,
Till drunkenness cease, and the battle is won.

Oh ! now for a band of the fearless and brave
Our country to free, and our drunkards to save,
That their households may bask, and their homes may wax
    bright
In the sunshine of peace, and the smiles of delight.

Oh ! now for a phalanx of warriors indeed ;
With truth for their swords, and goodwill for their creed ;
Who trust in their God, and for payment can find
A golden return in the joy of mankind.

Our long, rayless prospects begin to improve ;
Our conquests have hallow'd this labour of love ;
The dawn of a moral millennium appears :
Wake, Christians ! and shake off the slumbers of years.

LET'S REASON TOGETHER.

Too long you poor drunkards have lavish'd your gains,
As wages to "Jerry" for stealing your brains,
For picking your pockets, for sapping your lives,
For starving your children, for killing your wives,
For stripping you naked, like sheep that are shorn :
But "that's a long lane which has never a turn."

Let's reason together! oh ! why should your brass
Turn the landlord in fortune's rich meadow to grass ?
Why should you keep his lady, his miss, and young spark ?
Why should you feed the "bum" and his master the "shark ?"
Why should your goods embellish "my uncle's" thick shelves?
You poor, silly noddies, look after yourselves !

I know you suspect they have used you like brutes ;
I guess you are sick of strong drink and its fruits,—
And you have not begun to be weary too soon ;
They have "pepper'd your bodies," they have to some tune.
Your freedom is near ; take our doctor's advice,
And you will be sav'd, without money or price.

Moderation pretenders would cure you by halves,
With "take-it-good" plaisters and "leave-it-good" salves.
Now, these bit-by-bit folks go the wrong way about—
The wound breeds "proud flesh," and it must be cut out,
Lest the poison should spread, and your vitals attack.
A doctor, indeed ! Moderation's a quack !

I pity your case, because I've felt the rod ;
I know you may, because I do, thank God.
Heaven knows what your bodies and minds have endur'd !
There is a physician, and you may be cur'd :
No fee is requir'd, and the worst may apply ;
The remedy's sure,—and God help you to try !

WE SHALL NOT TOTTER YET.

Tune—National Anthem.

WHAT though these topers all,
Madmen and mopers all,
    Make such a fuss ;
It is all vanity,
Drunken insanity :—
Friends of humanity,
    God is with us !

We shall not totter yet,
Though they wax hotter yet,
    Demon and man ;
Though they surround us now,
'Twould not astound us now ;
They can't confound us now,—
    God leads our van !

Drugs we have swill'd enough,
Men they have kill'd enough,
    Quit yourselves well !
Up and be doing, lads !
Stop all this brewing, lads ;
Till this wide ruin, lads,
    Settles in hell.

Zion's true soldiers, come !
Reason upholders, come !
    Fear not nor shrink.
Fight till these dandy shops—
Rum, gin, and brandy shops—
Beelzebub's handy shops—
    Shut up or sink !

AN ADDRESS TO A TEETOTALLER.

TEETOTALLER ! never mind the foe ;
Spurn their friendship—it's " no go ;"
Rise above each fat-paunch'd elf ;
Shun their doors, and mind thyself.

Comrade in this glorious strife,
Deck no more the landlord's wife :
She's too puff'd and overgrown ;
Deck not her—but love thine own.

Brother, feed no alehouse rats,
Nor enrich their upstart brats ;
Let not thy good-nature roam :
Thou hast children ; look at home !

We have been their " flats" too long ;
We are weak, but they are strong :
'Tis our brass has fed these pests,
But we'll cease to prop their nests.

Yes ! the day is breaking, when
Briton's shall be thinking men ;
When these rogues, Teetotal-sick,
All shall " cut their blessed stick."

Till the red-phiz'd Turpins, who
Beggar'd me and robb'd thee too,
Sigh, and cry, and whimper thus :—
" Temperance is bad game for us."

Serve 'em right ! for all the guilt
Drink has spread, and blood it's spilt ;
Serve 'em right ! and for this join
To pay the scamps in their own coin.

Teetotaller ! bless thee ! thou art rais'd,
Thou art sober—God be prais'd ;
Teetotaller ! onward ! stick like wax,
And we will throw them on their backs.

TRY, LADS ! TRY !

Tune—" Polly set the Kettle on."

I HAVE ventur'd out again—
From my cottage on the plain ;
And, despite of toil and pain—
  Hope in view.

I have come to take your part
'Gainst the tempter's wily art ;
Drunkards ! let us make a start—
  Do, lads ! do !

It is in the drunkard's power
To be rescued any hour,
Though the clouds of danger lower
  Thick and near.

Let him "bag" his "Jerry" pots,
Let him shun the place of sots ;
Drunkards ! if you'd mind your lots,
  Hear, lads, hear !

See the landlord ! he can thrive,
While with poverty you strive :
When you sigh—"Dear heart alive !"
  Watch him pass.

Nodding at you all the while,
In a Jack-and-Joan like style,
What's the meaning of his smile ?
  Brass, lads, brass !

Yes, he wants your brass, indeed ;
" Love thyself,"—aye, that's his creed,
When the rascal means to feed
  On your pelf.

Drunkards! do as he has done,
Keep an eye to number one,
Let your thoughts be turn'd upon
       Self, lads, self!

When will English dwellings be
Edens of felicity?
When will English workmen see
       As wise men?

When will truth and common-sense
Prove Old England's best defence?
When strong drink is banished hence—
       Then, lads, then.

It's as easy as "come out"
To bring this nice change about,
If you'd lay these good-for-nought
       Liquids by;

If, instead of "Jerry-dregs"
You would let roast beef and eggs
Occupy your munching-pegs.
       Try, lads, try!

NEVER TOUCH, LADS!

Thou look'st very queer; thou'rt sufficient to scare
  Whoever may see thee, poor fellow!
Thy "smeller" all o'er with red spots so sore
  Is pimpled, and thy skin is yellow,—
Besides thy red snout; thy shoes are out—
  Sad places are these "Jerry-wag" shops!—
And thy hat, and thy coat, and thy breeches have got
  To "my uncle's," or some of the rag-shops.

What an object drink makes thee! how sadly it shakes thee!
  Sot! art thou not tir'd of thy revels?
In fears thou'rt array'd—What makes thee afraid?
  Why, friend, thou hast got the "blue devils!"
The landlord won't thank thee for drinking, but rank thee
  With fools of the veriest class;
While thy "jink" he receives, he laughs in his sleeves,
  And calls thee a good-natur'd ass!

Dost thou know what has levell'd, and maul'd, and bedevill'd,
  And made thee the shame of thy race?
The *first glass* has done it—a murrain upon it!
  Poor drunkard, I pity thy case!

Whenever " Old Nick" wants to play thee a trick,
  The first glass will greatly assist him :
Oh ! do not give in to the " father of sin,"
  But, like a true soldier, resist him ! .

Let it stick in thy head, what friend Pollard once said—
  For a long-headed fellow he's reckon'd,—
" Don't quaff the first pot, and the devil cannot
  Compel you to swallow a second !"
Yes, that is the way to bid him "good day :"—
  His drugs we have guzzl'd too much, lads !
But no longer he'd brag, if we gave him the bag ;
  And how must we do't ?—*Never touch, lads !*

PINS APIECE.

Hie you ! hie you ! come with me,
And a curious sight you'll see ;
Come, without one if or but,
And inspect the drunkard's hut.
Pins apiece to look at a show,
Lots of nothing, all in a row.

Bring your bottles, lest by chance
You should faint as you advance ;
For as fame most soothly tells,
It is full of horrid smells.
Pins apiece to look at a show,
Spit and pick-up, all in a row.

Look within, and look without.
Look straight on, and round about ;
Isn't it supremely grand ?—
Straw for a bed, and grease for sand !
Pins apiece to look at a show,
Tallow for carpets, all in a row.

Torn with winds, and soak'd with rains,
Paper bags for window panes,
Which, when through the weather pops,
Are block'd up with sods and cops.
Pins apiece to look at a show,
Strange contrivements, all in a row.

Snails are creeping up the wall,
Round the windows spiders crawl,
A long-legged and grisly throng,
Weaving muslin all day long.
Pins apiece to look at a show,
Cobweb curtains, all in a row.

G

Where's the table ? That old door
In the middle of the floor,
Lash'd with sundry hazel sticks,
Propp'd with legs composed of bricks.
Pins apiece to look at a show,
Family fixtures, all in a row.

All the pots "my Uncle" sacked,—
All but two, and they are cracked,—
All the tools for dinner work,
Save one ancient one-legged fork.
Pins apiece to look at a show,
Tools on crutches, all in a row.

Where's the dish from which they feed ?—
"Bums" have dished it up, indeed—
Girl and woman, boy and man,
Stick their clutches in the pan.
Pins apiece to look at a show,
Two-legged grunters, all in a row.

Where the chairs on which they sit ?—
Swallowed in a drunken fit—
All below, and all upstairs—
Bricks are stools, and stones are chairs.
Pins apiece to look at a show,
Longridge cushions,* all in a row.

See that fender, as you stoop,
Made from an old barrel hoop ;
See that kettle on the hob,
Shedding tears for gipsy Bob.
Pins apiece to look at a show,
Jobs for tinkers, all in a row.

What's that stench that stops your breath ?
From a cat that's starved to death.
What's that "hobbuch" you behold ?
Heaps of bugs that died through cold.
Pins apiece to look at a show,
Swarms of brown-backs, all in a row.

Oh ! what high extatic bliss
To possess a home like this ;
Cleared of all its goods by some
Landlord, thief, or rascal "bum !"
Pins apiece to look at a show,
Swill-tub scrapings, all in a row.

---

* Longridge, near Preston : noted for its stone-quarries.

THE DYING DRUNKARD.

Stretch'd on a heap of straw—his bed—
 The dying drunkard lies ;
His joyless wife supports his head,
 And to console him tries ;
His weeping children's love, would ease
 His spirit, but in vain ;
Their ill-paid love destroys his peace :
 He'll never smile again.

His boon companions—where are they,
 Who shar'd his heart and bowl,
Yet come not nigh, to charm away
 The horrors from his soul ?
What have such friends to do with those
 Who press the couch of pain ?
And he is rack'd with mortal throes—
 He'll never rise again.

And where is mercy, in that hour
 Of dread, and pain, and guilt ?
Though Jesu's blood, of matchless power,
 For man's sear'd soul was spilt.
If justice spurn the fear-urg'd prayer,
 That stream has flow'd in vain ;
And lock'd in thy embrace, Despair,
 He'll never rise again.

———

THE DRUNKARD RAISED.

What numbers for the deadly glass
 Sell soul—and body—too ;
Forgive them, Father, for, alas!
 They know not what they do.

Assist us, Lord, these souls to win,
 The drunkard's soul to save,
To crush the land's besetting sin,
 And free the struggling slave.

Display thy arm, Almighty power,
 And strike a winning blow ;
The captive free—and from this hour
 " Loose him, and let him go."

THE DRUNKARD'S WIFE.

Tune—" The Soldier's Tear."

BEFORE the altar stood
    The bridegroom and the bride,
With willing hands and blended hearts,
    The holy knot was tied ;
And when he spake the words
    So welcome and so dear,
There glistened in her mild blue eye
    That test of love—a tear.

And thus they liv'd and lov'd—
    Their hours were never dull,
And heaven had crown'd their happy love
    With pledges beautiful ;
And as her charge increas'd
    With each succeeding year,
The mother's heart rush'd to her eye,
    Which trembled with a tear.

But year has follow'd year—
    As wave succeeding wave—
The once-lov'd wife is joyless now,
    And he a drunken slave.
Vice o'er him holds her sway,
    And from his dark career
She tries to win him, and her eye—
    Her dimm'd eye drops a tear.

Her kindness pleads in vain—
    His heart is sear'd and hard,
And tauntings loud, and cruel blows,
    Are that fond wife's reward ;
He spurns her from his side,
    With look and word severe,
Yet for that ruffian's sake, her eye
    Is gushing with a tear.

Upon his dying couch,
    Fear wraps his soul in gloom,
When common friendship hides her head,
    She never leaves the room ;
She kneels, and if faith can
    Compel the Lord to hear,
She opens mercy's gate, and melts
    The sinner with a tear.

That wife's a widow now ;
  The star of hope shall rise
No more for her ; her bosom lord
  Died as the drunkard dies!
God help this bruised reed,
  Her load of woe to bear ;
For none but Thou can rest her soul,
  Who cannot shed a tear.

AN APPEAL TO THE TRUE FRIENDS OF ZION.

Lo ! Zion droops—in vain—in vain,
  Her temple gates are open'd wide ;
Intemp'rance blights her fair domain,
  And lures ten thousand from her side.

In vain her watchmen cry aloud,
  And urge their plea with many tears ;
They cannot pierce the drunken crowd,
  Who shun God's house and close their ears.

They cannot see, intemp'rance blinds
  The hoary sire and beardless youth ;
And how can their bewilder'd minds
  Perceive or feel the force of truth !

To Salem's courts they never wend ;
  Far from her sacred fane they rove :
To Jesu's shrine they never bend,
  Nor list " his still small voice of love."

And well may Zion hang her head,
  Griev'd for her trump's neglected sound,
When such an Upas tree can spread
  Its mortal taint on all around.

Yet, fallen as the drunkard is,
  Though fallen he's our brother still ;
For him our Lord left heaven's bliss,
  And bled on Calvary's rugged hill.

Hark ! heard ye not that woe-fraught cry ?
  From Jesu's lips that wail proceeds :
Eli—Lama—Sabacthani—
  The sinless for the sinful bleeds.

If He, who was all free from sin,
  From yon bright climes of bliss withdrew,
To welcome even drunkards in,
  Shall we not love the drunkard too ?

And if the truths of Scripture are
　　Impervious to his clouded mind ;
'Tis ours to wage incessant war
　　With the foul sin that makes him blind.

For never till this foe be driven,
　　Shall Sharon's rose the world perfume ;
Nor hope, the beacon light of heaven,
　　The drunkard's darken'd soul illume.

Lovers of Zion ! foes of hell,
　　Ye who for Christ count all things loss ;
Strengthen our hands ; we seek to swell
　　The bloodless triumphs of the cross.

Rouse from your slumber, catch our zeal,
　　Our weapon is the written word ;
Our only guerdon Zion's weal ;
　　Our aim, the glory of the Lord !

INTEMPERANCE IS OUR COUNTRY'S BANE.

CHRISTIANS awake ! for still the foe
O'erwhelms the earth with grief and woe,
And tears in prostrate reason's eye,
" Haste to our aid," incessant cry.

Yes, drunkenness is still the bane
From which vain man will not refrain ;
And prejudice and custom bind
Their " swaddling bands" around his mind.

And every hamlet, every town,
Cries, " pull the nest of sorrow down ;"
And Jesus, from His throne above,
Weeps for the object of His love.

They're lost, for ever lost, if we
Cannot their minds from passion free—
Free from that wide-absorbing bane
Which crushes hope, and steals the brain.

Intemperance we aim to crush,
Oh, let us, Christians, make a rush
Upon this giant sin, and free
Lost millions from its slavery.

Go on, go on. and may that God
Whose word can make sin's temple nod—
May He expel this curse of men,
And save our land ! Amen, amen.

CHRISTIAN EXPEDIENCY.

PART FIRST.

When death unties the gordian knot,
  There is, beyond life's dwindling span,
An after state—a dateless lot—
  A long eternity for man.

Yet mortals, plung'd in blackest crime,
  Abuse the span in mercy given—
And "sell eternity for time,"—
  As if there were no hell—nor heaven.

For pleasures that repentance brings,
  For joys that tarry not a day,
Our drunken fellow-sinners fling
  Life—everlasting life, away.

And Zion wails her heavy loss,
  And Lebanon her cedars fell'd ;
For by deserters from the Cross,
  Damnation's reeling ranks are swell'd.

Can we this moral havoc view
  And feel no pain and shed no tears ?
Nor weeping, ask " What shall they do,
  When Christ, the righteous judge, appears ?"

Does not, as on these slain we look,
  The still small voice of conscience cry,
"Our own examples bait the hook,
  Which weaker brethren seize and die ?"

PART SECOND.

We cannot pray dead drunkards back,
  But lives in self-denial spent,
May lure the living from the track
  That thousands, now in torment, went.

" I'll not eat flesh," writes generous Paul,
  (Who knew and did his duty well),
" Lest by my right one brother fall,
  Or drunkard stumble into hell."

As he abstained—we likewise must
  Dash from our trembling lips the bowl,
And trample on that " fleshy lust,"
  Which wars against the drunkard's soul.

Weak is the Christian's faith who deems
  These—dead alive,—too deeply gone—
Blood—blood enough to save them streams
  From the rent heart of God's dear Son.

But, oh ! a parting must take place,
  The drunkard from his deeds obscene,
Before the troubled pool of grace
  Can wash the filthy leper clean.

Lord, teach us our course to shape,
  That our pure living may inspire
Our brethren with a wish to 'scape
  The vengeance of eternal fire.

TO THE DRUNKARD.

Besotted slave, by lust o'erpower'd,
  Repent, or dark thy doom will be ;
The dullest cloud that ever lower'd
        Now bursts on thee.
Souls die not with departing breath,
  And wilt thou trust that sceptic prop ?
There is a worse, a second death.
        Stop ! madman, stop !

There is another after life,
  Where hope is swallowed in despair ;
And bootless is the sinner's strife
        For mercy there.
Time flies, life wanes, and demons wait
  To bear thee off, a helpless prize ;
Oh ! ere the effort be too late,
        Rise ! drunkard, rise !

THE TEMPERANCE HOTEL.

We've built an hotel, and, behold, it is here,
But Jowitt will sell neither strong nor small beer,
For John is teetotal, and knows very well
What's fit to be sold at a temperance hotel.

Hurrah ! for friend John, and success to the cause,
Good luck to our friends and bad luck to its foes,
Destruction to liquors invented in hell,
For this is our aim with the temperance hotel.

And when we are wed,—"if that ever will be,"
As our friends will all look for a teetotal spree,
We'll have a nice party, and cut a real swell,
At neighbour John Jowitt's—the temperance hotel.

WE'LL BEAT 'EM.

THE landlords, alarmed at our panoply strong,
  Are striving to crush us ; well, let 'em !
They fight in a cause, which is grounded in wrong,
  And we'll beat as we've hitherto beat 'em.

Let 'em come with their paunches, as bulky as tubs,
  Huge lumps of corporeal lumber ;
Our abstinence fire-arms shall scatter the grubs,
  And gloriously lessen their number.

Moderation, (out on it), its out of our line,
  And shall we uphold it ? No, never !
No Jerry-wag gravy for us, nor malt brine,
  But beef and spring water for ever.

These, these are our pistols, fresh primed for a fray ;
  Present, and make ready, and cock 'em,
And then if the landlords assail us,—huzza !
  We'll let go our triggers, and sock 'em.

LITTLE-DROP SAINTS.

WHY do the little-drop men drink,
  Drink where they can pike it ?
What's their motive, do'st thou think ?
  'Tis because they like it.

Why is drink so sweet to such ?
  Why so fond on't is he ?
'Tis because the sparkling "lush"
  Makes his thinkers busy.

'Tis because the "slimy posh"
  Makes a man quite stupid ;
That's the motive, or, c'gosh,
  Cupid is not Cupid.

"Love thy neighbour as thyself,"
  That's the rule of duty ;
But the moderation elf
  Cannot see its beauty.

Love his neighbour?   Him, indeed!
 Love his weaker brother?
" Love thyself's " his darling creed,
 " Care not for another."

Though the lust of drink has sent
 Thousands unforgiven,
To their graves—their faces bent
 Far from God and heaven.

Fraught with apathy enough,
 Quite enough to freeze us,
He will calmly drink this stuff,
 And he'll talk of Jesus.

Out upon him ! while he drinks,
 (Though he does it snugly),
Selfishness in saints, methinks,
 Looks confounded ugly.

Well may worldlings closely eye
 Such an one's transgressions,
While his actions give the lie
 To his fair professions.

Drunkenness is hell's own car,
 Laden with lost millions,
And these " back door " drinkers are,
 Beelzebub's postillions.

Block its way, impede its course,
 " Scotch" no wheels, but " smash them ;"
On these drivers hurl your force—
 Floor, expose, and thrash 'em.

We can do without their helps,
 Can't we lads?   We'll try for't ;
Shame these moderation whelps,—
 Conquer, lads ! or die for't.

HANDLE NOT, TASTE NOT !

HANDLE not, nor touch, nor taste ;
 Lest your ranks be in disgrace,
By the careless walk of those
 Who seem zealous in the cause.
Let your words and actions be
 Models of propriety ;
Round your passions build a fence,
 Grounded upon abstinence.

Slave of custom and of lust,—
Man! thy station is the dust ;
If thine eye be not too dim,
God is power—confide in him.
On that God thy burden roll,
He can save thy feeble soul ;
Under mercy's pinions hide
All thy guilt, for Jesus died !

VALUE OF WATER.

As water ranks, by all the world confess'd,
Of nature's boons the greatest and the best,
So, in the catalogue of ills, the first
Is fierce, unmixed, unmitigable thirst ;
Lo ! when the fleshy pores too widely gape,¹
Through which the streams of vital juice escape,
The vital heat. which nothing then restrains,
Rolls the hot blood like lava through the veins ;
And thick eruptions on the parched skin
Are symptomatic of the pangs within ;
A raging Etna of intense desire,
Whose flames are hotter than material fire.
Oh! dread sensation,—restless, maddening, wild,—
Compared with which, stern hunger's tooth is mild.
Oh ! wretched state, of human woes the chief,
When man would swallow poison for relief ;
And one cool draught from nature's sparkling rills
Is worth " the cattle on a thousand hills."

A TEMPERANCE HYMN.

WRETCHED drunkard ! there is not
On our race a fouler blot ;—
Not above, around, below,
To himself so great a foe :
Not on earth's polluted sod,
Such a traitor to his God !

Ah! what fiend can so transform
Man, into a scrawling worm ?
In yon tiny vessel lurks,
That which all this ruin works !
Drug—than juice of henbane worse :—
Man and Britain's greatest curse !

Yes, the sot,—like one possess'd,
Spurr'd by lust,—by habit press'd ;
For the contents of that bowl,
Risks the safety of his soul ;
Barters Heaven, and Hell defies ;
Mocks his God,—and, mocking, dies !

Honour'd with our Master's name,
Zeal for souls should ours inflame ;
He is not of Christ, who can
Tamper with this bane of man :
Lax professors,—(mark it well !)
Slope the drunkard's path to hell !

Conscience whispers in alarm—
" Do thy brother's soul no harm !"
Rouse ye, brethren, from your sleep,
Hear your God, and blush, and weep :
" With your meat,"—He long has cried,—
" Kill not him, for whom Christ died !"

Drunkard ! can thy soul forget,
Him,—who paid thy mighty debt ?—
Him,—extended on the tree ;—
Stretch'd, and pierc'd, and nail'd, for thee /
Thou art sick, and He can cure ;
To that Fountain, deep and pure,
Crimson'd with Redeeming Gore,
Brother, " Go and sin no more !"

———

KESTER'S BOTTLE.

A TALE.

I, who so lately sang your praise,—
  Preachers of Vauxhall-road—
And, in my poor but honest lays,
  Sounded your fame abroad,—
I take my harp and sing again ;
But ah ! how different is the strain
  To what it was before!
From naked truth I weave a song,
Reckless if slander's venom'd tongue
  Should blacken my name o'er.
The truth, the truth I do revere,
And by that chart my course I'll steer :
Corruption, from her winding maze,
I'll drag before the public gaze ;

And now another trump I'll blow—
Another truth the world shall know.
Hear it, ye treacherous Vauxhall crew!
And from your filthy entrails spew
That gin, which met the eager throttle
Of some of you from " Kester's bottle."
The march of intellect brings forth
New characters of passing worth :
For instance, " The Free Gospel Preachers"
To fame's hill top are nearest reachers.
These men, who, though they rant and prate
'Gainst hirelings, with relentless hate ;
And cry, in language trite and nice,
" We preach the gospel, without price !"
Yet in their deeds they are so queer,
That Christians eye, with jealous fear,
Their motives,—crying, " Their chief wish is
Not souls redeem'd, but 'loaves and fishes.' "
And so think I ; for I know one
I look with jealous eye upon.
By trade this man's a c——— maker,—
Known better as a great snuff-taker.
Readers, full well ye ken, I ween,
By what I've stated, who I mean.
This man once, on a Sabbath eve,
Of wife and children took his leave ;
He pass'd by many a street and ward,
And came at last to N—— C——— yard ;
He paus'd not, till he stood before
J—— G——'s ; when he found the door,
He open'd it, with trembling hand,
Saying, " Night-preaching I can't stand ;
See how my feeble body shakes !
Oh dear ! how my poor belly aches !
John, has ' Old Kester's bottle' in
A drop or two of chapel gin?"
" No," John replied, " a drop there's not ;
But, if there's any to be got,
I or my wife can get you some :
Whether will you have gin or rum ?"
" Get which you will," the preacher said ;
So John to buy the liquor sped.
O, preacher ! preacher ! did you right,
In acting thus that Sunday night ?
A man, and after that his spouse,
To send into a public-house,
To buy you gin ! The Scriptures say,
" Remember, keep the Sabbath day,
And keep it holy." You did not,
You canting, greedy, snuffy sot !

Ye Vauxhall people, you did pay
For what this fellow drank that day :
And yet, O people, this is he
Who said, "We preach the gospel free!
To tell Redemption's wondrous story,
Without a fee, is our chief glory.
Brethren, we are not your wealth craving ;
The thing we want is your souls saving !"
I do not say he preach'd for cash ;—
He loves rum, gin, and such like trash
Too well ; and in this thought, no doubt,
My simple tale will bear me out.
This circumstance so roused the ire
Of T—— and G——w, in the fire
Of their just wrath, they, with fell stroke,
Old Kester's bottle broke.
Now, you who I had face to face,
Near Banks's stand, in th' Market-place ;
Who said that I had wrote a libel
On you yourselves, and on your tribe all ;
When you see I have wrote another,
You'll do your best my voice to smother.
Well, 'gainst my head your fury knock,
For I can stand the tempest's shock.
Corruption I'll expose; and you
Have got your share of it.—Adieu !

DRAM-DRINKING REFORMERS!

YE champions of freedom, oppressions out-wormer's,
Who would roast every tyrant on liberty's spit,
Ye air-castle stormers, ye dram-shop reformers,
"Give ear," for I want to "chop logic" a bit.

Political drunkards are all "losing stakes" men,
Who take losing methods to get what each craves ;
You're poor as March rabbits, and poverty makes men
What drunkards deserve to be, Paupers and Slaves!

One talks of "repealing the taxes on knowledge,"
Sufficiently loud "the deaf adder" to vex ;
Yet he must have been taught at a learn-nothing college,
For the gobbin can't tell a big Q from an X.

And one, because some turn their coats, keeps a-mourning,
And if he could catch 'em, the scamps he would "muz ;"
Yet, I think in my heart he had better be turning
His own, for it cannot look worse than it does.

Another would " wipe off our national debt," and
  He'd dot with the " sponge " of which Cobbett could talk,
Yet to wipe of his own debt a sponge he can't get, and
  He still is the dupe of the two-for-one chalk.

Another would get out of tyranny's books, but
  He's down in his grocer's, who gives him a squeeze,
For he gets not a penny, by hook or by crook, but
  Goes there for " trust" bacon, and maggotty cheese !

Another would make " freedom get on her legs," but
  His thoughts must be rank " topsy-turvyish " grown ;
He might doctor poor liberty's " sish-shashle " pegs, but
  The sot has quite lost the use of his own.

One will never desert those who live by their labours,
  The struggle with him will but end with his life,
Yet the wretch (and it's very well known to his neighbours)
  Has been " cribbed " above once, for " deserting his wife!"

Another would " kindle a radical bonfire,"
  To burn up the trash and the dross of the state,
Yet for one week, at least, he has never had a fire,
  To warm his blue nose in his own rusty grate !

Another would " patch up our laws," and he itches
  To mend 'em wherever a rent place appears ;
Yet he can't pay his tailor for mending his breeches ;
  Just look ! what a couple of leg sleeves he wears.

Another would " loose all the slaves in the nation,"
  And till he has loos'd 'em he never would stop ;
Yet, he must have glanced o'er his own situation,
  For the fellow can't loose his own shirt out of pop.

When election time comes, these men chatter like parrots,
  And if bawling would win, then would tyranny fall ;
But they live in unregistered cellars and garrets,
  And, having no votes, they are nothing at all.

Are you blind, or aught worse, drunken champions of
      freedom ?
  Hear me out, I beseech you, I know what you'd say ;
You would give their full rights to the millions who need 'em,
  " Amen !" I reply, but you go the wrong way.

We've had talkings sufficient, and now we want actions ;
  Your cups have undone you, lay these on the shelves ;
Leave the shell of reform unto parties and factions ;
  Seize the kernel at once by reforming yourselves.

Let our joiners and spinners, mechanics and founders,
  Keep the brass they once spent on their bowls in their
    fists ;
Their money thus saved, what a crowd of "ten pounders"
  Might rally round Freedom, and swell out her lists !

Teetotal's your engine ; it looks but a puny one ;
  But, work it, you'll find it gives strength to the weak,
For, thus knit, we shall form a Political Union,
  Which tyrants may hack at, but never can break.

CHRIST DIED FOR DRUNKARDS.

Ye, who for souls immortal strive,
  Arise, and form a temp'rance band,
By Jesus led, equipp'd to drive
  The horrid monster from the land.

How many feel his gripe, and lo !
  The Priest and Levite pass them by,
And Christians self-securely go,
  And cast aside a pitying eye.

Yet left as drunkards are, alone,
  Their souls were bought with Jesu's blood ;
For them the garden heard His groan,
  And gush'd for them the purple flood.

But led by drink—accursed drink—
  What crowds their hell-ward journey take,
And madly sport on ruin's brink—
  Lead, lead them back for Jesu's sake.

Oh ! teach them "not to touch nor taste,"
  Lest hell should seize what Mercy claims ;
Haste to their rescue—Jesus—haste,
  And snatch thy purchase from the flames.

WHAT IS A DRUNKARD?

What is a drunkard ? A lust serving devotee
  To his own belly, and Satan a slave ;
Fill'd with a wild idiotical levity,
  Crushing his hopes on the brink of the grave.
Waken him ! waken him ! Friends of Humanity !
  Let not his danger affect you in vain ;
Rouse him ! and shew him his reckless insanity,
  Lead him to safety, and bid him abstain !

What are the landlords? The patrons of revelries,
 Vendors of poison, and jackalls for sin ;
Cursing the world with their death-breeding devilries,
 Bearing the name of rum, jerry, and gin !
Men who think rightly, that drunkards are crazy men,
 Rul'd by a nod, like the wives of a Turk !
Humble the pride of these Turpin-like lazy men,
 Stop the supplies, and compel them to work !

What are their spirit vaults, 'dram shops, and brewing
  holes ?
 Dens where the engines of mischief are crammed, ·
Famine, and sickness, and folly, and ruin holes,
 Mammon's high places, where millions are damn'd.
Soldiers of godliness, arm ye, and scatter these
 Haunts of despair, of terrific renown ;
Brandish the weapons of reason, and batter these
 Babels of guilt, till they crash and come down.

Recommend abstinence ! Practice it too, my lads !
 Give none occasion for foemen to sneer ;
Labour ! Unite ! to the good cause be true, my lads ;
 Reckless, like Hampden, of danger and fear !
Back your exertions with spotless sincerity ;
 Charity calls you—arise at her nod ;
Strike ! for man's weal, and your country's prosperity ;
 Battle with hell, for the honours of God !

SHUFFLE THE CARDS !

OUR cause is a good one ; depend upon that !
 Come and join us, ye " Jerry-wag" buyers !
Never mind what the publicans say, nor "Old Scrat ;"
 For I'm sure they're a parcel of liars.

While you give 'em your brass for their brown-colour'd suds,
 They'll call you " free," " easy," and " funny ;"
But they'll treat you no better than lumber-room goods,
 When they've physick'd you out of your money.

Then, then will the landlady twitch up her snout ;
 Then, then will the " Jerry-lord" mask all
His nods and his " thank ye's," and cry, " Get thee out !
 Begone, thou poor penniless rascal !"

This is all the reward (except hunger and sighs)
 Which the landlord returns for thy kindness ;
Unless the fat rogue aims a blow at thy eyes,
 And requites thy good-nature with blindness.

Thy money all gone, and thy moveables "popp'd,"
   Thy carcase and character stinking ;
For labour unfit ; or, if able, "unshopp'd"—
   These, these are the pleasures of drinking !

Go then to the landlord who smil'd upon thee :
   Will he let thee lie down in his pasture ?
Will Boniface open his pockets ? Not he !
   But lock 'em a thousand times faster !

Appeal to his wife :—will she open her purse,
   To lessen the evils that lash thee ?
Will she crown thee as like ! With a sneer and a curse,
   She'll call up her bullies to thrash thee!

While this termagant swears, how the devil will laugh,
   Till hell's caverns resound with the titter,
At thee, whose bright hopes they have scatter'd like chaff,—
   Confound 'em ! they're all of a litter !

Oh ! what is this drum-bellied crew at such pains
   To hoist their fine signs in the air for ?
To put in their pockets thy hard-gotten gains :
   "Number One" is the chap which they care for.

Let's shuffle the cards ! they've gull'd us enough ;
   Too long they have finger'd our pelf, lads !
Learn a lesson from them—yes, abandon their stuff,
   And strive to do something for self, lads !

"We cannot," you say, "give up draining our jugs :"
   Try again ! and you'll learn to abhor it ;
Join us ! and, unlike the vile vendors of drugs,
   We'll cure you, and charge nothing for it !

The following lines were suggested to the mind of Mr.
Anderton, after the public meeting at Warrington had
commenced, on Saturday evening, June 11th, 1836. Mr.
A. being the second speaker on this occasion, he began his
speech with the following poetic effusion, which is copied
from the *Liverpool and Warrington Temperance Herald.*

TO THE TEETOTALLERS OF WARRINGTON.

   We are not tired,—our cause is good,—
   And to our pledge each feels a debtor ;
   Joys pour upon us like a flood,—
   And every day we like it better.

Just now we've had a two days' spree,
And yet we are not "fagg'd" or "weary,"—
Nor penniless,—but full of glee,—
And "flush" of brass,—and fresh and cheery !

About this very time last year,
" Us chaps" were trudging from the races,*
Without a penny—seen quite clear
In our stretch'd eyes, and lantern faces ;—
Our breeches soak'd in ale and spew,—
No "chewing stuff" within the platter :—
Our lips daub'd o'er with stuff like glue ;—
Our porridge bags—than pancakes flatter.

This was, last year, our woeful case ;—
Our pinched guts, like thunder, rumbling ;—
And hunger show'd his pale green face ;
And, oh ! our wives, like cats, kept grumbling !
And what was worse than all besides,
(Just as it is with all carousers),
Our "yellow boys" had cut, to hide
Their noses in the landlord's trowsers !

But blessings on our blessed cause ;—
We stand upon a better bottom :
The landlords are our mortal foes ;
And we have found it out,—'od rot em !
Our aspects tell a different tale :—
Strong drink is bad and we forsake it.—
Good night brown stout, and nut-brown ale,—
And Jerry—may the devil take it !

SONG.

Ye enemies of drunkenness,
    Who sneer at moderation ;
Who rather would go " Jerry"-less
    Than brutalise the nation,—
Press on ! and, though the greedy clan
    Of landlords hotly press you,
While working for the good of man,
    Be firm, and God will bless you.

While hypocrites cry, " Dear, ah ! me,"
    And take a little sup, lads ;
Pester the knaves continually,
    Until they give it up, lads.

* Held at Newton.

'Tis true they may not like your jokes ;
　But, if your arrows hit 'em,
Let 'em abstain, like fair-up folks,
　And then the cap won't fit 'em.

As for the devil's slaves, who sell
　The stuff which breeds confusion ;
Who get their licenses from hell,
　To spread the great delusion ;
If Truth will grant us elbow-room,
　If landlords must be smitten,—
Let's grasp you huge Teetotal broom,
　And sweep them out of Britain !

Procure a pair of moral scales—
　Let Love's firm hand adjust 'em ;
Heed not, though Mr. Mammon rail ;
　Nor dread the jeers of Custom :
Fill one with thousands freedomless,
　With thousands freed the other ;—
And which weighs heaviest—selfishness,
　Or safety for a brother !

Custom, indeed !　If it has propp'd
　The Bacchanal's loud riot,
From reason's laws it must be lopp'd,
　And saints must change their diet.
The one-glass saint may close his eye,
　While sanctioning the revel ;
But does he act consistently ?
　What think ye ?—Does the devil !

The true-bred saint will spurn the " nast,"
　Far from his lips he'll toss it ;
He will not eat it in puff paste,
　Nor drink it in a posset.
Whate'er his sect, it matters not—
　A bishop or a Ranter,—
Ale will not sparkle in his pot,
　Nor wine in his decanter.

If "little drop" men rail at you,
　Laugh at the bootless gammon ;
If landlords, to their pockets true,
　Raise one cheer more for Mammon ;
And if their chief this question puts :—
　" In that case, what must we do ?"
Bid him sweat down his bulky guts
　By working, same as ye do !

While drunkards, without number, steep
  Their souls in torpor,—snoring
On ruin's brink!—can Christians sleep,
  Unhelping, undeploring!
To arms! to arms! for earth and heaven!
  Let Truth's artillery rattle!
The plot is ripe,—the signal's given,—
  May God decide the battle!

ENGLAND'S CURSE!

YES, England pants beneath the weight,
  The dead weight of her greatest bane;
The ship is sinking with her freight,
  And hell usurps where heaven should reign.

Man's direst foe—the drunkard's drink—
  Spreads far and near its horrid fires;
Yet, yet professing Christians shrink
  From fighting when their God requires.

Hell's deepest caverns burn e'en now
  With souls by drunkenness undone:
Before that idol millions bow,
  Which damns the wretch it glares upon.

While down they send their drunken hosts—
  Men, for whose souls God's Son was giv'n,—
Should Jesu's captains quit their posts,
  While hell is thus defrauding heav'n?

We charge you, in the Saviour's name,
  Who for your sake His own life gave,
Your drunken brothers to reclaim
  From doom more wretched than the grave.

Fight, wrestle, struggle with the foe;
  One effort for the drunkard make;
Give this huge vice its mortal blow,—
  And do it now, for Jesu's sake!

DRUNKARDS SLEEP!—THE SWORD HANGS O'ER THEM!

DRUNKARDS sleep!—the sword hangs o'er them!
  Brethren! your example give;
Let your light so shine before them
  That they may repent and live.

Habit, with her mountain barriers,
  Chokes their path : without delay,
Break them down, ye gospel warriors !
  Take the stumblingblock away.

Fathers, husbands, sons, and brothers,
  Laden with this heavy doom ;
Sisters, daughters, wives and mothers,
  Sinking hopeless to the tomb ;
Sin's broad way with victims crowded ;
  Homes despoil'd ; and millions, too,
By the winding-sheet enshrouded,
  From their graves appeal to you !

By the ties this vice hath riven,
  By the homes this sin hath marr'd,
By the souls this curse hath driven
  Unreclaim'd to their reward ;
By the earth which it is thinning,
  By the hell which ends its track,—
Use your influence with the sinning ;
  Guide your Father's stray sheep back.

What, though for these lost immortals
  Blood from Calvary's fount may gush,—
Thousands perish— hell's wide portals
  Gape for them, and down they rush !
Lo ! through error's devious turnings,
  See what fearful speed they make !
From the everlasting burnings,
  Save them, for your Master's sake !

ALBION ! THY FRIENDS HAVE CAUSE TO MOURN.

ALBION ! thy friends have cause to mourn :
Thy bosom is gored, and thy vitals torn ;
One giant sin, beneath a sea
Whose billows are fire, is 'whelming thee !
Mourn, England ! mourn !—thou land of tombs,—
Thy laurels are dead, but the cypress blooms.

Salem weeps o'er—and weeps in vain —
Her Sabbaths contemn'd, and her slighted fame :
In Belial's fold her flock is penn'd ;
Beneath his foul shrine her wand'rers bend.
Weep, Zion ! weep ! With conquest flush'd,
The mockers exult, and thy songs are hush'd.

Drunkard ! thy life is deeply stain'd,
Thy beauty is marr'd, and thy home profan'd ;
Thy wife's fill'd eyes reveal her tale,
Thy little ones breathe their hapless wail ;
Turn, drunkard ! turn ! thou lost one, see,—
In mercy's wide ark there is room for thee.

Lovers of God the crucified !
Who suffer'd for you, for the drunkard died :
Then gird your loins,—one effort make
To rescue the lost, for Jesu's sake.
Help, brothers ! help ! the lost to save,
From ruin on earth, and beyond the grave.

O Jesus ! fan the dying flame
Of mercy, in all who bear Thy name ;
Shine on our cause, and in Thy sight
May thousands emerge from sin's dark night.
Speak, Jesus ! speak ! for, at Thy nod,
The sleepers will wake, and return to God.

Deserted by my dearest friends,
Strong drink despair and sorrow sends ;
O'er children, wife, and lonely cot,
There hangs a sad and threat'ning lot.
Hark ! hark ! some footsteps hither stray !
But joys can't soothe the drunkard's day.
Is there a hope ?—strangers, quickly tell !
Abstain, repent, believe,—all's well.

Enlisted in the Temperance band,
With drunken sots on every hand,
Our careful watch explores the lanes,
To snatch the slaves from Satan's chains ;
And oft we hear the cheering voice
Of homes reform'd, where all rejoice :—
" What cheer, neighbours ?—quickly tell !
Abstain'd, believ'd Christ died,—all's well !

SUNG ON LAYING THE FOUNDATION-STONE OF
THE TEMPERANCE HALL, BOLTON,
MAY 24TH, 1839.

Vice lords it o'er this Christian land ;
Her man-traps set and baited stand,
  To catch unwary souls ;
And, " seeking whom he may devour,"
With serpent guile and boundless power,
  The " roaring lion" prowls.

Till late, the servants of the Lord
Forbore to wield the two-edg'd sword,
    In blameful slumber laid ;
Though every drunkard, dead and lost,
Was purchas'd at so great a cost,
    On Calvary's summit paid.

Awaking from that guilty trance,
Behold our Temperance ranks advance,
    Our cross-mark'd banners wave ;
And on this spot we pitch our tent,
The schemes of hell to circumvent,
    And liberate the slave !

Yet, firmly though the stone we plant,
Unless the Lord the increase grant,
    How barren our employ.
Lord ! make the truths proclaimed here,
To hapless drunkards far and near,
    " Glad tidings of great joy."

A life-boat may our temple be,
For thousands toss'd upon the sea
    Of lust, and shame, and sin ;
For them and theirs a refuge prove,
A stepping-stone to Jesu's love,
    For all who enter in.

From drunkards who have mercy found,
Oft may our Temperance Hall resound
    With shouts of holy mirth ;
And Bolton, now so sunk in crime,
Become, like Zion of old time,
    A praise in all the earth.

AFTER LAYING THE STONE.

The stone is laid, whereon we trust
    A refuge shall be built,
To which the frenzied sons of lust
    Will fly from chains and guilt.

Here contrite reprobates shall mourn,
    Who never wept before ;
And, trembling for their souls, return,
    Resolv'd to sin no more.

Here shall their wives and children meet,
To speak of joys restor'd ;
And join their neighbours in a sweet
Hosanna to the Lord.

Here shall backsliders, sick in soul,
Bewail their guilt and loss ;
And, yearning for salvation, roll
Their burdens on the Cross.

Thy glory, and the weal of man,—
To these our hopes aspire :
Our efforts, Lord, with favour scan,
And grant our heart's desire.

Are not the souls of drunkards Thine—
Thine, for a price paid down ?
Lord ! fit them evermore to shine,
Bright jewels in Thy crown.

TO CHRISTIANS.

DID Jesus die to pay our debt ?
Then such as feel the sprinkled blood
Will, like Him, ease and self forget,
And part with all for Zion's good.

Love bade Him quit the joys above ;
Love brought the Father's firstborn down :
And we must show our faith by love,—
No love, no bliss ; " no cross, no crown."

For us He left a shining heaven,—
Unbought, unbidden, undesir'd ;
And, where so much is done and given,
There must and will be much required.

Why stand ye idle all the day ?
While drunkards—an unnumber'd host—
Madly with their perdition play,
Die without mercy, and are lost.

The true saint never thinks of self,
When battling with a damning vice ;
But gladly parts with fame and pelf,
If God demands the sacrifice.

As Christ for him, so he, for such
As have by guilt Heaven's anger brav'd,
Will give up all, nor deem it much—
Nothing,—if drunkards can be sav'd.

H

Diseas'd without, diseas'd within,—
  Their case a heart of flint would melt :
Have pity on these slaves of sin,
  Ye, who the Saviour's power have felt.

He paid your debt's extreme demands,
  When hell's dread prison gap'd for you :
For Christ's sake, seize your brother brands,
  And snatch them from the burning too.

Oh ! while the sot to ruin drives,
  Point out to him a different track ;
And, by the magnet of your lives,
  Attract the lust-born truants back.

Poor Zion mourns her scatter'd sheep ;
  And can her shepherds sleep supine ?
" The fields are white," and who shall reap ?
  Servant of God, the work is thine !

ELEGIES, &c.

TO MARGARET.

WHERE is thy sister ? Not on earth,
  In this low vale of tears ;
That voice of sweet and guileless mirth
  No more shall bless thy ears ;
And thou may'st weep as one bereft ;
  Then, let thy grief-drops flow :
And thou may'st smile, for she has left
  Her heritage of woe.

She has "shuffled off this mortal coil,"
  And her deserted clay
Is made the last destroyer's spoil,
  In mouldering decay.
Her earthly tortures were extreme,
  And her mortal eye wax'd dim ;
But Jesus suffer'd to redeem,
  And her mind's eye gaz'd on Him.

Then treasure up her dying words,
  Let them thy heart revive ;
That retrospect a hope affords
  That Jane is yet alive.
Before thy beauteous sister died,
  Ere yet her soul was freed,—
" He ever lives above," she cried,
  " For me to intercede."

Margaret, where is thy sister now ?
  With the shining ranks of grace ;
The crown of life relumes her brow,
  And glory decks her face.
Oh ! may that soaring soul be fraught
  With energy divine,
To make her Saviour and her lot
  For ever, ever thine.

Margaret, I have perus'd her life,
  Whose matchless zeal these pages prove :
An angel in a world of strife,
  A martyr in the cause of love.
She was a chosen one of God ;
  She felt the Saviour always near ;
She prov'd the power of Jesu's blood ;
  She found the love that casts out fear.

Where is she now ? Where Jesus is ;
  Where sin and sorrow may not come ;
In heaven —that heritage of bliss ;
  In Zion—her abiding home.
Oh ! in our life's short, fleeting, day,
  We have a glorious work to do ;
Then let us track her shining way,
  That we may dwell with Jesus too.

TO —— AND HIS SISTERS, ON THE SUDDEN DEATH OF THEIR PARENTS.

Poor orphans—twice bereft !
With all your living troop of friends, no other
  Can fill the gap left by the cherish'd dead—
  Your kind, dear father, with the silver'd head,
And your sweet mother.

The grave's serene eclipse,
As with a sable curtain, shadeth
  From your tear-laden and corporeal glance
  Those dearest ones, in bright inheritance
Which never fadeth.

How sorrowful to you,
How beautiful to them, was this transition !
  When, as they pass'd the dim and shadowy maze,
  The golden city's clear and glittering blaze
Fill'd their rapt vision.

Children, your grief repress,
Nor yield that deep, excessive scope to sorrow :
  Like them, for your mysterious change prepare ;
  That, after death's brief midnight, ye may share
Their bright to-morrow.

Would ye the lost recall
To this dread Golgotha and weeping,
  From a retreat so tearless, calm, and pure,
  Where Jesus hath the little flock secure
In His own keeping ?

Excessive grief is vain :
Ye know earth's seeming evergreens must wither.
Beyond time's limits, and the dark'ning foam
Of Jordan, is your parents' happy home—
Go, track them thither !

TO THE WIDOW AND DAUGHTER OF THE LATE RICHARD STEPHENSON.

WHY do those heavy floods of sorrow gather,
In eyes where late bright smiles were seen to play ?
They flow for him—the husband, friend, and father,
By death's stern summons rudely snatch'd away.

A husband faithful to his first embraces,
A father sway'd by gentleness benign,
A man whose earthly love and moral graces
Were fashion'd in the mould of love divine.

Oh ! bitter stroke,—all power of words excelling—
To lose a husband, father, friend, like this :
For never soul resign'd the fleshly dwelling
More loving or more fondly lov'd than his.

Yea, while you raise the voice of lamentation,
I, too, will grieve because that tongue is mute
Which, tun'd by Jesus and His great salvation,
Hath match'd Isaiah's lyre or David's lute.

But what though death all human ties can sever,—
The soul defies the tyrant's stern embrace ;
Believers only die to live for ever,
With Jesus, their Redeemer, face to face.

The way to life lies through the grave's dim portal ;
And oh ! what joy doth this sweet truth afford :—
Our buried friend survives,—a free immortal,
Cloth'd in a glorious body like the Lord.

Poor, lonely widow ! toss'd by every billow—
Why grieve for one so honour'd, safe, and blest ?
The Lamb is now thy husband—go, and pillow
Thy throbbing heart upon His bleeding breast.

Thou weepest, Anne ! and reason cannot blame thee ;
Yet, doff that sackcloth for a garb less wild :
The orphan's Father will adopt and claim thee,
When thou art willing to become His child.

Oh ! would you share the home that he inherits,
Whose spirit hath just dropp'd the cumbrous clod,—
Make good your claim, through the Redeemer's merits,
And, strong in faith, "prepare to meet your God."

ON THE DEATH OF MARY ——.

When Mary's spirit, panting for the skies,
    Left tenantless her fair abode of clay,
I dare not watch the grave-side obsequies,
    I dare not look where her discarded relics lay.
And now—when two long years have fleeted by—
    A keen remembrance will sometimes awaken
My startled soul, and force a heaving sigh,
    And shake a heart by aught besides unshaken.

"Time tempers sorrow;" it may lull awhile,
    But not eradicate, the sense of grief;
And even I, who smile when others smile,
    Have sorrows which admit of no relief:
For so ill-starr'd has been my destiny,
    My brightest prospects in the bud were blighted;
And cheerfulness and pleasure fly from me,
    As one to dark despondency united.

ON THE DEATH OF A YOUNG FRIEND.

Why should you mourn, with unavailing sorrow,
    The loss of one whom skill nor prayers could save?
Why load your souls with hopelessness, and borrow
    The black and dismal aspect of the grave?

If by this life man's destiny were bounded;
    If like the brutes your dear departed slept;
Reason might own your sad complaints well-grounded,
    Nor blame the sigh you heav'd, the tear you wept.

If, by Death's irrespective slaughter,
    Our dreams of something after death were cross'd;
Then might her parents mourn their vanish'd daughter,
    Their sleeping child, as one for ever lost.

But, if at Death the unharm'd spirit smileth,
    Your mourning hush, your bitter tear-drops spare;
For there, where nothing enters that defileth,
    Your young immortal breathes her native air.

Even while I muse, with that glad, chasten'd feeling
    Which hopes like this to trusting souls impart,
Methinks I hear sweet consolation stealing,
    Like heaven's own music to my ravish'd heart.

'Tis her dear voice—for it can be no other:
    "Let not your hearts," she cries, "so troubled be;
Rejoice, my father, and be glad my mother;
    For all is well; arise, and follow me!"

ON THE DEATH OF ANN BROWN.

HER soul is from the body fled,
  To Him from whom at first it came ;
That humble, fervent one is dead,
  Who set our meetings in a flame.
Ann Brown has ceas'd with us to meet,
To worship God in Jordan-street.

No more her "class" will hear her say :—
  "I feel encourag'd to go on !"
Dissolv'd is her frail house of clay,
  Her spirit to its rest is gone—
Gone to enjoy the rich reward,
To be for ever with the Lord.

What though, till the last trump shall sound,
  Her frame (as every mortal's must)
Lies withering in the clay-cold ground,
  Commingling with its native dust,
Enwrapt in black, sepulchral night :
Her soul is with the saints in light.

Methinks I hear the ransom'd cry,
  "Worthy the Lamb who died for us !"
And, seeing Ann, our sister, nigh,
  They greet her happy spirit, thus :—
"Come, sister, to our blood-wash'd throng,
And join in our eternal song."

Well, Ann is safe—safe from the snares
  Of hell, the world, and sin : yes ! she
Is gone, from death, and pain, and fears,
  To be where she must ever be.
May we, at last, like her arise,
And meet her spirit in the skies.

ON THE DEATH OF MISS JANE WARING
(HIS COUSIN.)

IT is a heart-affecting thing to see
  A youthful female sink by slow decay :
She fights in vain with her last enemy ;
  He saps her health and takes her life away.

A careless eye will shed a tear for such ;
  But unto friends how will that friend appear
Who prematurely dies ? It is too much—
  Too great a burthen for their hearts to bear.

Betsy and Anne, a friend has died of late ;
 You ne'er must see her in this world again :
Edward, how sad and lonely is thy fate !
 For death has parted thee from thy dear Jane.

But ye—her friends, and thou—her only love,
 If virtuous, shall meet with her among
The ranks of the redeemed ones above,
 And swell, with her, their everlasting song.

She was a lovely being here ; my eyes
 But rarely met with one so sweetly fair.
What is she now ?   A spirit, o'er the skies, ·
 Basking in bliss and cloth'd with brightness there.

ON THE DEATH OF A FRIEND.

Our brother is gone ! with solemn tread,
 We bear him to the gloomy spot,
The narrow house, the dreamless bed,
 Where we must shortly sleep and rot.

So runs the sentence—" Dust to dust ;"
 So earth to earth is now restor'd :
Peace to his ashes ! and, we trust,
 His "better part" is with the Lord.

Ah ! sadly would his soul have fared,
 If Heaven to mark had been severe ;
Or if compassion had not spared
 This barren tree another year.

Long, long he slighted grace received—
 Almost too far God's power defied ;
And, but for mercy, as he lived
 This once-a-drunkard would have died.

Oh ! may yon bell's deep, warning sound,
 That moans our brother's last farewell,
Beget a wish, in all around,
 To miss the "bitter pains of hell."

Oh ! may his death some drunkard win
 From the broad way, by millions trod ;
That living, he may die to sin ;
 And dying, he may live with God.

ON THE DEATH OF A FEMALE FRIEND.

Your grief is her due, and I share in your sorrow;
  Yet we who have known her can never despond:
Our tears, as they drop on her sepulchre, borrow
  A ray of the glory that greets her beyond.
By wishing her here, we unwittingly wrong her :
  No gulf divides her from Him she ador'd ;
A fetterless spirit—a captive no longer—
  A mother in Israel sleeps in the Lord.

We lose, for a season, that friend so endearing,.
  So lavish of kindness, unconscious of guile ;
The tones of that voice, to the mourner so cheering,
  The ring of her laugh, and the gleam of her smile :
How meekly she pass'd through the period allotted,
  Sweet proof with rejoicing afford ;
And, closing a pilgrimage pure and unspotted,
  A mother in Israel sleeps in the Lord.

The Saviour she lov'd to His servant, in pity,
  Reveals the dear friend His compassion had lent ;
And sorrow subsides, as we muse on the city
  To which in glad triumph she recently went.
Behind her the robe of mortality casting,
  A native of Eden—to Eden restor'd ;
O'ershadow'd and pillow'd by love everlasting,
  A mother in Israel sleeps in the Lord.

---

*TO MR. JOSHUA PHILLIPS, ON THE DEATH OF HIS DAUGHTER.

*Written at the request of the poet's sister, then Miss Ellen
Anderton.*

Thy heart was sad, thy looks were wan,
  Thy faith and patience sorely proved,
When death cut short Rebecca's span ;
I could have wept with thee, old man,
  The loss of thy beloved.

Oh ! 'twas a bitter drop to part
  From one with thee so closely blended :
No wonder if the fatal dart
Had likewise reach'd thy aching heart,
  And all its throbbing ended.

---

* Mr. Phillips lived and died a firm Teetotaller and a Christian.

In fancy I could hear thee say,
　　As death perform'd the deed of slaughter,—
"She is too young to be thy prey ;
Take me, for I am old and gray ;
　　But spare, oh ! spare my daughter !"

Yet was thy lost Rebecca fain
　　To shuffle off the mortal fetter :
Life was to her a load of pain ;
But now she feels " to die is gain,"
　　To be with Christ far better.

Before she plung'd in Jordan's tide,
　　A glimpse of Paradise was given ;
As, waking from her dream she cried,—
" I've seen my Joshua !" and died,
　　And join'd her babe in heaven.

Then hush that sob, and dry those tears ;
　　She's left a Sodom, false and hollow,—
Its guilt and anguish, grief and fears—
And gone where, in a few brief years,
　　Old pilgrim, thou must follow.

The future claims thy care ; arise !
　　With faith unwavering, clear, and steady,
Take up thy cross, obtain the prize—
A home beyond the starry skies—
　　For all things now are ready.

Earth is no long abiding-place
　　For one whose hairs are hoary :
Up, then ! for, at bright Canaan's gate,
Rebecca and her children wait,
　　And beckon thee to glory.

———

*ON THE DEATH OF MISS HANNAH PHILLIPS.

"There is a time for all things :" joy and sadness
　　Will, in their turn, the eye and memory steep ;
And, though philosophy may count it madness,
　　When friends depart, 'tis Nature's time to weep.

Nor are we bidden by our God to smother
　　Tears for kind hearts to death's embraces crept ;
For David mourn'd for Jonathan his brother,
　　And at the grave of Lazarus " Jesus wept."

---

* This poem was lithographed, framed, and presented to the poet by
Miss Phillips' friends.

Sweet is the sob that bruis'd affection heaveth;
   And oft I muse how bitter death would be,
If, when my soul its tabernacle leaveth,
   No brimful eye could spare a drop for me.

No wonder, then, that sorrow's briny traces
   Have in your cheeks worn many a channell'd spot;
For, from the circle of familiar faces,
   One hath departed, and returneth not.

No marvel if your quivering lips should falter,
   And sounds of wail mix with the voice of prayer,
When, kneeling round the dear domestic altar,
   Your lifted eyes behold no Hannah there.

Weep on, weep on! yet mingle faith with sorrow,
   And Hope's sweet balm will mitigate the sore;
For death is but the prelude of a morrow,
   When souls shall reunite and part no more.

Paint not your loss to me—I know the story:
   Why Hannah here to Hannah there prefer?
Though she may never leave her rest in glory,
   Through the strait gate you may go home to her.

Why look on earth for lasting habitations?
   This place is not your rest; awake! arise!
Haste to the city which has no foundations,
   " Not made with hands, eternal in the skies."

Then seek the cure for hearts with grief oppress'd,
   Then find your dead alive, your lost restor'd:
There dwell the ransom'd, glorified, and bless'd
   And there she is, for ever with the Lord.

ON THE DEATH OF AGNES POLLARD.

My dear fellow-teachers, our band has diminish'd;
   That fate which Jehovah alone can retard
Has robb'd us of Agnes—her labours are finish'd,
   And now she is reaping her glorious reward.

The disbanded abode of her spirit lies under
   That ground over which she so frequently trod;
But her spirit is sharing, with pleasure and wonder,
   The exquisite sweets of the city of God.

May the deeds of her short but bright pilgrimage fire us
    With zeal to devote to King Jesus our breath ;
And her life's peaceful close with a good hope inspire us
    In Him who makes stingless the conqueror Death.

She is parted from us, but I hope not for ever ;
    Our warfare will soon be accomplished, and then
We shall meet where the pain of a parting shall never
    Throw a chill o'er the joys of the chosen again.

TO MISS MARY RICHARDSON,

AS A TOKEN OF RESPECT TO THE MEMORY OF MISS BETSY
FERGUSON, HER FRIEND.

On, Mary! well may tears flow from thy eyes ;
    For, in the climax of her youth and bloom,
Thy well-belov'd and heart's companion lies
        Low in the tomb.

Yes, Mary, never more on earth wilt thou
    Behold thy Betsy's sweet endearing form :
That frame, deserted by the soul, is now
        Food for the worm.

Oh, Mary, sure thou canst not have forgot
    The words which dying Betsy spoke to thee :
They were important words—O may they not
        Be lost on thee :—

"We've been companions long," she said, "and sweet
    Thy friendship is,—but breaking is that tie :
How awful, Mary, if we should not meet
        At last on high !"

It would be awful, Mary ;—but, when death
    Shall claim thee as his own, mayst thou, forgiv'n,
Without a sigh resign thy mortal breath,
    And rise to join thy lovely friend in heaven.

ON THE DEATH OF MISS RUTH JOHNSON
BLAND, AGED 21.

Death is sin's penalty ;
    Nor youth, nor hoary hairs,
Can claim exemption from his shafts,
    Who pities not nor spares :

He smites the sweet and guiltless babe,
    The sinner, old in crime ;
The maiden in her morning bloom,
    And manhood in his prime.

The cloud which hung o'er Chesham Mount
    Has deepen'd into gloom,
Since beauty, youth, and gentle worth
    Have glided to the tomb ;
Nor father's groans, nor mother's tears,
    Nor lover's bitter sighs,
Could longer keep the captive here,
    This angel from the skies.

The painful strife is ended now,
    The weary voyage o'er ;
And, long ere this, her love-borne steps
    Have touch'd a brighter shore.
Past the dim outlet of the grave,
    Souls breathe their native air ;
And faith assures her wailing friends
    That Ruth is shining there.

Ah ! cruel was this wrench of hearts ;
    Yet mercy dealt the blow ;
For lingering years were lingering pain,
    A heritage of woe :
But shiver'd is the golden bowl,
    The worn-out frame is still ;
And, pillow'd in serene repose,
    She sleeps on Bircle hill.

A sure retreat, a glad escape
    From sorrow, death, and pain ;
From racking cough, and languid pulse,
    And throbbing heart and brain.
The Saviour woo'd the stricken lamb
    To His own fold above :
Oh ! what a shelter are the arms
    Of Everlasting Love.

Her happy soul has thrown aside
    The garments of decay ;
This fragrant flower, which wither'd here,
    Blooms in eternal day.
A chrysalis has burst its shell,
    And upward, God-ward flown ;
Another glittering gem is set
    In the Redeemer's crown.

Her early doom should startle us
  Who sadly linger here ;
Health hopes a longer lease of life,
  Yet Death is lurking near :
The frequent hearse, the daily bell,
  The hourly-lifted sod,
In solemn, thrilling accents cry,
  " Prepare to meet thy God !"

ON THE DEATH OF TWO CHILDREN.

Written for their Sister.

FAREWELL ! my brother Thomas ;
  Yet, wherefore should I weep,
Though he be taken from us,
  In Death's cold arms to sleep ?
From tears and pain to save him,
  From bonds of sin and clay,
The Lord—the Lord who gave him—
  Hath taken him away.
By God's free grace forgiven,
  His servitude is o'er ;
Our Thomas is in heaven,
  And lives for evermore.

Good bye ! my little sister ;
  Ah ! little did I fear
How soon, when last I kiss'd her,
  She'd leave me lonely here ;
Yet glad that death o'ertook her,
  For she's alive and well,—
Free from the " overlooker,"
  And harsher factory bell.
The grave her bondage closes,—
  Poor Mary Ann's at rest ;
The weary lamb reposes
  Upon the Shepherd's breast.

Dear Saviour, meek and lowly,
  Affliction makes me bold ;
I'm vile, but Thou art holy ;
  Oh ! take me to Thy fold.
My playmates have departed
  To better worlds above ;
And I am broken-hearted,
  And pining for their love.
Kind God of the oppressed,
  Whose death has set us free,
Oh ! in that hour so blessed,
  Let there be room for me !

ON THE DEATH OF JOHN ———.

How just the plea of sorrow,
  When friends resign their breath ;
If man had no to-morrow,
  Beyond the night of death.

Mother ! on thee, while weeping,
  The word like manna falls :—
" He is not dead, but sleeping,"
  To wake when Jesus calls.

Father ! why art thou wearing
  A visage so depress'd,
When angel arms are bearing
  Thy darling to his rest ?

The beams of glory gather
  Around his placid brow ;
And, with his heavenly Father,
  Dear John is happy now.

The casket there lies darkling ;
  The precious gem is flown ;
And faith can see it, sparkling
  In the Redeemer's crown.

ON THE DEATH OF M———.

Though she is dead, I will not grieve,
  Nor loudly speak my moan ;
In seeming carelessness I'll weave
  The web of life alone ;
Yet not the less I'll think of her
Who made me her idolater.

Still I can gaze upon the fair,—
  Their beauty and their bloom ;
But unto me they are no snare—
  My love is in the tomb :
For even death has fail'd to part
My Mary from my love-lorn heart.

Then, fare ye well ! ye things of earth,—
  My sky is overcast ;
My hopes, with her who gave them birth,
  Like joyous dreams are past.
I care not if I cease to be—
To live or die is one with me.

ON THE DEATH OF MISS ELIZABETH AINSCOW.

To her Brothers and Sisters.

She is not dead ; her relics are but sleeping
   Till Jesus makes His chosen band complete :
Then cease your plaints, and stay your bootless weeping ;
   For yet a little while, and we shall meet.

Her soul, emancipate from fear or doubting,
   Has safely reach'd that bright, unsullied sphere ;
And Salem's courts reverberate the shouting
   Of angels, welcoming your sister there.

Oh ! when the separating pang shall seize us,
   And nothing from that clammy grasping save,
The free and sinless sacrifice of Jesus
   Shall join our sever'd links beyond the grave.

TO MISS JANE WESTRIE, ON THE DEATH OF HER LOVER.

The smiles are flown which lately deck'd thy face,
   And left those burning teardrops in their stead,
Because thy lover's earthly dwelling-place
   Is chang'd for the cold regions of the dead.

Thy loss is great ; for he was none of those
   Whose flippant spirits ever love to stray ;
But one whose love flam'd brightest at the close,
   And death's cold grasping could not scare away.

" Thee," cried his quiv'ring lips, " I've often told,
   That nothing but the hand of Death should tear
My heart from thine ; and mine is waxing cold,—
   But thou art graven, deeply graven, there.

" My life is ebbing—Jane, my love, farewell !"
   And his imprison'd spirit bade adieu
To time and sense.   Oh ! it were hard to tell
   Where breathes a heart so kind, and good, and true.

But cheer thee, Jane, thy lover is with Jesus ;
   Yet something lacking dims his radiant eyes :
He wants thee purified in Jesu's blood,
   And fitted for thy birthright in the skies.

Oh ! when thy sin-freed spirit reaches home,
   How rapturous will be your first embrace !
Oh ! shortly may some bright conductor come,
   And bear you safely to that happy place.

GENERAL POEMS, &c.

FLEETWOOD-ON-WYRE.

" The age of miracles is past. '—Common saying.

SO says some old graybeard, who turns up his nose,
And shutteth his spectacled eyes as he goes ;
Who, when he first heard of a steam-engine, sighed
At man's growing folly, or laugh'd till he cried ;
Who stuck to his text,—though he stared aghast
When, swift as a comet, a train hurried past ;
And in his sage pate drew this inference pat :—
" I'm sartin Owd Nick has a finger in that !"

Have miracles ceas'd ? Are the workers all dead ?
Before ye affirm it,—just think where ye tread !
Five brief years ago, and on this very spot
All nature ran wild, and improvement was not ;
The chill wastes of Lapland could only compare
With wild Rossall Warren, unshelter'd and bare ;
And here, where the sole of man's foot found no rest,
The rabbit had house-room, the sea-gull a nest.

But see, what have talent and enterprise done !
A beautiful town from the wilderness won :
The streets, which the proudest in Britain may vie ;
The spire of the temple salutes the blue sky ;
Her baths so unrivall'd—enough to impart
Ineffable joy to a Mussulman's heart ;
And—wonder of wonders—the glorious hotel,
Where royal Victoria (God bless her !) might dwell.

How vainly our neighbours her overthrow seek—
Upcrying the Ribble—that pitiful creek :
(If offer'd as wages, their clerk would refuse
The yearly amount of their custom-house dues !)
As vainly the anger of ocean is sped
Against the town's bulwark, her noble pier-head ;
Her harbour is studded with funnels and sails,
And snug in her berth is the huge *Prince of Wales.*

Ye dwellers in towns, to whom seldom is given
To breathe, as God gives it, the free air of heaven,—
Haste, haste ! to our newly-form'd paradise flee,
And quaff it in puffs, as it blows from the sea.
The railway invites ; and, if marvels you crave,
Your track lies through valley, o'er mountain, and wave :
Go on, and—redeem'd from the seaweed and mire,—
Behold that true miracle, Fleetwood-on-Wyre.

THE MARCH OF INTELLECT.

TALK as they will about the "march of mind,"
Still we have mortals mentally stark blind.
    Witness the following little story,
Which happen'd in the glorious days
That loggerheads are wont to raise
    As high as heaven—the days of mental glory.

    In Preston town,
    A conjuror of great renown
    Pasted his papers up and down,
    Which stated that the man would show
    Such things as only devil-dealers know.

These wondrous words attracted people's eyes
And fill'd them with surprise ;
    They thought the man a bedlamite, or madder,
And said it was a sin
To say a man could balance on his chin
    A living ass upon a ladder ;
And as for all the stuff about a lady and a bird—
To think that he could do so, was exceedingly absurd.

Two fellows from a neighbouring village, bent
On seeing such strange feats performed, went :
    When they got there,
    How he made them stare ;
For, while they stayed, they could not sunder
Their sweating fear from gaping wonder ;
And, when the time to close the scene was come,
Like blades of shaking-grass they waddled home.

Relcas'd from fear, around a blazing fire,
One of the other ventur'd to enquire :—
"What dost thou think of each and every sight
Which thou and I have witnessed to-night ?"

"Why," quoth his friend, "I think that every trick
Proves him to have some commerce with Old Nick."
"Fudge !" said the first ; "but I'm a silly elf,
If this is any but Old Nick himself !"
His wife confirm'd it,—roaring out " Alack !
It is Old Nick,—for he was drest in black !"

WRITTEN IN AN ALBUM.

MADAM, what can you have to do
    With such a mass of gilt-edg'd lumber?
We've scribbling nincompoops enow,
    Nor do I wish to swell the number.

An album is a precious bore,
    And oh ! it makes me melancholy,
To see such rhymers wish to store
    Your pages with ridiculous folly !

You'll think I've written *quantum suff.*,
    But madam, burn your book this minute,
With all its wealth of mental stuff,
    Though "reverend" fools have written in it.

Can English wives find nought to do
    Save filling albums ? Have a try, ma'am ;
Instead of scribbling—bake and brew,*
    And mend your stockings.   So good-bye, ma'am.

RAILWAYS.

SOME fifty years since, and a coach had no power
To move faster forward than six miles an hour,
Till Sawney Mc.Adam made highways as good
As paving stones crushed into little bits could.
Then coachee, quite proud of his horseflesh and trip,
Cries, "go it, ye cripples," and gave them the whip ;
And ten miles an hour—with the help of the thong—
They put forth their mettle, and scampered along.
The present has taken great strides of the past,
For carriages run without horses, at last ;
And what is more strange—yet it's truth, I avow—
Hack-horses themselves are turned passengers now.

---

* This was written before Mr. Anderton became a Teetotaller.

These coaches alive go in sixes and twelves,
And once set in motion, they travel themselves ;
They'll run thirty miles while I'm cracking this joke,
And need no provisions but "pump milk" and coke.
With their long chimneys, they skim o'er the rails,
With two thousand hundredweights tied to their tails ;
While Jarvey, in stupid astonishment stands,
Upturning both eyes, and uplifting both hands ;
"My nags," he exclaims, betwixt laughing and crying,
"Are good'uns to go, but you —— are flying."

A PEACE-EGG SONG.

(FROM A FRIEND'S MEMORY.)

OLD Harry Smith has a bitch named Sal,
And it goes a hunting with Brambley's Moll ;
As for these two bitches, I think they are to blame,
For into Calrow's wood they go a-killing game.
                    Singing, Fal-der-dal-der-I-do.

These two bitches, one moonlight light.
Into Calrow's wood they took their flight,—
Into Calrow's wood they speedily went,
And killed a hare there, on the second day of Lent.
                    Singing, &c.

Then Sally brought it home to Barrett Hall,
And barked at the door to let Harry know :
Harry opened the door as quick as a mouse,
And laid hold of the hare, which he flung into the house.
                    Singing, &c.

Harry look'd at the hare, saying, "thou'lt just do ;
I must go to Mr. Brewer's in another day or two :"
So, early in the morning, Harry he did rise
To go to Mr. Brewer's, to tell a pack of lies.
                    Singing, &c.

When he got to the Chapel door, there he made a stop,
And his finger in the holy-water pot he did pop ;
Then up to the altar, and there he kneels him down,
Puts his hand into his pocket and pulls out half-a-crown.
                    Singing, &c.

He put it on the pillow, thinking nothing was the worse,
And then he look'd up and made a sign of th' cross :
And, standing up, the Priest drank of grapes a solution,
And pronounced to old Harry the fullest absolution.
                    Singing, &c.

Now absolution's over : from sin thou art set free,
If thou hast only faith to believe in me ;
And for those sins of thine, I havn't charg'd thee dear ;
And now thou art set free only for another year.
Singing, &c.

Now to conclude and finish off my song :
Who would not be a papist, that never could do wrong—
Who never could do wrong in country or in town,
But pay for their sins with the sum of half-a-crown ?
Singing, &c.

TO JEMMY FEILDING.

A P.S.

Now, 'tis high time for me to stop,
 For, give me leave to let you know, sir,
That I must off to Rochdale pop,
 You coaxing, rhyme-requesting grocer.

You're a teetotaller, 'tis true,
 That's why my tired hand yet lingers
Upon this paper, though the blue
 Cramp has laid hold upon my fingers.

You're welcome to these rhymes, my boy,—
 Not often is my pen so yielding ;
Grocer, good-day, I wish thee joy
 In life or death, dear Jemmy Feilding.

TO MASTER JOHN FALLOWFIELD,

OF WALTON-LE-DALE.

WELL, John, the playing time is o'er,
And you must off to school once more,
To take your book and pen in hand,
And what you learn, to understand.

You say you like the school,—I'm glad ;
Nor will it make your father sad :
The more in learning you improve,
The more it will increase his love.

Oh ! never let a dunce's shame
Get link'd and coupled with your name :
'Twould cause your dearest friends to mourn,
And wiser boys to laugh to scorn.

Obey your master—feed your mind
With food for that great use design'd ;
While others think of kite and ball,
Read, learn, and get before them all.

I'm sure, John, this is sound advice,
Then set about it in a trice ;
And let us see how high you'll climb
Up learning's hill, by Christmas time.

For John, I should be pleas'd to hear
Your father whisper in my ear :
" Henry, what think you's come to pass ?
Our John stands first in Laing's first class."

Remember, Christmas time will come,
When we can stay at " home, sweet home ;"
And then, if all your tasks are done,
We'll play, and we'll have lots of fun.

Then farewell school, and farewell toil,
And farewell " *hic, hœc, hoc,*" awhile ;
Farewell the boys you've struggled with,
And farewell Messrs. Laing and Smith.

For Christmas is a holiday,
On which we should not work, but play ;
And father, mother, thou, and I,
In your new house will eat mince pie.

TO MISS ANNE ATHERTON,

ON RECEIVING FROM HER A PRESENT FOR MY MOTHER.

To you, dear Anne, this scrawl I send ;
    I trace in it my mother's name,
Who bids me thank the gentle friend
    From whom those free-will offerings came.

The pleasure their possession gives
    May form the sole return she'll make ;
But she will keep them while she lives,
    And prize them for the giver's sake.

I feel I should prove uncommonly slack,
In receiving from any young lady " the sack ;"
Yet, truly, my tongue did with gratitude wag,
When my dear friend Miss Atherton gave us "the *bag.*"

And won't little Jim be delighted—my eyes !
And his heart be brimful, and run o'er ?
When he tosseth his shuttlecock up to the skies,
With a jerk from his brave battledore.

So, after all, the tale's no puff ;
And Mag intends to "splice" with Duff !
Believe me, 'twill sound queer enough
To call your sister "Mistress Duff."
Would *you* (the question's rather rough)
Receive a beau whose name was Duff ?
Alas ! dear Anne, there's many a maid
   Would give a chap a stern rebuff—
No matter what he did or said—
   If once he sign'd himself, "Your Duff !"

TO ANNE.

STRANGE thoughts, dear Anne, would fill your head,
When told that Fanny Snape was wed ;
You'd be in tune to laugh or cry ;
You'd think your friend was very sly,
And feel dispos'd to take this text :—
"I wonder what will happen next !"

Yet, though she bears another name,
Poor Fanny's heart is still the same
As when ye went, with converse sweet,
Link'd arm-in-arm, up Cannon-street ;
Or leaving tracts, ye pass'd away
The ever-welcome Sabbath day.

"And is she happy ?" you will ask :
Yes, Anne, beneath God's smile we bask ;
And, urg'd by love, we gladly share
Each other's joy, each other's care ;
Our life runs smoothly, like a rill,
And we are busy courting still.

Go search the whole creation round,
Two more united can't be found :
Me to the world our Fan prefers ;—
My life is fast bound up in hers ;
As cheerful as the birds are we,—
And, if you doubt it, come and see.

"Come, Anne," says Fanny, "and admire
Our home at Fleetwood-on-the-Wyre ;"
"Come Anne," say I, "and gaze upon
A home where truly two are one ?"
Thus, may God's blessing ever dwell
With you and yours ; and fare-ye-well !

TO LITTLE HANNAH.

Thou art a pet, 'tis very clear,
To both thy parents very dear;
In their fond eyes, a sparkling pearl—
Thou little tinety, tinety, girl.

And thy aunt Mary doth delight,
To hear thee sing at morn and night;
And says, " 'Tis wonderful, how soon
Thy cherry lips could learn a tune."

Thou hast a better friend than these,
I'll tell His name, if that will please:
His name is Jesus; and says He,
" Let little children come to me."

Once, for thy sake, this good Friend died;
For Hannah He was crucified;
And He expects thee up above,
To dwell with Him in light and love.

And, oh! that will be joyful, grand,
To sit with Him at God's right hand;
To meet thy friends on Canaan's shore,
And ne'er lose sight of Jesus more.

TO THE SAME.

Dear Hannah, you learn from your aunt to conceal
The things which your parents do bid you reveal.
'Tis true I am Henry, and Anderton too;
But that's not an answer expected from you.
You, yesterday, call'd me a very dear name,
Which set my poor pit-a-pat heart in a flame:
Speak! am I your "uncle?"—the truth I would know;
I wonder who taught you to speak to me so!
I'm not so by nature;—then how can it be?
Perhaps your aunt Mary could satisfy me!
Go, ask her if she will explain how it is;
And then, Hannah ———, I'll give thee a kiss.

TO LITTLE PETER LANGSHAW.

They tell me that eyes can distinguish and trace,
Some old-fashioned folks in thy young-fashioned face:
That a look of thy grandmother Langshaw is clear;
And the features of grandmother Philips appear.

If this be correct, them I am nothing loth,
To say thou must be a pet with them both ;
But strive, my dear boy, to deserve all their love,
And not theirs alone, but thy Father's above.

Thy name is the name of a man great and good,
Who battled for truth, and for that shed his blood ;
Yet the faith of thy namesake too hardly was tried,
When with curses, thrice told, he his Master denied.

May'st thou, little Peter, be valiant and bold,
Like Peter, the famous disciple of old,
When he followed Jesus—oh ! copy it well ;
But pray that thou fall not as Peter once fell.

A P.S.

PETER LANGSHAW continues uncommonly fat,
And he looks very well, in his Quaker-like hat :
His wife is much thinner ; but, if I may tell,
The thin one and fat one agree very well.
She's three or four sisters ; and one, I avow,
Persists to my teeth that I call'd her "reet fou' :"
To silence her clapper I never will try ;
But I'll stick to the fact that she tells a big lie.

TO LITTLE MARY LANGSHAW.

THEY say you're kind-hearted—then learn to forgive
The wrong done unto thee, as long as you live ;
Remember that Jesus forgave thee thy debt ;
Oh ! learn that hard lesson, " forgive and forget."

They say you are firm—then quite resolute be
In learning far more, love, than A, B, and C ;
Resolve not one chance of improvement to miss,
And father will give his good scholar a kiss.

Good bye, Mary Langshaw ! good bye for this time ;
May God, in His mercy, preserve thee from crime :
May grace, unto thee, little Mary, be given,
Begun upon earth, and continued in heaven.

l

TO A LADY ON HER MARRIAGE.

Sure fancy is dull, or I'm not so clear-headed,
  With words at command, as in days passed away ;
I promised some rhymes when Eliza was wedded,—
  And married thou art ; but the rhymes—where are they ?
And Jane, the dear bridesmaid—exacting as beauty—
  Demands the unflinching discharge of the debt ;
And seals the despatch which recals me to duty,
  With love's sweet remembrancer—" Dinna forget."

From the arms of thy mother at length thou hast ventured,
  To a coveted home, with the man of thy choice ;
In him all thy hopes and affections are centred,
  And in that decision I greatly rejoice.
Remember thy vows, and adhere to the letter ;
  Nor give thy affianced one cause to regret :
Constrain him to bear the conjugal fetter—
  I urge this upon thee, and—" dinna forget."

I pray that thy lot may be speckless and cheerful,
  As friend the most sanguine can ask for a friend ;
In regions like this, where the gay and the tearful,
  The storm and the sunshine, so frequently blend,
The married have power to repress and to smother
  The cares that annoy, and the sorrows that fret ;
And earth will be heaven, if ye love one another ;
  Then act on the precept,—and " dinna forget."

New ties may await thee—a mother's sweet title
  Perchance may be thine, though procured with its smart ;
But the lisp of thy child will be ample requital
  For bodily pangs and misgivings of heart.
What draughts of pure rapture a woman is quaffing,
  When first she embraces her first little pet ;
As prone on her lap he lies crowing and laughing ;
  Then haste to possess one,—and " dinna forget."

Alas ! we exist in a scene of mutation,
  Where causes most trifling our love can estrange ;
Yet, faith knows an Eden of bright consummation,
  Where life is perennial, and hearts never change.
Earth's buds of affection, so fragrant and vernal,
  The blight of unkindness may wither them yet ;
Yet, heaven may be thine,—and its joys are eternal,
  Oh, strive for admission,—and " dinna forget."

THE "NILE."

What craft is that in Morecambe bay,
 So faultless in her rig,
Which onward speeds her placid way,
 As lively as a snig !
I ken her fairy fabric now,—
 I mark her dashing style :
Behold ! with Nelson on her prow,
 The gallant little " Nile."

How fearlessly the tide she braves,
 How well she does her work,
She bounds above the swelling waves
 As buoyant as a cork ;
Though four-feet shallows hem her round,
 Her crew serenely smile,
For she can float when others ground,—
 The saucy little " Nile."

The smoky towns their crowds disgorge,
 I hear the train's loud hum ;
From heated mill and deafening forge,
 Their pallid millions come ;
And sickly frames with health are stored,
 And spleen forgets her bile,
And joy entrances toil, on board
 The merry little " Nile."

Here's three times three, and one cheer more,
 And still may fair winds waft.
This waterwitch from shore to shore,
 Well crowded fore and aft.
Long may her owner watch her skim
 The sea, in dashing style,
And feel that she has been to him,
 The grateful little " Nile."

A NEW PEACE-EGG SONG.

Kind neighbours ! do not turn us out,
And you shall hear a song about
The pranks that our police did play,
On Walton Cop, last bonfire day.
 Right-tol-la, &c.

Last bonfire day, as Britons should,
We heap'd up sticks, and turf, and wood ;
And lighted bonfires, bright and hot,
In memory of the Popish Plot.
Right-tol-la, &c.

We shouted and had lots of fun,
With cannon, pistol, squib, and gun ;
And show'd the neighbours round, we hope,
That Walton hates both priest and pope.
Right-tol-la, &c.

Now, though there was no harm in this,
The Rurals took it much amiss—
Those chaps as stiff as barbers' blocks,
With hats japann'd and leather stocks.
Right-tol-la, &c.

These rogues are Irish—nearly all,
And this provok'd their popish gall :
To see that we were wide awake
For Church and State, and no mistake.
Right-tol-la, &c.

So, led on by a puppy vain,
Who styles himself " Inspector Maine,"
The Rurals came, in their glazed hats,
And seiz'd a lad from Walton Flats.
Right-tol-la, &c.

They let him go, for higher game :
James Tomlison a-walking came ;
When Maine exclaim'd, " This *is* a prize !
You b——d b-——, d—— your eyes !"*
Right-tol-la, &c.

" John Fowler," cries this Irish tup,
" This is your prisoner—lock him up !"
" Nay," answered John,—a Churchman true—
" If there's a kick-up, it's through *you !*"
Right-tol-la, &c.

So they were forc'd, by eights or twelves,
To take the man in charge themselves ;
But James's heart was firm and light,
Though he in th' lock-up was all night.
Right-tol-la, &c.

We knew, when he his case should state,
That any English magistrate
Would sift, and probe, and know what's what,
And baffle this new Popish Plot.
Right-tol-la, &c.

---

* This shocking language was, we believe, used by the Inspector.

The case came on ; and, though they swore
And lied, as rogues ne'er lied before,—
James left the court without a stain,
And laugh'd to scorn Inspector Maine.
Right-tol-la, &c.

And, when November Fifth comes round,
The note of war again we'll sound,—
In spite of law, and wind, and rain ;
And, crack that nut, Inspector Maine!
Right-tol-la, &c.

And, if you cannot put us down,
With thund'ring word or threat'ning frown,—
Go, fight and run away in Spain,
As you did once, Inspector Maine !
Right-tol-la, &c.

Hurrah ! for Hornby—Swainson, too—
And Calrow—Livesey—all our crew !
Throughout the strife they did not flinch,
Because they're English, every inch.
Right-tol-la, &c.

Hurrah ! for all the neighbours poor,
Who crowded round the prisoner's door,
And heap'd above a curse apiece
Upon the Whigs and their police.
Right-tol-la, &c.

Hurrah ! for England's noble church ;
May honest soldiers guard the porch,
Who'll bring to light each plot and trick
Of Rurals, Red-necks, and Old Nick !
Right-tol-la, &c.

Our song is done ; but, ere we pass,
We wish to beg a little " brass ;"
For we deserve it for our pains ;
And we'll buy powder with our gains.
Right-tol-la, &c.

We thank you kindly for your mite ;
And, while we bid you all good night,
We pledge ourselves, next bonfire day,
To load, and ram, and blaze away !
Right-tol-la, &c.

MYSTIC BABYLON.

When mystic Babylon unfurl'd
Her bloody banner through the world,
When nought appear'd to block her way,
But all was subject to her sway ;
When Kings were at her Pontiff's bidding,
And all her votaries Priest-ridden ;
When fire and sword and inquisition
Were us'd to teach her foes submission ;
When the poor fabric Christ had rear'd
Had altogether disappear'd ;- ·
Wycliffe the gospel trumpet sounded,
And Babel's mighty hosts confounded ;
And from her ashes rose a new one,
Which I'll denominate the true one.

Adversity and persecution
Kept this awhile free from pollution ;
But in prosperity and case,
This Church grew lukewarm by degrees,
Which caus'd the Wesleys (men of knowledge),
To emanate from Oxford College ;
And publish through the British nation
A present and a full salvation ;—
And now, with Father, Son, and Spirit,
They everlasting joys inherit.

But sin's insinuating ways
Succeed, in these degenerate days.
In conference, where preachers meet,
(Lo ! aristocracy complete),
It is as if I heard them say ;—
" We can, and will, have our own way ;
Though they of Preston keep beseeching,
And say they don't like H——'s preaching ;
Yet, be his motives pure or sinister,
This same R. H. shall be their minister ;
N——n to Preston take this pill,
And ram it down against their will."

Pray, who are these, who, stride by stride,
Are rais'd to such a pitch of pride ?
I don't know what they would or could be,—
But Wesleyan Methodists they should be ;
These high-flown upstarts are the same
Who preach redemption through the Lamb ;—
They show to us that we should be
Possess'd of deep humility ;

They point to Jesus as a sample,
But are themselves a bad example :—
Oh ! single eyed (if there be any,
Which I would hope among so many),
Oh ! guard against th' impending storm,
And cry aloud, " Reform ! Reform !"

But mark yon man, whose prayers arise,
Like holy incense to the skies,—
Who, 'midst such rottenness, is found
A Christian,—sterling, honest, sound ;
Who dares to raise a great eruption,
In this big mountain of corruption :
God's Spirit, does this man embolden ;
Our reader, it is Moses Holden.
The world opposes might and main,
And hell asserts her rage in vain !
The mild J. H. did with him grapple,
And tried to wrench from him his chapel ;
But Moses this mild Lawyer tended,
And went and got his chapel rented.

This mild aristocratic fellow,
Did like an Indian savage bellow !
" The pulpit's in my hands" cried he,
You demagogues must bow to me ;
" Though earth should this, my system, batter,
And all should disapprove the matter—
I'll not retract from what I say,
But will persist in my own way."
Thus spoke the great imperious Jack,
He heard a rumbling at his back.
'Tis the bold voice of freedom sounds—
The cry from earth to heaven resounds :—
" No more will we, a servile group,
Obedience yield to Preston's pope ;
To Vauxhall-road we will repair,
And worship our Redeemer there."
The cry re-echo'd, and again
'Twas answered by a loud " Amen."

Behold yon crowds in holy strife,
Wishing to hear the Words of Life ;
Not a fine-worded, splendid sermon,
But doctrine, pure as drops from Hermon,
Deliver'd in a homely diction :
And carrying with it deep conviction ;
Behold him pointing to the Lamb,
And preaching pardon in His name ;
Watch him, to faith's admiring eyes,
Make clear a vista to the skies !

'Tis in this man, that human weal
Has burned with a steady zeal ;
This is the man, whose bowels move
Towards mankind with honest love.
Moses, may'st thou continue still,
Subservient to thy Master's will,
Till, summon'd by a call from heaven,
May'st thou then meet thy Judge forgiven ;
And up to glory rise to dwell,
And sing eternally, " All's well."

———

TO MR. A—— H——.

Was it manly, Sir A——, or just to betray
The girl who had cast her affections away :
And cast them on you, sir ! Why did you offend
That beautiful being, by calling her friend.

Does friendship consist, sir, in breaking a heart
That joins in your joys, and partook of your smart ?
Was it friendship to make that fond being believe
Her heart was your object,—and then to deceive ?

If this is your friendship, repair to that place
Where Satan resides with the "outcasts of grace ;"
And as you are plunged into brimstone and fire,
Acknowledge yourself an unprincipled liar.

———

PROTESTANT METHODISM.

An assembly of treacherous men.—JER. ix. 2.

Through deceit do they refuse to know me.—JER. ix. 6.

Both' Prophet and Priest are profane, yea in my house have I found their wickedness, saith the Lord God.—JER. xxiii. 11.

Since Adam brought us in the scrape,
Vices of every size and shape,
Of every hue, and every shade,—
Their way to human hearts have made ;
A fact so generally known,
'Twould be sheer madness to disown ;
For none but fools, will dare gainsay
A truth they witness every day.

Of all the vices which infest
Poor mortals, one above the rest,
Proudly, pre-eminent, leads along

A vast incalculable throng :—
I think I need not be so nice
As name that soul-absorbing vice ;
For every one knows something of it,
Who does, in any measure, covet.

Oh gold !—'tis for the lust of thee
That merchants travel o'er the sea !—
For thee, will patriot rebels sing,
" True to our country and our king."—
For thee, will counsellors appear,
With all their lies, to look sincere !—
For thee, will preachers preach and pray,
In a disinterested way.—
Oh Gold !—thou wert the root of evil,—
For thee will saints lie like the devil.

Know ye from whence yon sound proceeds ?
The turn-out Methodists of Leeds.
Amongst the many clashing noises,
And thousand different human voices,—
I recognise old J*hn***s ; loud
He thus harangues the gaping crowd :—
" We will not drain the poor man's purse,
'Twould dub us with a hireling's curse;—
We will not seek to fleece the sheep,—
We will our hands from lucre keep.
And now, to that blood-sucking crew,
The conference, we bid adieu !
Farewell to N*wton, W*ts*n, B*nt**g ;
Bishops, who Bishops pay are hunting;
This day henceforth our sect shall be
From you, ye human leeches, free.—
And now, ye long neglected poor,
Thrice welcome to our temple door,
We seek your good, we seek no more."

The speaker ceas'd : from man to man
The words as quick as wild fire ran ;
A token of consent burst out,
From those assembled, in a shout.
Nor blaz'd at Leeds alone the flame ;
The neighbouring counties felt the same,
Preston, at once lost all affection
For those attach'd to th' old connection.
" Free preaching," R*b**t L***st*r cried,
" Is that in which ourselves we pride;
We'll not (pretending souls to cure),
The good things of this world secure
Ourselves,—'tis for this cause we ply

Lune-street, the venal watchman's stye.
This curse from us we mean to sweep ;
We will no lazy parsons keep !"
O L****st*r ! you can lie as quick
As one related to Old Nick.
Four shillings, L****st*r, was a deal
For giving Leyland folks a meal
Of gospel truth ! Fie, L***ster, fie !
Oh ! cease to preach, or cease to lie !

They're all alike,—for those at Leeds
Are capable of dirty deeds :
Their preachers are to have, I hear,
Fifty and eighty pounds a-year !
Eighty a year !—a goodly trade
Free preaching by these men is made.
Free preaching ! it my soul doth fill
With rage—that name is us'd so ill.

Ye new-sect preachers, if I had
A name above all others had,
That you should have ! 'twas your intention
At first to kindle up dissension ;
That (after you had got a set
Of fools to join you) you might get
A living out of them ; which throws
A light upon your deeds, and shows
Your motives, in the whole transaction,
Were built on lucre, cant, and faction !

Yes, my anathema is weak,
To what my soul would fainly speak.
Oh ! that I had a Byron's power !
I'd tan your hides for half-an-hour,
Strip you of all that seeming fair,
And lay your very bosoms bare ;
Then would your naked spirits tell
Themselves to be as black as hell.

But here my muse must drop her wing,
For further I forbear to sing.
This dull monotony, I fear—
Or friends or foes—will tire your ear ;
Yet, though at best I can but bungle,
Still, " gold is gold—though in a dunghill!"
And truth is truth, though in a poor
Unletter'd ————, unknown, obscure ;
And here plain facts have been my faggots
To fire these undermining maggots.
I've done my best—no more this way
I'll venture,—friends and foes, good day !

TO W. HARRIS.

A few days since, dear Harris, it was my lot
To read your second letter in the *Pilot;*
From which I learnt how fancy had deceiv'd you,
And how some late occurrences had griev'd you :
For, notwithstanding your long canvass list,
The president's a non-phrenologist ;
And, writhing with this sore and sad defeat,
Your body still must take a common seat.
No wonder, then—though hearts at ease may smile—
At your epistle, and its acid style ;
No marvel, with your mind in such a state,
If what you scribble smacks of Billingsgate :
For shame breeds strife ; and, therefore, words severe
Are what from you we may expect to hear,—
For ah ! " a wounded spirit who can bear ?"

'Twere bitter mockery to console thee now,
When *Ichabod* is written on thy brow :
Thy glory is departed ; thou art cross'd
In thy ambition, and thy labour's lost ;
Thy long and deep acquaintance with the science
On which was plac'd thy strongest, sole reliance,—
Thy friends have suffer'd this prime prop to fall ;
Oh ! " this was the unkindest cut of all."
Does not the ancient British proverb say
That " where there is a will there is a way ?"
'Tis false ! for most determin'd was thy will
The chair of the phrenologists to fill—
Alas ! thou art a private member still.

Yet surely, doctor, 'tis of no great use
To seek by lies your rival to traduce,
Or bring him from his perch to this low level,—
For falsehood is the weapon of the devil ;
Yet thy whole letter with the truth at war is—
Did some she-demon whelp thee, Doctor Harris ?
Are not thy statements of the council's acts
At shameless, barefac'd loggerheads with facts ?
Why soil good paper, and why waste good ink ?
A world so wide awake as soon could think
That hell is quite as fair a place as heaven,
As that six anythings are more than seven :
By common numeration thou art " done,"—
For all arithmetics through which I've gone
Make seven nor more nor less than 6 + 1

And by that one thy foeman was elected,
And by that one poor Harris was ejected ;
For that one's sake, let figures be respected !

Still, you will not this humbling truth confess—
You strive to prove the greater is the less.
Oh ! what more glaring could your foes require,
To dub you blockhead, and to brand you liar ?

In pity to your cranium's conformation,
Accept, dear sir, my deep commiseration.
You are a fool in deed, as well as name,
And this your skull's developments proclaim :
Your frontal regions are depress'd, sir, but
The right and left sides of your occiput
Are grac'd with organs of tremendous size—
Just where the " love of approbation" lies ;
And nearer to the centre, sir, you seem
To own above your share of " self esteem ;"
And lower down, no hat, however wide,
Could your huge bumps of " combativeness" hide ;
And on the top sits " firmness," thron'd in state—
The crowning wonder of your wondrous pate !

Hence, sir, your previous canvass, zeal, and fuss,
And whence they sprang, were manifest to us ;
And your mad movements, after the division ;
Impell'd by self esteem, your thoughts ran thus :—
" The chair is vacant, and thou art the man ;"
" Rise," mutter'd Love of Approbation, "rise ;
None is so fit ; and, if I may advise,
Make no delay, and never rest content
Till thou art 'William Harris, president !'
In the requir'd attainments you excel,
And spectacles become a chairman well."
" Yes," you replied, " the post is mine,—I'll win it,
And fill it like a gentleman—when in it."

The great day came—the fav'rites were propos'd—
The members voted—the election clos'd :
Oh ! that which follows in my gizzard sticks—
Lomas had seven, and Harris only six !
Smarting, as you then did, at this defeat,
Pierc'd in your love of praise and self-conceit,
Up to your aid your " combativeness" starts,
And at the victor like a bulldog darts.
" Again," you cried. " I do and will insist
That none preside but a phrenologist ;
And for that honour I will struggle yet,
In spite of Corless and his chuckling pet."
So your first letter, hot with its own fervour,
Hiss'd in the *Pilot*, blaz'd in the *Observer*.
In sooth it was a matchless paper bullet,
Though ill adapted for the public gullet :

Yet pass'd it not unheeded; for thy folly
Was answer'd by a well-directed volley,
Which did thy patience utterly confound,
And gave thy vanity a mortal wound.

Then stiff-neck'd "firmness" stood thy friend; and when
This organ influences a mortal's pen,
It renders him unwilling to draw back, as
An Irish hog, or stiffer English jackass;
And, prompted by thy "firmness"—grown self-willy—
Thy vengeance forg'd another sword, my Billy;
But in its *Pilot* sheath the weapon tarries,   .
Pointless and rusty as thy wit, dear Harris.

Lo! no man heeds thy worse than monkey tricks,
And though thou kickest, 'tis against the pricks.
This ceaseless, three weeks' ransack of thy brains,
These waking tremors, and these dreaming pains,
This constant racking of thy ruling bumps,
Have gain'd thee nothing but contempt and thumps.
The public voice thy selfish sphere derides;
Upon the private form thy —— abides;
And, worst of all, the cause of thy despair,
The pet of Corless, fills the presidential chair.

TO MISS D——.

I KNOW, dear Betsy, that thy heart
  Is stainless as the babe unborn;
And that a villain's oft-tried art
  Would meet thy unabated scorn!

Still, Betsy, with thy wonted care,
  This tender virgin flower defend,
Lest thou should'st fall into the snare
  Of her, thy false, discarded friend.

My careworn spirit could not bear,
  But sink beneath her load, to see
The fame of one so truly dear
  The sport of base malignity.

Beware of her! for thou hast prov'd
  That slander strikes a surer blow
From one we once have dearly lov'd,
  Than from an old, acknowledg'd foe.

If she smile on thee, heed her not,
  But fix'd in thy aversion stand;
And show her thou hast not forgot
  The spirit of thy father's land.

TO A YOUNG LADY FROM INDIA

(AN ORPHAN).

Oh ! welcome, lonely stranger,
　To the island of the free ;
For where thy earliest years were pass'd
　Thy home shall never be.
The deep sea rolls between thee
　And that unforgotten shore,
Which thou, with lisping Indian girls,
　Were 'custom'd to explore.

Yes, thou hast look'd thy latest
　On that ever-cloudless sky,
And thou hast sought thy father's home,
　To breathe awhile, and die.
But ah ! how barren and how cold,
　Compar'd with that bright land
Where, far as mortal eye can pierce,
　Her sunny vales expand.

But thou art not alone, sweet girl ;
　Thy orphan sister dear
In thy rejoicing will rejoice,
　And give thee tear for tear :
Her strong affection rivals thine,
　And will not let thee prove
The nameless grief of those who love
　When none are left to love.

What though our clime be changeful,
　And our mountains bleak and bare ;
What though our skies with India skies
　We never may compare ;
What though our feeble solar beams
　Scarce sever day and night ;—
Yet we have hearts, and view your love
　With limitless delight.

Then welcome, lovely stranger,
　To the island of the free !
For where thy earliest years were pass'd
　Thy home shall never be.
The deep sea rolls between thee
　And that unforgotten shore,
Whose beauteous bowers of evergreen
　Will bless thy heart no more.

TO MISS D——, FROM INDIA.

A RANGER art thou, and a beautiful ranger,
  From the sunshiny land of thy birth ;
And welcome art thou to the land of the stranger,
  Though barren our portion of earth.
We cannot, affectionate fair one, invite thee
  To walk through the flower-scented grove ;
But oh ! we can love thee: and won't it delight thee
  To live in the sunshine of love ?

Oh ! dash off that teardrop, so bright and so pearly,
  And clear that ingenuous brow ;
From parent and kin thou wert sever'd so early,
  Thou canst not remember them now :
But, if they are fresh in thy warm recollection,
  Their absence no longer deplore ;
For, Anna, we love thee with equal affection
  To those who can love thee no more.

TO MISS HODGSON, OF FRECKLETON,

While on a visit to Miss Anderton.

I HAVE sever'd from friends without caring or sighing,
  And heard without shrinking their final adieu ;
But now thou must leave us, 'tis painfully trying
  To part with a being so loving and true.

I would that prosperity alway may cheer thee ;
  But should o'er thy prospects adversity lower,
Throughout the dark hour may that Being be near thee
  Whose love is as great as His wisdom and power.

Not long, my dear Ellen, not long shall we wander
  On earth, ere our sun of existence is set ;
And then we shall meet, love, all glorified yonder,
  Where cloudless enjoyment will banish regret.

TO MARY AND HANNAH HORSFALL,

While on a visit to his Mother.

I'M glad to see my lovely friends once more,
Who us'd to make my cup of bliss run o'er ;
While you are with us, joyful be your stay,
And peace attend you when you go away.

But, while I joy to have you here again,
That happiness is closely link'd with pain :
Oh ! how can I, when gazing upon you,
Forget your mother, and her last adieu ?

For you are very near the well-known place
Where death releas'd that "monument of grace ;"
And you are very near that dear abode
From which her soul ascended unto God.

I do not this afflicting theme advance
The pang of separation to enhance ;
I only wish to lay before your eyes,
A mother who has gain'd the upper skies.

Oh ! tread her steps, and keep her in your view ;
As she believ'd in Jesus, so may you !
As she was meet for death, so may you be,
And reap the glories of eternity !

WHAT HATH THE SAINT TO DO WITH GLOOM !

WHAT hath the saint to do with gloom ?
    The willing slave of sin
May tremble at his coming doom,
    The danger he is in.

'Tis just that our Redeemer's foes
    Should feel his flaming sword ;
But safety is the lot of those
    Whose trust is in the Lord.

Does not our God, in accents mild,
    This declaration make :—
" The soul which grace hath reconcil'd
    I never will forsake ?"

Joint heir with Jesus of that place
    Which never can decay,
Rejoice ! for thine's a happy case,
    And dash thy tears away.

TO MR ENOCH PRESTON.

RIGHT?zealous art thou in the effort sublime—
The task of instructing mere sucklings to climb
The ladder of faith to the mansions above,—
And Jesus will prosper thy labour of love.

Thy heart's in the school ; and no wonder the young
Receive with affection what falls from thy tongue :
Their souls and God's glory divide thy regard,—
Their welfare thy aim, and His smile thy reward.

We own thee the fitting preceptor of youth,
By patience, and faith, and thy love of the truth ;
Thy power to persuade, to incite, to appal ;
Thy " word in due season," for each and for all.

We own thee a " teacher in Israel" indeed ;
Thy life is a copy which children may read ;
Thy mind is quite wean'd from this perishing sod,
And, like holy Enoch, thou walkest with God.

His triumph how great who successfully wins
One dear little pilgrim to leave off his sins,
And leadeth him gently to mercy divine !
And often, through Jesus, this joy hath been thine.

And she, by whose kind and persuasive command
These lines are now willingly traced by my hand,
Prays God that of thee a wide channel He'd make
Of mercy to thousands, for Jesus's sake.

On ! on ! Christian friend, till the race thou hast won,
When Jesus shall say, " Faithful servant, well done !"
And thou in the presence of God shalt sit down,
To sing the new song, and to claim the bright crown.

Oh ! that will be joyful ! and certain I am
Thou wilt raise an additional " Worthy the Lamb !"
While joining the myriads so sinless and fair,
When scholars from Cannon-street welcome thee there.

TO GEORGE LAMB,

*On his entering on the work of the Ministry in the
Primitive Methodist Connexion, July 20th,* 1829.

GEORGE, I would write a word or two,
By way of bidding thee adieu.
I would not write in friendship's name,
Because it is a threadbare theme ;
It is so prostituted,—know,
Upon that ground I would not, dare not go.

But I would write as to a soul
Who, pressing towards the heavenly goal,
Through good or ill, through gain or loss,
Fights on the battles of the Cross ;
Who now is striving to secure
A heaven that shall eternally endure.

Call'd to the vineyard of the Lord,
Thou now must go to preach the Word :
O may the Holy Spirit guide
Thy steps, and o'er thy heart preside !
O may He all thy labours bless,
And give the Word preach'd by thee great success !

Dangers and trials may assail,
But God to help thee will not fail ;
Diseases dire and death may come,
But there's a home beyond the tomb !
O may this cheer thee on ! may this
Assist thee to ascend the road that leads to bliss !

There mayst thou see Him, face to face,
Who sav'd thee by unaided grace !
And I, too, who have lov'd thee here,
May I meet thee, my brother, there—
Where grief, and all that can alloy,
Give place to songs of love and harps of joy !

GOD BLESS YOU ALL, AMEN !

On, ye lovely, faithful few,
    Who, sincerely,
Are to my dear preacher true,
I love every one of you,—
    And that dearly !

I know some designing men,
    Who endeavour
To make you and Moses twain,—
But the links of that sweet chain
    They can't sever.

Oh ! how pleasant 'tis to meet
    Sisters, Brothers !
At his house in Jordan-street ;—
'Tis a joy, the most complete
    Of all others.

Preacher, brethren, sisters all,
    When we're driven
From this sin-marr'd, fleeting ball,
May I recognise the whole
    Of you in heaven !

TO MISS D——, MANCHESTER,

In remembrance of her kindness to Josiah Johnson.

When sickness laid hold of the flaxen-hair'd stranger,
  And bow'd down his comfortless head :
Like an angel of mercy in season of danger,
  You tended the languisher's bed.

No cold, no oblivious slumbers came o'er you,
  While the hour-panting wanderer slept ;
But sadly you gaz'd on the dreamer before you,
  And thought on his sorrows and wept.

That soldier loves me with the love of a brother,—
  Impassioned, devoted, and true ;
And warm as the friendship we feel for each other,—
  The friendship I cherish for you.

A mother may lose her maternal affection ;
  But life is too transient to prove,
That withered in us is the dear recollection
  Of you and your labour of love.

TO MISS MARY H——.

I've watch'd you very narrowly, since you
That card beneath the work-room table threw :
Because you prov'd yourself by that foul trick,
As great a rogue as cloven-footed Nick.

But thou art worse than hell's great ruler,—for
He has a form which all mankind abhor ;
But you have such a fascinating face
As would a throne of cloudless glory grace.

But all thy seeming goodness is deceit ;
Thy eye informs me that thou art a cheat :
I could this very moment prove you so,
And 'tis my duty to let Watson know.

You little blackleg,—if you do not try
To look less sidelong with that roguish eye,—
I'll make Will Morland Watson leave thy arms,
And seek more honest, though less perfect charms.

TO HIS SISTER ELLEN, ON HER WEDDING-DAY.

Thy lot with mine is cast,—
  Our hearts are plighted ;
And if we be as fast
  To Christ united,

We shall enjoy below
What worldlings never know,—
A heaven before we go
  To dwell in glory.

And though on earth we meet
  With stormy weather,
Where bitter things and sweet
  Are mix'd together ;
My voice shall lull thy fears,
My hand shall dry thy tears,
While Faith our vessel steers
  Straight home to glory.

Misfortunes may come on,
  And sickness seize us ;
But if we two are one,
  And " one in Jesus,"
His Word this truth maintains,—
That, after all our pains,
A sweeter rest remains
  For us in glory.

Weep not ! though death at length
  Our ties will shiver ;
For faith will lend us strength
  To cross the river ;
And we shall recognise
Each other in the skies,
When Christ shall say, " Arise !
  And share my glory !"

IMPROMPTU, ON SEEING SOME LINES
IN AN ALBUM.

These lines on prayer are very well,
But they belong to L. E. L. ;
And this, to be as true as brief,
Will prove that Ellen Ward's a thief.

THE CHRISTIAN POET.

Sweet chords in sounds abhorrent
  His listening fancy hears
In the roaring of the torrent,
  In the clashing of the spheres,

In the elemental battle,
  In the hoarsest wind that raves,
In the thunder's loudest rattle,
  And the din of tossing waves.

Far, far as fancy wanders,
  Bright shapes the earth assumes ;
Where the rippling stream meanders,
  And the mountain daisy blooms ;
In the liquid drop that staineth
  The violet's purple dye ;
And the rich gem which raineth
  From woman's sparkling eye.

On, on ! as fancy dashes,
  Fresh glories strike the sight :
In the blue electric flashes,
  And the glow-worm's silvery light ;
In the thickly-studded alley,
  In the wrack through ether driven,
In the soft, reposing valley,
  And the blazing pomp of heaven.

Religion from creation,
  Like honey, he distils ;
And sacred contemplation
  The raptured gazer fills,—
As step by step ascending,
  He spurns the earth's green sod ;
And flesh and spirit bending,
  He blesses Nature's God.

NATURE.

" How beautiful is all this visible world."—*Byron.*

There's something bright and glorious
  In the sun's first earthward glance,
When from his bed he riseth
  Like a giant from a trance ;
Or when, the eye o'erpowering,
  With his full meridian ray,
O'er heaven's cerulean pavement
  He hurries on his way.

There's something vast and glorious
  In the sea—the deep profound,—
Who claspeth, like a lover,
  The earth, his mistress, round ;

As an infant's sleep unruffled,
  Or tossing the glittering brine,—
Dark dread, and pathless ocean,
  What majesty is thine !

There's something fair and glorious
  In this little speck of ours :
In the plumes of her winged warblers,
  And the painting of her flowers ;
In her fresh and vernal carpet,
  In her pebbled, troubled rills,
In her wild, untrodden forests,
  And her everlasting hills.

There's something far more glorious
  In the faith that says " I know,
From the void and formless chaos,
  Who bade these wonders grow !"
Bend, reverently, my spirit,—
  Before that Being fall,
Whose wisdom first created,
  Whose power sustaineth all.

TO A FRIEND WHO TREMBLED AT THE THOUGHT OF DYING.

True, Christian, true, we all are dying mortals ;
  The sentence pass'd on all of woman born
Will force us through the grave's terrific portals,—
  For "dust thou art, and shalt to dust return."

Alas ! and must we leave the scenes we cherish,—
  Our homes and friends, affectionate and fond,—
And in the tomb sleep like the beasts that perish,
  Without one glimpse of happiness beyond ?

Nay, Christian, nay ! not thus we read the promise,—
  " The woman's seed shall bruise the serpent's head :"
Here is a hope which death can ne'er take from us—
  The Saviour liveth ! He liveth who was dead !

He liveth who was dead ! Let this reflection
  Wipe any tear from sorrow's glistening eye ;
He conquer'd death ; and, by His resurrection,
  He that believes in Him shall never die.

Death, friendly Death, unlocks a bright hereafter ;
  And, seen by faith, his sharp, relentless knife—
Despite the worldling's sneers, the atheist's laughter—
  Clears the soul's passage to eternal life.

Lo ! Christ is risen, beyond the grave's dominions ;
    And, through the power of His victorious love,
We His joint-heirs, upborne on Hope's strong pinions,
    Shall mount to Eden, our sweet home above.

Poor, trembling saint, let not thine heart be troubled,
    Nor with the dread of death thy mind oppress'd ;
But be thy faith, and love, and patience doubled,
    For time is short, and this is not our rest.

Read and believe Redemption's wondrous story :—
    To him who fights and conquers shall be given,
For conflict here, the victor's crown of glory ;
    For death's cold box, a blood-bought throne in heaven.

THE SABBATH.

How barren, how cheerless, how hopeless our lot,
    And earth what a prison unblessed,
If He, who is rich in compassion, had not
    Appointed these portions of rest :
Loved seasons, exempt from the toils and the cares
    With which our journey is rife ;
Sweet flowers springing up in a wild field of tares,—
    Green spots in the desert of life.

O ! loud let our praises ascend unto God,
    That one day is granted in seven,
On which—while forgetting the perishing clod—
    Our soul may hold converse with heaven ;
Dear moments of peace and external repose,
    When man talks with God as a friend,
Bright types of a service which never shall close,
    A Sabbath which never shall end.

We claim of the Lord what his conflict hath won,—
    That ultimate fruit of his love ;
The rest which remains for his people alone,
    A Sabbath eternal above ;
O, that we may reach that blessed shore,—
    The seat of the glorious I AM,
And join the great multitude who sing evermore,
    "Salvation to God and the Lamb !"

FOR ME, IN CRIMSON DROPS, THAT SWEAT RAN DOWN.

Thou Son of David and his Lord,
  Where shall a sinner rest ?
Where hide his load of guilt abhorr'd,
  But in Thy willing breast ?

For me, in crimson drops, that sweat
  By Kedron's brook ran down ;
And on Thy head in mockery sat
  The sharp and thorny crown.

Thy limbs were rent by Pilate's lash,
  For me—a child of hell ;
And on Thy head the lightning-flash
  Of God's displeasure fell.

Thy merits magnified the law,
  That God might man forgive ;
Thy richest blood did freely flow,
  That these dry bones might live.

Thy death left hope where none was found,
  Made peace where there was strife ;
And on Thy dying pangs I ground
  My claim to endless life.

No other refuge, Lord, have I,
  But in Thy gushing side ;
My Jesus lifted up on high,
  Emmanuel crucified !

Extend to me Thy mercy now !
  By Thy dear cross and pain,
Thy smitten face, and bleeding brow,—
  Let me not see in vain !

Grant me the boon bestow'd on him
  Who, stretch'd upon the tree,
As life's last glimmer grew more dim,
  Cried, " Lord, remember me !"

Remember me, thou Source of Grace !
  And, guided by Thy love,
My soul shall reach her native place,
  Our " home, sweet home" above.

RESOLVE, RESOLVE !

Why lag ye, sinners, on the road,
  So burden'd with that heavy load ?
Awake, awake ! delay's a crime,
  Make for the Refuge while there's time !

This way conducts to joy and peace,
  And that to woes that never cease :
Resolve, resolve ! begin the strife
  For hell or glory, death or life !

Yet, never on that journey start
  With guilty mind and lep'rous heart ;
The Cross, the Cross ! to that repair,
  And hang your burdens boldly there !

Strait is the way,—and long beside,
  But Jesus is a matchless guide ;
" My blood, my blood !" our leader cries,
  " Is a sure passport to the skies !"

Then, free from sin's detested yoke,
  Your mind at peace, your shackles broke ;
March on, march on ! to that bright shore,
  Where sheep and Shepherd part no more !

TO MR. ROBERT SNAPE, ON HIS BIRTHDAY.

" Three score and ten !" such is the span
That measures out the life of man :
Not long, then, must thou here abide ;
For God, thy Father, Friend, and Guide,
Hath led thee eight-and-sixty years
Through this low vale of sin and tears.

The time of thy departure's near,
Nor dost thou wish to linger here ;
Thy weary spirit does not shrink
From Jordan's fast-approaching brink ;
For Jesus—good and strong to save—
Can bear thee safely o'er the wave.

Eternal life, the long-sought prize,
Beyond that gloomy river lies ;
And wildly though its billows roll,
They will not overwhelm thy soul ;
For, after all thy trials past,
God will not fail thee at the last.

K

Thus saith the Lord, and says to thee,
" Where I am you shall also be."
As sure as He thy peace hath made,
As sure as He thy debt hath paid,
His work in thee He can defend,
And will perform it to the end.

Thy trembling steps, thy hair so gray,
Proclaim thy mortal frame's decay ;
Thy sin-sick soul, by cares oppress'd,
Like thy poor body, pines for rest ;
And Simeon's words are in thy heart,—
" Lord, let thy servant now depart."

Thy time is near, yet there's one thing
That chains thee here, and clips thy wing ;
And thus thy thoughts break out afresh,—
" Lord ! save my children in the flesh !
Let all like me Thy mercy find,
And let not one be left behind !"

God is a God that answers prayer—
Then leave thy children to His care ;
The grace that pull'd the father through
Can reach and bless his children too,
Graft them to Israel's chosen stock,
And add them to His little flock.

Then give thy doubtings to the wind,
Leave earth and earth-born cares behind :
Thy Saviour calls, by day and night,—
Press to that "land of pure delight ;"
And, when at " home, sweet home," prepare
To welcome all thy children there.

A GRACE.

STILL kept by Thy kind power, we live,
Unworthy though we be ;
And still, dear Father, we receive
Our daily bread from Thee.

Oh, sanctify, indulgent Lord,
The bounties Thou hast given ;
And grant that all who crowd this board
May taste Thy love in heaven.

A GRACE.

By our merciful Creator,
  We, poor helpless worms, are led
To the banquet-house of nature,
  Kindly to be cloth'd and fed ;
    Heavenly Father,
  Give us still our daily bread.

For the bounties amply given,
  Help us some return to make ;
Grant that of the bread of heaven
  Freely we may now partake ;
    Make us welcome
  To that feast, for Jesus' sake.

GOOD NIGHT !

To weary man repose is sweet,
  A blessing we'll not slight,
But give to God the praises meet,
  Before we say "good night."

We thank Thee in this peaceful hour,
  Thou Source of grace and might,
By whose one offering we have power
  To bid the curse "good night."

Should'st Thou Thy favour Lord, remove,
  How helpless then our plight ;
But trusting in Thy covenant love,
  We bid our fears "good night."

Oh, Lord, our cold, dark hearts inflame,
  And fill with heavenly light,
That we, in Thy most holy name,
  May bid the world "good night."

If we are Thine,—approaching death
  Will not our souls affright ;
But joyfully our dying breath
  Shall bid our sins "good night."

And when at length—the struggle o'er,
  Our spirits take their flight,
We'll meet in heaven to part no more,
  And never say "good night."

ATTRIBUTED POEM.

LINES ADDRESSED TO MISS A—— W——.

THINE ! yes, for ever thine I'll be,
    However worldly things may go :
Whether serene prosperity
    Her golden beams upon thee throw,
Or poverty, and grief, and pain,
Shall cleave thy tender heart in twain.

Wast thou a queen, and didst thou move
    Deck'd with a thousand diamonds bright,
I still would view thee as my love;
    And, turning from the gaudy light
Of glittering gold, would, in thine eye,
Look for a ray more heavenly.

Wast thou as destitute, as poor
    As e'er was Afric's vilest slave,
Or orphan at the miser's door,
    Or tar escap'd the stormy wave,
To perish on a desert shore,
'Gainst whose rude rocks wild waters roar,—

Would I forsake thee ? No, I would not,
    But round thy bleeding bosom twine.
Could I forget thee ? No, I could not!
    Though wretched, thou shouldst still be mine !
My words, my sighs, my tears should prove
I lov'd thee with a *lover's* love.

TOULMIN, PRINTER, CANNON-STREET, PRESTON.

www.ingramcontent.com/pod-product-compliance
Lightning Source LLC
Chambersburg PA
CBHW031955060726
47497CB00016B/2304